BOBBY NASH'S
SNOW
BEN
BOOKS

First BEN Books Edition 2018

SNOW SERIES 1 VOLUME 1

First BEN Books Printing.

Book Production and design by Bobby Nash.
Snow Falls edited by Gary Phillips
Snow Storm, Snow Drive edits by Ben Ash Jr.
Snow Cover Art by Dennis Calero

Printed in the USA

Published by BEN Books, PO Box 626, Bethlehem, GA 30620

http://BEN-Books.blogspot.com

And so it begins…

This one is dedicated to all the fictional heroes I grew up idolizing.
And to the real-life heroes I discovered along the way.

SNOW FALLS

BOBBY NASH

BEN BOOKS

Abraham Snow knew he was about to die--

--and the thought of it pissed him off to no end.

Everything had been going according to plan.

Before it all went to hell, everything was moving forward as laid out. The meet was set. All of the details had been checked and rechecked. Every *i* had been dotted, every *t* crossed. It had taken him years to get this far inside, but he was finally getting a face to face with Miguel Ortega. The man was a ghost, a legend. Ortega was a phantom that law enforcement operatives all over the world had been chasing for decades. No one had even come close to catching the elusive Miguel Ortega despite the fact that he was rumored to have his hands in everything from the drug trade to arms dealings and human trafficking to murder for hire. There was a good reason for this, however, and Agent Snow was one of a select few people alive that knew the truth.

Miguel Ortega was an alias.

It was a code name frequently used by less than reputable men and women who preferred to remain anonymous while keeping their questionable business dealings close to the vest. This alias provided the Ortega's of the world with a sense of security. Snow had finally made it past the middlemen and low-level goons inside the organization belonging to the Miguel Ortega he was after.

That's how Abraham Snow, in his alias as James Shepperd, found himself standing on the blisteringly hot tarmac of a tiny smuggler's airfield in the middle of a South American jungle in a suit, sans tie, standing next to a beautiful woman named Daniella Cordoza. She was Ortega's right hand and was as dangerous as she was alluring in her formfitting custom dress. They both stood out of place against the jungle backdrop. Snow didn't trust her, but he needed Cordoza to get to her employer.

One minute everything was going according to plan.

The next-- well, the next minute was not so good. Time moved as though it was trapped in amber. The man in the white suit was all smiles as they walked to meet one another across the airstrip's tarmac. Snow was finally getting his face to face. It was the first step in the final chapter of his undercover operation.

"Agent Snow." the man said once he was within earshot.

It took half a second to realize what he had said. Snow did a double take. Ortega had called him by his real name, Abraham Snow, not the James Shepperd alias he had been working under the past eighteen months. *How the hell does he know my name*?

"I think you've got me mixed up with someone else, Mr. Ortega. My name is…" Snow started, but it was no use. He could tell by the man's demeanor that there would be no fast-talking his way out of this one.

His cover was blown.

Somehow, someway, someone had sold him out. The list of possible rats was small. Only a handful of people knew his true identity and most of them he had known and trusted for years. His mind raced through the possible scenarios-- a leak inside the Pentagon or the CIA, a compromised asset, or a mistake he'd made himself, a slip up that had given him away. Each of these played across his mind in less time than it took to realize how deep in the shit he was at that moment.

He was all alone.

There was no backup close by, no one to swoop in and save the day.

Snow reached for the gun tucked into his belt behind his back.

Ortega moved faster.

Still smiling, he pulled the Glock-30 from a shoulder holster and squeezed the trigger.

Snow felt the first impact, but it wasn't until the second that he realized he had been shot. The next thing he knew, he was knocked off his feet, flying backward through the air. Snow dropped to the asphalt, unmoving, blood leaking out of two very large holes in his body. A tingling sensation in his extremities told him that the blood loss was substantial. Despite the humid clime, he felt a chill run through him.

He was dying.

Ortega had only fired three shots. The first clipped Agent Snow's arm, spinning him around. The second missed completely. The third hit its mark, center mass.

Snow stared up into a brilliant blue sky punctuated with a few fluffy white clouds as blood pooled beneath him. Above him, Ortega and his companion stood and looked down at him. He was smiling, but she wasn't. That surprised him. Although they had been intimate with one another, neither of them had pretended it was anything more than a physical convenience. For him, she had simply been another asset to get him closer to his target.

Mission accomplished.

He had found Ortega.

Surprisingly, he didn't finish the job. After a moment, Miguel Ortega shook his head, turned and walked away, out of Snow's line of sight, presumably back to his plane. Daniella Cordoza stayed a moment longer and he thought he saw sadness in her eyes, although he couldn't be sure of anything as he lay there gasping for air.

And then she was gone.

He assumed she had a plane to catch.

Snow's vision grayed around the edges as he struggled to catch his breath. Then, surprisingly, followed the sensation of flight, as if gravity no longer held sway over him. Trees and clouds flashed past his vision at dizzying speeds until gravity reasserted itself and he crashed back to Earth.

And just like that it was all over.

All that remained was darkness--

--and pain.

SNOW FALLS

1.

The view was gorgeous.

Nineteen weeks had passed since Abraham Snow had been left for dead on a smuggler's airstrip in South America. The week of surgery and follow up procedures had been bad enough, but eighteen weeks of physical therapy and recovery time had almost driven him mad with boredom.

Now that he was finally free of the treatment center and all of his former obligations, Abraham Snow was unattached, unemployed, and happier than he had been in years. Waiting for him at the check out desk was a small box and a note. He smiled as he read the short note scribbled there in familiar handwriting. Sitting outside the treatment facility was a candy-apple red 1961 Chevrolet Corvette convertible and it was waiting for him.

Thought this might lift your spirits, the note had said and boy did it ever. Snow had loved this model car since he was old enough to dream about driving. His grandfather had once called this car the greatest achievement in man's history. Although he could probably cite a few other examples, he couldn't deny how great this car was to drive.

He couldn't get on the road fast enough. All he wanted to do was put the shooting, the treatment center, and his old life behind him. All he had handy was in a duffle bag tossed in the back seat. He really hadn't given much thought to where he would go after his release from the treatment center, but now he had a destination. He decided to take the scenic route to get there.

After reorienting himself to the Greater Atlanta area, Snow marveled at how much his city had changed, but he also noted with a small hint of pride how much of it had remained the same. He was enjoying his drive, but fatigue had started to set in. It was a sensation he was unaccustomed to feeling, but one his doctors had told him he would have to get used to, at least for the foreseeable future. No matter what the surgeon told him, he would never accept this limitation.

He pulled onto the interstate and headed north. The Greater Metro Atlanta area was easily divided into two sections: Inside The Perimeter and Outside The Perimeter. The Perimeter was Interstate 285, a giant loop around the city. Snow had grown up in the city, but spent a lot of time at his grandfather's farm just outside of Atlanta. It was a small oasis from the hustle and bustle of city life, but was still close enough for a short car ride.

Snow hadn't seen his grandfather in years. Such was the nature of undercover work. When you go under as deep as he had, you had to divorce yourself completely from your old life. It wasn't easy, but Snow had learned how to compartmentalize the disparate parts of his life. He just hoped he could return to the life he'd had before.

The farm looked pretty much as he remembered. He turned into the long drive from the road to the farmhouse. To most people, a farmhouse was a small, modest dwelling, but the Snow family rarely did anything modest. Calling it a mansion would probably downplay the definition. All brick and rock, Grandpa Snow's house had always looked like a castle to him when he was younger. Now that he was older, it looked less like something out of a fantasy novel, but was no less impressive.

He parked next to the porch on the side of the house, the one that was used more often than the front door. The side entrance had always felt less formal, which suited Snow just fine. To his thinking, only visitors rang the front porch bell. After all this years he had been away, he supposed he was a visitor now. As he reached up a hand to knock on the door, it opened to reveal a broad shouldered man in jeans, shirtsleeves, and a cowboy hat. He also wore a very broad grin.

"There he is!" the big man shouted and scooped up Snow in a big bear hug.

Snow winced under the embrace, tried to stifle a grunt.

"Oh, I'm sorry, boy," Archer Snow said, suddenly remembering where his grandson had spent the past five months. He released his grip.

"It's okay, grandpa," Snow said. "I'll live."

"It's just so damned good to see you," Archer said, motioning Snow toward the deck off the back of the house. "So glad to have you home."

"It's good to see you too," Snow said. He pointed toward the white hair poking out from beneath his grandfather's hat. "When did this happen? Last time I saw you this was a lot darker?"

Archer removed the hat to reveal a head full of white hair. Like his grandson, Archer's hair had that unruly quality that no comb could defeat. "You've been away a long time, kid. The snowy top comes with the territory." He smiled. "Besides, I can see you're sporting a few salty gray streaks as well."

Snow unconsciously ran his hand through his dark mop of unruly hair. Thanks again for the loaner," he said, motioning to the car and hoping to change the subject. "That's one helluva car you've got there."

"You like it? It's yours."

"You don't have to do that," Snow said, grimacing. Unlike some members of his family, Snow rarely accepted gifts from his grandfather and even on those odd occasions when he did, he did so reluctantly. Snow did not want their relationship to be built only on what the old man could give him. That was probably why they got along so well.

"Still a stubborn cuss, I see," Archer said. "I wonder where you get that from?"

Snow chuckled. "Yeah. I wonder."

"Must run in the family. I blame your father."

So do I, Snow thought, but instead shook his head. "Guilty as charged," he said.

"We'll call it a loaner then. You feel free to drive it as long as you need to, okay?"

"Fine, grandpa," Snow said, surrendering. "Fine. You win."

"I usually do," he joked. "So, how are you feeling?"

"I'm really getting tired of being asked that question."

Archer waved it off. "We don't have to talk about it," he said. "I should have known better than to bring it up this soon. I'm sorry, kid."

"No. It's okay, Grandpa. Really. I'd rather get it from you than from strangers," Snow said and offered a pained smile. "It hurts. Bad, but I'll live."

Archer nodded, but said nothing. He knew that sometimes the best way to get information was not to ask for it, but to say nothing and let the other person fill the silence. It was a trick he had learned as an interrogator years earlier when he had been in the same kind of business his grandson had followed him into. He was thankful none of the other grandchildren took that path. Worrying about one was more than enough for him. He hated using interrogation techniques on his grandson, but he also knew full well the danger of keeping his thoughts bottled up inside. The kid had to let it out sooner or later.

Snow ran a hand gently over the wound. "Do you know what the difference is between life and death?" he asked.

"What's that?"

"Half an inch," Snow said, holding two fingers the same distance apart. "That's it. That's how close I came to checking out. If that bullet had been just half an inch over that would have been it, you know? Just half an inch."

"I do," Archer said. "I've seen more than my fair share of death, kiddo. You were lucky, I'll grant you that. Or maybe you got a guardian angel sitting on your shoulder. Either way, I'm just glad to have you back home."

"Thanks."

"How long you back for this time?"

"For good, I think," Snow said.

"They benched you?"

"No, but I'm thinking about benching myself."

"Oh?"

"I think I'm done, grandpa," Snow said. "I've had a lot of time to think while I was recuperating. I suddenly… I realized that I really haven't lived my life, you know? I've been pretending to be somebody else for the better part of my adult life. I think I might enjoy being me for awhile."

"I can see the appeal," Archer said and waited. He knew what was coming next.

"How did you know when it was time to hang it up?"

"Pretty much the same we you did," Archer said. "I realized that I had spent so much time in countries that were not my home, pretending to be someone I wasn't while dealing with people who did bad things. It wears on your soul, son, chipping away at the part of you that makes you *you.* I pulled the pin while there was still enough of me left inside that I could recognize."

"I think I'm there now," Snow said. "I just wish it hadn't taken getting shot in the chest to make me realize what I was missing."

"God talks to each of us in unique ways," Archer said.

"I wish he had spoken a little softer."

Archer smiled. "Well, it takes a lot to get through that hard head of yours, kid. You always were a little too stubborn for your own good."

"I don't know what you're talking about," Snow joked. "I've not been stubborn a day in my life. Now, my grandpa on the other hand…"

"Please, kid. Don't even start. I know all your childhood stories, remember?"

Snow's smile faded as he stared off into the distance. "I think it might be time to get out of the game while I'm still ahead."

Archer squeezed his grandson's shoulder. "Abraham, this is one of those life moments that no one can choose but you. Just know that, whatever you decide, I'll support you." He shrugged. "Besides, you could always come to work for me."

Snow's brow creased. "Yeah. No. I don't think so."

"There will always a place for you," Archer said. "Not just because you're my grandson either. A man with your record of service would bring a lot to the table. Don't discount the possibility out of hand. Promise me you'll at least consider it."

"I will and that's nice of you to say, but there's one very important factor you seem to be forgetting in al this."

"What's that?"

"The president of your company hates me."

"Hate is such a strong word, kid."

"But an accurate one," Snow joked. "We're all probably better off if I keep my distance."

"I think you're oversimplifying things, son," Archer said. "If you just talked to him I'm sure you two could come to some kind of understanding. Who knows, maybe now that you're both older and more mature you can sit down and hash out your differences like rational adults."

"Oh, I think we understand one another just fine," Snow said. "Trust me, nothing's changed."

"You never know until you try."

"Then I doubt we'll ever know," Snow said. "Can we just let this go?"

Archer held up his hands in surrender. "Okay. Okay. I'll drop it. For now."

"Thank you."

"But not for good. We will talk about this eventually."

"Of that I have little doubt," Snow said.

"The job offer still stands though."

"Thanks, grandpa, but I think I'll pass if it's all the same to you."

"And if it's not," Archer said. "All the same to me, that is."

Snow's smile grew. "Then I'll still have to pass. I'd just feel bad about it."

"Consider it an open-ended offer. Anytime you're ready, kid, it's waiting for you," Archer Snow said. "Now, come on. Let's get you settled in and go grab something to eat. I'm starved and I want to hear all about your travels."

###

"This is great," Snow said.

"I thought you might like it," Archer said as they stepped into the apartment over the shop/garage. "I had it fixed up a few years back as an office, but now that I only work part time I hardly ever come up here. I thought you could crash here during your recovery." He smiled. "Unless you'd rather stay in the main house?"

"No. This is perfect."

The apartment was spacious, running the length of the shop below, which held fifteen cars easily on one side while leaving workspace on the other. A collector of classic cars, Archer Snow had a rather immaculate collection. He also bought, restored, and sold a number of cars as well. It had become a nice sideline business for him. Some of his favorite childhood memories were of him and his brother attending classic car shows with their grandpa.

The large sliding glass doors at the far end of the apartment led out onto a deck that looked out over a picturesque view of the lake. As a kid, he had spent many summers swimming, canoeing, and fishing in that lake. He and his cousins had named it *Lake Snow*, which seemed appropriate for a private lake. In later years, it became a recurring in-joke among the family.

"Perfect," Snow said again. "You know, I wasn't going to let you talk me into staying. I even prepared an argument full of good reasons not to stay."

"I figured as much."

"You don't play fair, old man," Snow said.

"Where would be the fun in that?" Archer joked.

Snow laughed in spite of himself. "I guess you've got yourself a new tenant." They shook hands.

"You consider this home for as long as you like." Archer looked out over the lake, inhaled. "I can't think of too many better places than this to get your mind back in order," he said. "I've always loved this view."

"What's not to love?" Snow said. "Lake, trees, just a hint of the mountains in the distance. It's perfect."

"Great. Let's go grab some lunch. I'm starving."

"Now there's a plan," Snow agreed and followed his grandfather down the stairs leading into the shop floor instead of the ones leading down the outside of the apartment.

"I just need to make a quick stop, first, check in on my mechanic."

"No worries." Snow said. He looked out over the row of classic cars and whistled. "Looks like you've added a few jewels to the collection."

"You know me. Have to keep 'em moving. Right now, we're rebuilding a '57 Ford Fairlane. A lady I know found it rusting out in an old barn after her father passed. The deal she offered was too good to pass up." He pointed to the car in question. A pair of coverall covered legs jutted out from beneath the rust-colored body. "Come on, I'll introduce you to my chief mechanic."

"She's a beaut," Snow said. "You've got a lot of work ahead of you on this one though."

"This baby will be turning heads in no time," a familiar voice called out from beneath the car.

"John?" Snow said.

John Salmon slid from beneath the car, a big grin on his face. "Ham Bone!" he shouted, leaping to his feet to embrace Snow in a hug that squeezed him even tighter than his grandfather had earlier. He grunted under the strain.

"Oh, shit!" Salmon said when he realized. "Sorry, man. I forgot. I mean, your granddad told me about your… uh… you know…" he pointed toward Snow's chest.

"It's all right," Snow said, smiling despite the pain. "It's damn good to see you, Big John. You work here?" he motioned toward the room as if he couldn't quite process the news.

"Yeah. I know. I got in some trouble and did a little stretch. When I got out there weren't a whole lot of people willing to give me a shot," Salmon said. "The old man here helped me out."

"Ah, it was nothing," Archer said, smacking John on the shoulder. "You're like family. It was the least I could do."

Snow and Salmon had grown up in the same neighborhood. As kids they were inseparable. After high school, their lives drifted off in different directions. Snow had enlisted right after graduation and was recruited for deep cover work not long after that where he learned a new skill set. Big John, the nickname everyone called the tall, hulking teenager fell in with some new friends who taught him some new skills as well. He learned how to steal cars.

"We were heading out for lunch," Archer said. "Thought you might like to tag along, maybe catch up a little."

"Sure. Do I have time to clean up?"

"We'll meet you outside," Archer said.

"Give me two minutes," Salmon said, still smiling. "Glad to have you home, Ham."

"Bring the SUV around on your way."

"You got it, boss."

Once they were outside, Snow turned to his grandfather. "He works here?"

"Yeah. For a couple years now," Archer said. He noticed the puzzled look on his grandson's face. "What?"

"You know I love Big John like a brother, but he is a car thief. Isn't this like sending an alcoholic to work in a brewery?"

"He's a former car thief and it's fine," Archer said plainly. "We've had no problems since he got here. Not a one. He did his time, paid for what he did. I trust him."

"Glad to hear it," Snow said. "Thanks for taking care of him. I know you've always had a soft spot for the big lug."

"Of all the friends you and your brother used to hang out with, I always liked him the best," Archer said. "Better than that McClellan kid. He still bugs me."

"You've seen Mac? How's he doing?" Snow asked. "Don't tell me he works here too?"

"Not bloody likely," Archer said. "We run into him sometimes at work."

"Really? Grandpa, you're in the security consultant business. What possible business dealing could you have with Mac?"

Archer barked a laugh. "You really have been out of touch with everything, haven't you? Tom McClellan works for the FBI."

Snow felt his mouth gape open. "I beg your pardon? Are you seriously trying to tell me that Mac works for the Federal Bureau of Investigations?"

"Yep."

"As what?"

"He's one of their lead investigators, kid. Special Agent, if you can believe it."

"Seriously?"

"You really need to learn how to pick up a phone every once in awhile, Abraham. You're out of touch."

Snow scratched the side of his head, a gesture he did whenever he was working out a situation. "I guess I did fall way off the grid there for a bit. I'll have to give 'ol Mac a call," he said just as Big John pulled up to meet them. Snow climbed into the back seat.

Archer slid in the front passenger seat. "Just do me one favor, kid," he said.

"What's that?"

"Do it after we've had lunch."

"Yes, grandpa."

2.

That first day had been wonderful.

Spending time with his grandfather and friend had been just what Snow needed. It had been so long since he could be himself, to enjoy a friendly conversation without having to keep track of all the lies and half-truths he had crafted as part of his cover identity. For the first time in a couple of years, he could be Abraham Snow instead of James Shepperd. It felt good to simply be himself, to be Abraham Snow, and not having to worry about slipping up and letting the wrong detail slip out or doing one of a million things that could get him killed. He felt the weight of undercover work lift off his shoulders. It was freeing.

He'd spent the evening catching up with Big John before turning in for the night. It was the first peaceful sleep he had gotten in quite some time. There was something about being back at his grandfather's place that was very comforting. He felt safe there.

On the second day, his grandpa sneaked up on him and set the trap.

"Ride into town with me," he had said, all smiles and cheer. Still flying high from the great time he'd had the day before, Snow agreed. He should have known something was off when he saw his grandfather in slacks, shirtsleeves, and a jacket. Comparatively, he felt slightly underdressed in jeans and a button-down shirt so he grabbed his jacket as well. Neither man bothered with a tie.

Big John brought around a nicer SUV that the one from the night before. This one sparkled like new and was loaded to the nines with all the latest and greatest accessories. In hindsight, Snow would realize this should have been his first clue that the old man was up to something.

"I just need to swing by the office for a bit," Archer Snow said once they were on the road, springing the trap closed around him. The last place Abraham Snow wanted to go was to visit the family business.

Snow shot him a disapproving look. "You don't fight fair, old man," he muttered. "This is dirty pool."

"I've never played fair, kid," Archer said, still smiling. "And I'm too old to worry about changing my ways."

Snow Consulting occupied the top six floors of the twelve story Archer Building, named after Archer Snow's great grandfather, at least as far as Archer the second told the story. Snow had always ribbed the man about the coincidence that he just so happened to share the name of the man he named the building after. The headquarters of Snow

Consulting was just outside of Atlanta, one building over from the FBI field office, which made traffic a little less of a headache than if they had to head all the way downtown.

"Place hasn't changed much," Snow said as they parked in the spot reserved for the company's owner.

"What can I say, I like consistency," Archer quipped.

"It couldn't be that you're too stubborn to change, could it?"

"Not at all, kid. Not at all." Archer got out of the car and started toward the entrance. He stopped when he realized that his grandson had not followed suit. "You coming?"

Resigned, Snow climbed out of the car and joined Archer. "I was really hoping to avoid this," he said.

"I know," Archer said. "That's why I had to lie to get you here."

"Maybe I could just run next door and look up Mac, maybe say hello."

"Later," Archer said. "Besides, I know he's not there today."

"And how do you know that?"

Archer Snow smiled.

Snow waved him off. "I know. I know. You've got your ways."

After checking in at the security desk and getting him a visitor's pass, they rode the elevator to the top floor without speaking while a piano version of Queen's *Who Wants To Live Forever* piped through the speakers. Snow found himself humming along with the tune in spite of himself.

"Good morning, Mr. Archer," a receptionist said as soon as the men stepped off the elevator on the twelfth floor, where the public face of Snow Security Consulting lived.

"Is he in?" Archer asked.

"Yes, sir. I'll let him know you're on the way in," the receptionist said.

Archer waved her off. "Don't. I've brought him a surprise." He chucked a thumb in his grandson's direction.

If Archer noticed the receptionist's apprehensive look, he didn't acknowledge it.

Snow felt her pain. His grandfather was a force of nature. He was hard to corral. "Sorry about that," he said as he passed, offering her a shrug and a smile.

It had been years since Abraham Snow had visited the family business. He had hoped never to set foot inside the place again.

Although the outside of the building looked the same as it always had, the interior was a different matter all together. Everything was shiny and new, not to mention top of the line. His grandfather was not one to spare any expense to keep his people outfitted with the best equipment needed to do their jobs safely, but he also understood that the packaging was almost as important was what was inside. His time working for the Agency had taught him a few tricks that he brought with him to the boardroom. From what Snow had seen of his grandfather in action, Archer Snow was a shrewd businessman. He was firm and fair, but could be ruthless when the need arose.

Snow consulting knew their business. Nothing put a client's mind at ease with a security consulting firm than seeing all the latest and greatest toys. Little did the clients realize that the best security measures were those not seen, but most customers wanted the best equipment when what they should be asking for was the best people for the job.

Snow whistled.

"You like?"

"You do know how to put on a dog and pony show, grandpa," Snow said.

Archer clapped him on the shoulder and flashed that big smile he reserved for the customers. "Give the people what they want, kid. The shiny electronic gizmos make the clients feel better. Who am I to argue?"

As they walked down a hallway next to the offices and cubicles where the consultants worked, Archer slipped into tour guide mode. He explained what happened in each section they passed. Not only could they handle local security measures, but they were also mobilized to handle international client concerns as well. The company had grown from a local security firm to offering their services to a worldwide clientele.

Snow's grandfather was proud of the company he built, as he should have been. His success was a testament to not only his skills, but also his business acumen. Archer Snow projected a likeable good 'ol boy charm that instantly caused those on who opposed him to like him while underestimating his abilities. That was usually the start of their undoing.

"This is our bread and butter," Archer said as they reached the cyber-security division. "The world is a much smaller place than it was when I was your age. Dealing with someone on the other side of the world was a massive undertaking, and not usually something you did without going through a lot of hoops to get approved. Now, you can use social media to talk to people in war zones. There's probably only a handful of locations on this planet where you're truly off the grid."

"And even those are drying up fast," Snow said.

"Sounds to me like you've visited a couple of them."

Snow smiled. "One or two."

At the end of the hall, Archer entered the corner office without knocking. The man occupying the office was standing next to the window, the phone pressed to his ear. He did not turn at the intrusion. Instead, he simply held up a finger toward the newcomers so he would come in quietly as he paced back and forth behind the desk, tethered by the landline's phone cord.

"Yes, sir," the man in the expensive tailored suit said, his voice deep and commanding. He was in great shape/ If not for the thinning gray hair atop his head that was starting to show signs of going white, he could have passed for a man much younger than in his sixties. "I assure you that all necessary precautions have been put in place," he continued. "Yes, sir. I will be on hand personally to supervise security. No, sir. It is my pleasure. Very good. I will speak with you then. Goodbye, sir."

He dropped the receiver back into its cradle. Only then did he look up to see who had stepped into his office uninvited. He didn't seem all that surprised to see Archer Snow standing there. If seeing his grandson with him was a shock, he didn't show it. "When did you get back in town?" he asked as he turned to face the newcomers.

"Good to see you too, Dad," Snow said softly.

Dominic Snow straightened his jacket before taking a seat behind the antique desk that Snow assumed cost someone a lot of money. "You'll forgive me, gentlemen, but today is a rather busy day and I don't have a lot of time for a family reunion. The trade summit starts this afternoon and I'm juggling several ops related to that."

He tapped a spot on his tablet to reveal the floor plan of an upscale hotel that appeared on the wall-mounted seventy-inch flatscreen.

"You got all the angles covered, I take it?" Archer asked, walking closer to the screen for a better look.

Despite himself, Snow did the same.

"It's handled," Dominic answered without looking up from his tablet. "I'll be heading out in a few minutes to give everything the once over."

"You need any help?" Archer inquired.

"It's handled."

"Okay," Archer told his oldest son. "I'll see you there."

Dominic looked up from the screen. "Is there any particular reason you're joining us?"

"You mean beside the fact that I own the company?"

"Yes. Besides that," Dominic said. "You know I didn't mean any disrespect, Dad. It's just that I see you've got company. I thought you might have other things to do than watch me handle a simple security check."

"At ease, son," Archer said. "You know I have the utmost faith in you. I wouldn't have put you in charge if I didn't. I'm not checking up on you. That's a promise. I've got a meeting with one of the trade delegates to set up the possibility of us handling security for them on a more permanent basis. Once this new initiative passes, they will have a delegation living in the U.S. on an almost permanent basis. Hopefully, I can get a tentative deal in the books now. It could be a lucrative contract."

"Are you that certain the initiative will pass?" Dominic said.

"You know me, the eternal optimist," Archer said.

"Why don't you let me handle it?" Dominic said. "Spend some time with your grandson. You and Abraham can grab some lunch. I'm sure the last thing he wants to do is tag along on some corporate wine and dine."

"I've got it covered," Archer said, signaling that there would be no debating his decision. Once he made up his mind, it was all but impossible to change it. "Besides, you know I can't pass up an opportunity to see my one and only granddaughter, now can I?"

Snow had been uncomfortable from the moment he stepped into his father's office. He couldn't pinpoint exactly when their relationship had fallen apart, but it had been strained long before he took off for parts unknown on a deep cover assignment. Somehow, he suspected that their relationship, such as it was, was beyond repair. He wasn't even sure he wanted to try and patch things up. From the cool reception he had received, he could tell that Dominic Snow felt much the same way. He had all but tuned out the conversation until mention of his sister was made.

"Sammy's in town?" Snow asked.

"Oh, didn't I mention that?" Archer said, feigning befuddlement. It was a game he played to keep others off balance. In business deals, the bumbling old man act had worked to his advantage on more than one occasion. Snow hated when he used the tactic against him, however. Especially consider that the old man act was just that, an act. Archer Snow was usually the sharpest man in the room, including this one.

"Must have slipped your mind," Snow said.

"Yeah. Must be getting senile in my old age."

"Right," Snow said, drawing out the word.

Dominic stood. "I really need to get going, gentlemen," he said matter of fact. "I guess I will see you there."

"We'll be right behind you," Archer said.

"It was good to see you, Abraham," Dominic said before heading out the door.

"See? I told you he didn't hate you," Archer announced once they were alone.

Snow shook his head slowly as he followed his grandfather to the exit.

"It's going to be a long day," he muttered.

3.

“This place is amazing.”

Abraham Snow followed his father and grandpa into the lobby of the hotel and felt like he had been transported onto the set of a sci fi movie. The hotel’s interior could have passed for a futuristic city. Crosswalks crisscrossed over one another in different layouts on multiple levels. The hotel room floors stretched up as high as he could see, ending in a point. The floors were oddly shaped, not like any other standard square or round hotel he had ever stayed in before. The hotel had changed little in the years since he’d last been there to attend a science fiction convention with some friends the year he graduated from high school. His love of all things geeky had come from his mother, who also loved attending conventions dressed as her favorite characters. With her freewheeling spirit and his father’s lack of a creative side, the divorce was all but inevitable. Snow was twelve at the time and it hit him hard.

Snow and his grandfather fell back while Dominic and the rest of the team went on ahead to go over the last-minute preparations.

“You like?” Archer Snow asked.

“Yeah. This place is gorgeous,” Snow said. “Especially compared to some of the rat-holes I’ve been staying in the past few years. Must be a bitch to secure though. Look at all this…” he gestured. “You’ve got wide open space and plenty of blind spots. Not an ideal place for security.”

“I don’t disagree, but the people we’ve been hired to protect aren’t really the type to think about things like that,” Archer whispered. “Given the choice, they tend to choose aesthetics over security every time.”

“Sounds like every diplomat I’ve ever met. Too self-important for their own good,” Snow said.

“I hope that doesn’t include me,” a familiar voice called out from behind him.

“Sammy!” Snow all but shouted. He had a big smile firmly in place. In spite of being surrounded by her coworkers, he scooped up his baby sister in a big bear hug, lifting her feet off the marble floor and pinning her about. He laughed, and she did as well. He hadn’t realized exactly how much he had missed her until that moment.

“Hey,” he finally said once he set her back on solid ground.

"Hey yourself, Snowball," she said softly before turning back to her companions. "Why don't you go on ahead. I'll join you shortly."

"See you inside, Samantha," the head diplomat said with a nod. "Gentlemen."

"I was hoping to run into you before the meeting started," Samantha said.

"Really? You must have some good intel. An hour ago, I didn't even know I'd be here, much less that you were in town," he told her.

"Well, I do have an inside source," she said playfully.

"That would be me," Archer said, all smiles as he hugged his granddaughter.

"He texted me," she explained.

Snow snorted. "Why am I not surprised?"

"Are Dad and Doug here?"

"They're inside," Archer said. "Your boss has not been making things easy for him, you know."

"Don't start, Grandpa," Samantha said. "I'm just the mediator here. My client is responsible for making his own security arrangements. I simply suggested that Snow Security might be a good way to go."

"That's my girl," Archer said.

"I better get in there," she said. "I expect you to take me out to dinner tonight, buster," she told her brother. "We've got a lot of catching up to do."

"It's a date," Snow said. "Tell Doug to join us when you see him. It's high time the Archer Kids went out for a night on the town together."

"Done and done," she said. "See you two in a bit."

Once she walked inside to join her coworkers, Snow turned to his grandfather. "You're just full of surprises today, aren't you, old man?"

"Cluck all you want, kiddo," Archer joked. "My son and grandkids are all in the same building for the first time in God only knows how long. I plan to enjoy every minute of it."

"I can see that. Any other surprises I should be expecting?"

As if on cue, a boisterous voice cut through the air, bouncing off the walls. Snow turned, a big smile spreading across his face when he saw the tall slender man approaching. He wore a dark suit that complimented his brown skin tone. There was a FBI badge wallet tucked in the pocket and a Bureau issued sidearm holstered on his hip. His black-as-night hair was cut short and he wore a thin goatee and beard. Although he had changed much since they were kids, Snow recognized the man immediately. He couldn't help but laugh.

"Hambone!" the newcomer said, his arms spread wide. The two men embraced one another in a big bear hug and clapping one another on the back, which drew stares from the assembled dignitaries and their aides.

"How the hell you been, Mac?" Snow said when they parted.

"Better now that I've seen your sorry ass," Tom McClellan joked. "I was beginning to wonder if you were ever going to pop your head up from whatever hole you've been hiding in. You in town long?"

"For a bit," Snow said.

"Then you, me, and Big John are on for dinner and beers." He handed over a business card. "I've got to get back to work here but give me a call and we'll make a plan. Talk soon."

Snow took the card. "You bet, pal."

"Mr. Snow," Mac said to Archer Snow.

"Mr. McClellan," Archer replied as FBI Special Agent Tom McClellan jogged to catch up with the group he'd split off from to say hello. He sidled up next to his grandson. "What did I tell you?"

"This may be the first time I've seen Mac in a suit," Snow said.

"A lot can change in a decade, kiddo."

"Yeah. I'm starting to realize that. I missed a lot while I was gone."

"But now you're home," Archer said.

"Yeah," Snow said. "Now I'm home."

###

From a perch high above the ballroom level of the hotel, the sniper waited.

The contract was fairly straightforward. A photo of the target had been attached to an encrypted email sent along a secure server and routed through several different countries before being read through a temporary dummy account set up for this one assignment only and retrieved at a public computer in a library. The photo of the target, his name, a timeframe, and a place were all set up by the client. This was pretty standard SOP for a hit, but the client was not looking for collateral damage. In fact, the contract specifically forbade civilian casualties.

That ruled out explosives and poisons. The hotel was also a problem. The place was a maze of crisscrossing corridors, bridges, and people, all within a building with wide- open spaces making up its interior. While such a place was perfectly suited to conferences and conventions, it was not so easy for someone to lie in wait with a high-powered rifle until the target appeared.

This job required stealth.

And that cost extra.

The client was willing to pay the higher fee so long as the target was eliminated. The assassin assured the client, a fussy man who was used to broker deals with those who feared him. When faced with a professional, one that did not cower under his lofty position, he became demure. It was a common trait in men with supposed power. Take away their superiority and they became as malleable as clay.

The room in the corner closest to optimum firing position had been reserved under a false identity, courtesy of the client, who provided special documentation. All was ready.

All the sniper had to do was wait.

###

Abraham Snow was bored.

The first session of the day went off without a hitch, but he was already tired of listening to the delegates droning on and on before the first hour had passed. Quietly excusing himself, he slipped out of the ballroom that had been converted into a large conference room for the talks. He had never been good at sitting still for very long.

Since he didn't really have a stake in the trade talks, he decided to get out a stretch his legs with a quick walk around the lobby. He wanted a cigarette, but had sworn off the wretched things after waking up in the intensive care unit. Smoking had been part of his James Shepperd persona. Now that he had put that alias away, hopefully for good, the cigs went with it. The doctor had given him a shot that was supposed to help, but it only helped stave off the cravings a little bit. There were also his hands. He wasn't used to them being empty so he'd started carrying around an ink pen he could hold when the urge to smoke hit.

The hotel was a sight, like something out of a sci fi movie. Glass elevators moved up and down at the hotel's center, open to the surroundings. He watched as several guests zoomed skyward. With forty-three floors, he couldn't see them all the way to the top. From the elevators, you had to walk across one of four bridges to the lobby. The area surrounding the bridges was open so you could see into the lower levels.

The architect must have driven the builders made wit this layout, he thought. He'd never seen anything ,like it.

Snow had been worried about coming back to Atlanta. There were a lot of good memories here, but there were plenty of bad ones too. He missed his family, though, especially his sister and grandfather. Far more than he thought was possible. He looked forward to spending time with Sammy and Doug. They had been close growing up, but it had been a long time since he'd spoken to either of them. Granted, that was on him and he knew it. They weren't the ones who ran off to work under cover in the most remote places.

"You lost?"

Snow smiled. "More often than I should be," he said with a grin as his brother approached him. They hugged. "How have you been, Dougie?"

"I'm good, baby brother. I saw you duck out and thought this might be a good time to say hey."

"Yeah. I saw you earlier, but you were working so I didn't want to interrupt," Snow said. "I see you took to the family business, huh?"

"Yeah. Grandpa can be very hard to say no to," Doug said as they started walking the perimeter of the lobby.

"You don't have to tell me. I've been home less than a day and he's already working on me."

"Who knows, you might like it."

"I don't know. I'm not really sure I could work for Dad," Snow said.

"You two were always like oil and water."

"More like nitro and TNT," snow joked.

"I remember."

"Sammy mentioned the three of us getting together while she's in town. You in?"

"Hell, yeah," Doug said. "You tell me when and where and I'm there." His phone vibrated and he plucked it from his pocket and read the message. His smile faded. "Duty calls," he said.

"Go get 'em," Snow said. "We'll talk later."

"You bet. It's great to see you, man."

"You too."

Snow watched his brother head back toward the talks. Doug had always been more like their father while Abraham was more like their mom. Sammy was somewhere in between. Once Doug was back inside, Snow resumed his route.

The walk helped clear his head.

Sitting around listening to delegates discussing trade negotiations had passed boring five minutes into it. He had tried to pay attention as much as he could, but that didn't last long. He wasn't cut out for that type of inaction. He was the man of action type.

He would soon come to regret having that thought.

4.

Abraham Snow wasn't the superstitious type.

That said, but spending so much time undercover, always under the threat of being found out, had made him sensitive to his surroundings. It was little more that intuition, a hunch that started as a tickle at the back of his brain. He had learned to listen to those hunches. More than once they had saved his life.

Standing in the middle of the lobby of that beautiful five-star hotel, surrounded by enough security to protect a small nation, that familiar warning made itself heard. Whatever it was that set him on edge wasn't readily apparent. Maybe his subconscious had picked up on something that his conscious mind hadn't yet detected. He couldn't explain it, but there was danger lurking nearby. He scanned the floors above. The rooms ran down both sides of the hotel. There were no rooms along the front or back walls, save for the lobby and business center areas. Two restaurants, a copy shop, convenience store, coffee shop, a bar, the lounge, and a newsstand filled those spaces. Hallways lined the walls on the floors with guestrooms all the way up to the forty-seventh floor where the suites were located.

Nothing looked out of place, but the sensation of danger nagged at him.

The building was packed with people from all of the delegations on hand for the conference, their security personnel, local and federal law enforcement, not to mention the people who worked in the hotel. There were easily thousands of people around with small groups clustered on each floor and overlook. The elevators zoomed toward the upper floors and back down quickly, packed full of delegates for the conference. He recognized some of them, but before returning home there hadn't been a lot of time to keep up with world news unless it pertained to his case. He wasn't even sure what the ultimate purpose of this conference was to accomplish since he wasn't even aware of it until his grandfather shanghaied him there under false pretenses.

The latest session was just starting to break up. The doors opened and the room that had been quiet erupted with the murmur of several dozen conversations overlapping one another. A few delegates left quickly, but most stayed inside for more intimate group conversations and side negotiations.

Tom McClellan walked over to him with both Archer and Douglas Snow just a few steps behind. “I know that look,” he said. “What’s wrong?”

“I don’t know, Mac. Something’s just… not right. I can’t put my finger on it,” Snow said. “There’s something… off. I just don’t know what.”

“This place is about to fill up fast, Snowman. The next session starts in about fifteen minutes. Unless you can give me a good reason to lock it down. There’s still time to keep these people in that room, but I can’t sound the alarm without a damn compelling reason.”

Snow was about to say more when an elevator arrived. The security force, six men wearing black jackets over black suits with black ties flanked an older man wearing a white suit and his aide, wearing a gray suit. Another man dressed in a black business suit was also with them. Snow immediately recognized a familiar face in the crowd.

“What the hell is Owen Salizar doing here?” he said.

“Somebody I should know?” McClellan asked.

“Owen Salizar owns Salizar Biotechnix,” Archer Snow said before his grandson could answer. “It’s a worldwide biochemical corporation, if memory serves. Big money. Lots of influence in these negotiations.”

“Sounds like another rich prick to me,” McClellan noted. “Especially in that suit.”

“You have no idea,” Snow said. “It’s not widely known, but the U.S. believes that Salizar actively supports multiple terrorist groups and militant governments in exchange for business favors. He was on our watch list while I was under cover. We had leads against his company, but nothing actionable. Intelligence believes that his company is a front for laundering cash for several militant groups across the globe. I was tapped to go in as a UC in his company, but the assignment I was on took a turn and the mission went to someone else. What they hell is he doing here in the States?”

“He’s part of the negotiations your sister is working on,” Archer said.

“Salizar Biothechnix is scheduled to meet with Sam and her team during the next round of negotiations,” Doug said.

Snow felt his chest tighten. The thought of his sister being in the same room with Salizar was painful. “That man is a monster. What are they negotiating?”

"The details are hush-hush," Doug said. "Salizar and his brother are both major players in whatever it is they're working on in there."

"Is he what's got your gut twisted into knots?" Mac asked.

"No. I didn't even know he was here until now." Snow said. "This feeling's been gnawing at me for awhile now." He looked around the open space again, taking in the entire lobby.

A small spark, a reflection from above caught his attention.

"There," Snow said, but didn't point. "Third floor. Last room on the end."

"I don't see anything," McClellan said.

"What's going on?" Archer asked.

"Trust me, Mac."

"Okay." McClellan toggled his radio mic. "This is McClellan at zone alpha. We have a potential security breach. Keep everyone in the ballroom until we've checked it out. Send units three and five to the third floor, west end above check in."

"Make sure Sam stays put, huh?" Snow whispered to his grandfather.

"What's going on?"

"Maybe nothing."

"I know you better than that, kid," Archer started.

"Please," Snow said. "Doug, make sure they stay put."

"You got it," Doug said, taking his grandfather by the arm.

Archer made his way back to the room, unhappy about being sent out of harm's way, but content in keeping his granddaughter safe. As soon as he was out of earshot, McClellan shrugged.

"What are you thinking, Ham?"

"Shooter, maybe? Or it could be nothing. It's just a feeling."

"If it is a shooter, who's the target?"

"Your guess is as good as mine. This place is full of high profile targets. Any of them could be on a hit list. Or I could be wrong."

"I can't chance it," Mac said. "I've got to sound the alarm."

"Do it," Snow said, but it was too late.

The first shot sounded like a firecracker, the *pop* echoing off the concrete and steel. Snow caught a hint of the muzzle flash as the shooter fired and in that moment he knew who the target was. He started already on the move before he was even aware of it--

--but he was too late.

The sniper's bullet hit the black-clad security guard two steps ahead of Owen Salizar in the chest, spinning him around before dropping his body to the marble floor on the bridge leading from the elevator alcove to the lobby. Everything happened so fast that the screaming hadn't even started before Snow hit the bridge.

He vaulted over the fallen guard and slammed into Salizar and his security force as they rounded the corner out of the alcove onto the bridge. He pushed them to safety as a second shot echoed around them. The second bullet shattered the waist-high glass wall that ran along the sides of the bridge where the target would have been standing if Snow hadn't intervened.

"Who the hell are you?" the first security guard to recover shouted. He was a big man, his face reddening in anger.

"You're welcome," Snow said as he got back to his feet. "Keep your heads down." He pressed himself against the wall before the sniper fired again.

He didn't have to wait long.

The sniper opened fire, raining a hail of bullets across the lobby, focusing on the area near the elevators. Glass shattered and concrete debris filled the air as people ran for cover. Pandemonium reigned, which made it hard for the FBI and security to mobilize.

Instinctively, Snow reached for the gun that he had grown used to carrying on his hip, but there was nothing there. The last thing he had expected when he left that morning was to find himself in a gunfight. He would have to rethink his notion of what a quiet lunch with his grandfather meant next time the old man made the invitation.

"I need a weapon," he told the angry security man.

"I don't think so," the guard said, shaking his head. "I have no intention of giving you a weapon of any kind."

There was no time to argue with the man. Snow knew where to find a gun. The fallen guard's weapon was still holstered just a few feet away, which could have easily been twenty miles with a sniper targeting him. It was a sure bet that Salazar's security wasn't going to help-- a fine thing as he'd just saved their lives, not to mention the life of their boss. He needed a distraction.

He got it in the form of Tom McClellan and two other agents.

Mac and another agent took position behind the island bar that sat in the middle of the lobby. The third flattened against a column along the wall that was just wide enough to offer cover. None of them had a good angle on the shooter, but they did have weapons.

They used them.

Mac and his agents opened fire in the general direction of the sniper.

As soon as the first shot was fired, Snow was on the move. Taking off from a crouch, he pulled the dead guard's gun from his holster then dove over the body into a roll that brought him up on his back the gun leveled on the attacker's position. He squeezed off three shots in rapid succession. Two smacked the concrete barrier, but the third hit flesh. It was just a graze, but enough to take the sniper out of position long enough for the FBI teams on the third level to move in.

The stairwell door opened and two agents ran toward the sniper's position. Most snipers Snow had known were excellent shots at a distance, but up close and personal tended to be another matter. Unless he had misread the situation, the only course left open to the sniper was to run.

And that's exactly what happened.

The sniper leapt over the waist high barrier. It was a straight drop from the third floor to the lobby, but there was a lounge area even with the second floor that overlooked the lobby and the open lower levels. It was a long jump, but the sniper had an escape plan in place.

Snow got his first good look at the sniper. Still wearing a housekeeping smock disguise, the assassin hit the mark, landing in a roll on the carpet of the deserted lounge. The sniper was on the move almost immediately.

So were Snow and Mac.

"She's heading for the mall!" Snow shouted, already on the run.

Mac was only a step behind him. "She?"

"Sniper's a woman!"

They lost sight of the target as the sniper ran down the winding trail that connected the hotel to adjacent office buildings and the food court at the mall.

Mac was on his radio, shouting orders to the rest of his team. "I want a perimeter around the hotel and the mall! Now! Go! Go!"

The sniper was fast and Snow had trouble keeping up with her, especially with the tightness growing in his chest. His wounds were only recently healed. This much exertion wasn't good for him and he knew it, but he couldn't stop. He couldn't let her get away.

He headed up the ramp leading to the habit trail tunnel that crossed above the street into the food court of the Peachtree Center Mall. Once there, the sniper could disappear down any number of open avenues, including the street below. Normally, he would stop before rounding a blind corner and check to make sure he wasn't walking into an ambush, but in his haste to close the gap between him and his quarry, he barreled headlong into the tunnel without checking. It was a rookie mistake.

One that almost cost him his life.

The sniper had stopped halfway down the tunnel and dropped to one knee. She fired as soon as Snow entered the tunnel, but with both of them moving, she missed. Her first shot cracked the thick glass. The second smacked off the concrete wall. The third zipped past his head, a little too close for comfort, and ricocheted off the wall behind him.

Before he could return fire, Mac was there, pulling him out of the line of fire as the assassin fired again, just narrowly missing her target. The men were squeezed into the elevator alcove that accessed street level below.

"You go down and across," Snow said, depressing the call button. "I'll follow this way. Hopefully, we can cut her off."

"Be careful," Mac said. "I've got my guys closing down the mall. She might double back."

"Watch yourself, pal."

More cautious this time, Snow checked the tunnel. His target was on the move again and he caught a glimpse of her as she reached the end of the tunnel and headed into the food court. He took off in pursuit.

By the time he reached the food court, he had lost sight of her. "Dammit!" he cursed, which drew a few stares, although probably not as many as the gun in his hand. He tucked the weapon in the waistband of his pants and covered it with his shirttail. The last thing he needed was to start a panic or a riot. She was going to be hard enough to find without the extra pandemonium his charging in waving a gun would cause.

"If I were an assassin, where would I go?" he muttered as he cut through a line at the Chinese buffet.

He slowed, no longer running, scanning the cavernous space while trying to catch his breath. His body ached, the pain in his chest like someone had laid a concrete block on it. Stuffed in a nearby garbage can was a familiar piece of clothing, a housekeeping smock the sniper had been wearing. Now he had no idea what she was wearing. He wasn't even sure of her hair color. If she was good at her job, which seemed to be the case, then she was probably wearing a wig earlier. He checked the trashcan. No wig was inside, but that didn't mean anything. If it had been him, he would have dumped the wig in a different trashcan.

She was quick and had a head start, but she also wasn't stupid. He didn't see any one running and no shouts or screams of a person crashing through the throng of tables were heard. Why should she run? Once she ditched the disguise, all she had to do was blend into the crowd like the rest of the nine to five crowd gathered there for a quick bite to eat before heading back their offices.

There were too many exits to cover.

She was gone.

###

Snow was about to give up and head back to check on his family when he caught sight of her.

The shooter looked completely different, but he knew it was his target. She stared daggers at him across the crowded room. He started toward her, weaving around those milling about the food court. Surprisingly, she held her ground, not running. That unnerved him.

"What the hell are you up to?" he muttered as he navigated the crowd.

When he was within earshot she held a hand to keep him at bay. "That's close enough," she said.

"That's not how this works, lady." Snow was happy to slow down, not that he would let her know that. He tried to keep his breathing steady, but it was clear that the exertion was taking a toll on him. Once he would have been able to chase her down without so much as breathing hard, but now his breathing was labored and sweat ran down his face. Yet another thing to thank Miguel Ortega for when he found him.

But that was a problem for another day.

She flashed a pearly white smile his way. In any other situation, he would have found her attractive. Here, he found her scary. "You care to gamble if I had time to plant a surprise to cover my tracks?" she said, holding up her hand to show him the small trigger device clutched there.

"You've obviously got something you'd like to get off your chest," Snow said. He motioned toward an empty table nearby. "By all means, let's hear it. You have my undivided attention."

A smile crossed her lips. "Nice try. You sit. I'll stand."

Slowly, he complied and sat at the table. She stood nearby, just out of reach. This was clearly not her first assignment. If she was nervous or worried about being captured, she showed no outward sign.

"I know you're got people locking down the building," she said. "Something tells me you and I wouldn't be able to sit down and have a private conversation before your friends get here, would we Agent…"

Now it was his turn to smile. If she was fishing for his name then she was nervous. "I guess I didn't turn up in your homework, huh?"

"Not exactly. I do my research. The FBI lacks… shall we say, innovative thinking. Everything is either black or white with them. They like their plans and procedures and they rarely deviate from them. I've studied every man and woman on the detail, but not you. You weren't on it so I don't know who you are. And I'm pretty sure I'd remember you."

"It's the hair, isn't it?" he said, running a hand through his wild locks without taking his eyes off of her. "I never could get this stuff to stay in place. School pictures were a bitch when I was a kid."

"I don't like surprises."

"Really? I love 'em myself," Snow said playfully. In spite of the seriousness of the situation, he was enjoying himself. Until that moment, he hadn't realized how much he enjoyed being undercover. There was a freedom to playing a role that set him at ease. That revelation surprised him. He liked being in the thick of things.

"Who are you?" she asked again.

"Would you believe I'm just a guy in the wrong place at the wrong time?"

"No."

He laughed. "I didn't think so. Unfortunate, because it's true."

"Your name, agent?" She shook the detonator in her hand. The threat was clear. "Now, please."

He held up his hands in surrender. "Fine. My name's Abraham Snow and I don't work for the FBI. I really am only here to visit someone. Wrong place. Wrong time. You know how it goes."

"Right. And you just happened to be in the right place to interrupt my work?"

"Just lucky, I guess," Snow said.

"You're just dying to quote Die Hard, aren't you?" she said.

He crooked his head to the side. "Maybe a little."

"Don't let me stand in your way."

"You killed a man and tried to kill more," Snow said, the playfulness gone from his voice. "I couldn't stand there and watch."

"So you just decided to get involved in a shootout and then chase down the person doing the shooting? I find that hard to believe, Mr. Snow. No one is that stupid."

He chuckled. "I've been told I have impulse control issues."

"A little advice, Mr. Snow?"

Snow shrugged.

"Owen Salizar is not worth throwing your life away over. Trust me."

"Oh, you don't have to convince me," Snow said. "Salizar is as dirty as they come. I wouldn't be surprised that the rumors about him are true."

"And yet you risked your life to save his."

"I mentioned the impulse control issues, right?"

"Putting yourself in front of a man like Salizar will end badly for you, Mr. Snow. There's a very expensive bullet with his name on it. If not me, someone will collect. You don't want to be there when that happens."

"Considering you were the one shooting at me, I don't know what to say." He seemed to think it over. "Thank you… for, uh… missing?"

"I don't like killing people without being paid."

"Lucky for me," Snow said.

"I'm not so sure anyone would be willing to pay to much for you."

"You'd be surprised."

"Really?" Her eyes brightened. "I might just have to look you up," she said.

Snow smiled and changed the subject. "As much as I love sitting here having this lovely little chat, I have a dinner date to get to. So, I guess we should skip to the part where you tell me what you want so we can get out of here without getting any of these nice people hurt."

5.

Tom McClellan took the stairs in a run.

Once his men had the building surrounded, he headed up the steep concrete stairwell that opened up into the mall's food court. The first thing he noticed was that everything looks pretty much normal, which was not what he had been expecting. At the least, he expected screaming and running.

"All sites, report in," he said into his hand mic. A flurry of short checks piped in his ear. "Keep one agent on each door," he said once all of his men had checked in. "Everyone else, move in. Holster your weapons until we have eyes on the shooter or Abraham Snow."

"Who, sir?" a voice called back.

Following his own order, McClellan holstered his weapon and stepped into the bustling food court. "Snow is a private contractor. Jeans and a black suit jacket. Look for a guy with black hair that looks like it hasn't been combed in a week or two. He was last seen in pursuit of the shooter so remember, he's on our sides, boys and girls."

"This is Ellison. I've got a visual," a voice said in his ear.

"Where?"

"East end of the food court… near the sandwich shop."

"What's he doing?" Mac asked, stepping up his pace.

"He's talking with someone," Ellison reported. "Female. Could be our shooter. Moving in for a closer look."

"Be careful," Mac warned. "If it is the shooter, she's armed and dangerous."

"Understood."

Agent MacClellan could see the sign above the sandwich shop. He was close. With a hand on his service weapon, he eased through the crowd until he caught sight of his men. When they saw him they pointed and he followed to see his friend sitting at a table talking to a woman. He assumed she was the shooter, although he hadn't gotten as good a look at her as Snow had so he couldn't be sure.

He held up a hand signaling his men to hold position. If the woman hadn't seen them yet, she would soon enough. The last thing he needed was a shootout with so many innocent bystanders around. Her back was to him though, so the agent eased forward, slowly, carefully.

Snow saw him and waved him off with a simple hand signal.

Agent MacClellan didn't know what was going on, but he trusted his friend. He would give him a few minutes before he had to move in.

He thumbed his mic. "All agents… hold position. Move in on my signal only."

"Your move, Snowman," he whispered.

###

Snow saw Mac heading his way.

He made a soft gesture convinced his friend to keep his distance for the moment. When he saw his friend on the mic, he hoped he was telling his men to do the same. He wasn't sure what would happen if the shooter saw federal agents approaching with guns drawn. He suspected it would not end well for any of them, especially if her threat of planting an explosive device was genuine. He wouldn't afford to take the chance that it was a bluff.

"Looks like your friends are here," she said, shattering his hopes.

"Let's don't do anything rash," Snow said. "There's still a way out of this."

"Of course there is," she said. "You and I are going to walk out the door behind me and your friends are going to back off."

"You know they aren't going to let that happen."

"Yes they will. Unless they want to try and separate your remains from the mess it'll make if I let go of this." She shook her fist for emphasis. "Get up."

Snow stood slowly. He held out a hand, palm out in that *just give me a minute* way to signal Mac to stand down. "If I do this, you promise me nothing bad will happen to these people?"

"You have my word as a professional."

"Well, then, one professional to another, I'm going to hold you to that."

"Whatever," she said, grabbing him by the collar and pulling him close. "Come on."

The moment she grabbed him, the FBI moved in. "Federal Agents!" Mac shouted as he pulled his gun and aimed it at the shooter. "You need to stand down and let him go!"

"Tell them to back off or this place goes boom," the shooter whispered in her captive's ear.

"Mac," Snow said. "Give us some distance, okay?"

"What's going on, buddy?"

"She's not playing around," Snow said. "Look at her hand."

She held up the trigger so everyone could see it.

"We're heading outside. Once we're out she's going to give it to me and this will all be over."

"We can't let her go, Ham. You know that."

"I know what will happen if we don't," Snow said.

###

Agent MacClellan stood in the center of the food court.

"Okay. You win, pal. I'm standing down," he said, holstering his gun as a show of good faith.

The shooter moved faster, dragging Snow along with her as a human shield. They were only a few steps from the exit when Mac opened the channel on his radio mic. "All units, clear the food court and mall immediately. We have the threat of a possible explosive device on the premises. Get all of these people out of here and get the bomb squad in here a.s.a.p."

"Copy that."

"Let's keep the delegates inside the conference area," he added.

He turned back in time to see his friend pass through the doors out into the street. As soon as they were out of sight he ran to catch up, leaving his men to clear the area. Mac was almost to the door when he heard the first sounds of panic behind him. It was inevitable. Even without using the word "bomb," it was hard to clear an area the size of the food court without scaring someone.

Mac pulled his gun once they were out of sight and ran to catch up. He stopped at the door. Beyond the frosted glass he could just barely make them out as they moved down the one way street against the flow of traffic.

"This is MacClellan. Do we have eyes on the target?"

"Copy that," a voice called. "No good shot. The hostage is in the way."

"If you get a shot, you take it," Mac ordered. His glimpse of the device in the sniper's hand was brief, but he suspected the signal range was short at best.

"What about the hostage?"

"If there's no other way, take the shot."

"Sir?"

"You heard me."

"Yes, sir."

"I'm sorry, buddy," Mac whispered.

###

Snow held position at the curb as a car squealed to a stop.

"I think this is where you and I part company, Mr. Snow," the sniper said. "You'll forgive me if I say I hope to never see you again."

"Oh, I think it's a safe bet we'll see one another again," Snow said plainly. "You can pretty much count on it. You see, I'm a professional too and I keep my promises just like you do."

"That would be a pity. You get in my way again and, contract or no, I won't be so charitable." She opened the car door and moved him closer to block her from the obvious sharpshooter nests. She was good.

"The detonator," Snow reminded her once she was inside the car.

She smiled and held up the device between two fingers. "You mean this?"

"We had a deal. I held up my end," he reminded her. "Hand it over."

With a flick of the wrist she sent the small plastic piece flying as the driver of the car zoomed away. He reached for it and missed. She had purposefully thrown it where he wouldn't be able to catch it. The tiny plastic rectangle snapped into two pieces on impact with the concrete sidewalk.

Snow grabbed it, hoping it wouldn't go off--

--and let out a sigh of relief to see that it was empty.

Snow looked up in time to see the getaway car take a hard left at the next light just as Mac and a couple of his agents ran over to him. There was only one place that road went. Freeing the gun from his waistband, he started running down the one way street that paralleled the one used by the sniper's getaway vehicle.

"She's headed for the interstate!" Snow shouted to Mac as he crossed the street to the glare of honking horns.

Mac pointed to one of his men. "Call it in. Lock that car down. I want to know where it's going! Go! Now!" Then he took off running after his friend.

Growing up in Atlanta, Snow once knew the streets like the back of his hand. Unfortunately for him, there had been a lot of changes while he was away. Thankfully, he had been reminded the day before that the one thing that remained constant in this city was Interstate 75/85, which merged together in Atlanta, but then split off into their own separate directions on both the north and south sides of the city. The route the sniper's car took would put her on the bridge to the northbound lane. It was a one-way street that went nowhere else.

If he was fast enough, he could get ahead of her by following the road that ran alongside the mall. For once, Atlanta's one-way streets worked in his favor.

He was almost completely out of breath when he reached the end of the street, trying to ignore the pain in his chest. He hoped the fence and slid down the grassy embankment to the bridge just in time to see the car he was chasing turn onto the ramp.

He was too late.

If there was one constant to Atlanta traffic, it was how bad it was. Snow cursed. It was just his luck that today was not one of those moments. Of course, he realized that Mac's guys had probably stopped traffic, which worked against him. It did, however, leave him a clear shot.

Snow opened up with the gun and fired the remaining shots at the sniper's car. The rear window shattered, as did the taillight. He'd scored several direct hits, but it wasn't enough to do more than superficial damage to the car.

"You okay?" Mac asked as he came to a rest next to him.

"I'll live." He clutched at his chest. "I think."

"Did you get her, at least?"

"No," he said, panting around gulps of air. "Ran out of bullets."

"I've put out an APB. We'll get her."

"I hope so." Snow eased down on the grass, his chest aching from the exertion.

Mac sat down next to him. "The bomb?"

Snow held up the plastic pieces and dropped them into Mac's hand. "It's a dummy," he said. "Just like me."

Mac blew out a breath. "That's a relief, at least." He shook his head and laughed. "The fake bomb part. Not you being a dummy."

"Yeah. Well, she suckered me good."

"You weren't the only one, pal," Mac said. "My SAC is not going to be too happy with me."

"I'll back you up with the special agent in charge," Snow said.

"I appreciate that," Mac said. "Not sure that'll do much good. You aren't Bureau."

Snow smiled. "No, but I do have a connection or two."

Mac laughed. "Sit tight. I'll call us a ride. I'm not anxious to hike back up that hill."

"Neither am I," Snow said. "Neither am I."

6.

Matters hadn't quieted down at the hotel by the time they returned.

Agent MacClellan had used his fancy FBI badge to commandeer a taxi to get them back to the scene without waiting for someone official to come pick them up. Abraham Snow was happy to get out of the cab. He knew that Mac was worried about him. He couldn't blame him. Snow was worried too. The pain in his chest, brought on by the exertion, no doubt, had eased, but was not gone completely. Mac's insistence on calling a medic to check on him had grown tiresome before they had made it even halfway back to the hotel. Snow finally agreed to talk with one of the paramedics just to shut his friend up.

Mac badged them through the crowd and vouched for Snow. They were ushered through the barricade with no fuss. One of Mac's men came over to him as soon as he caught sight of them.

"What's going on here, Fitz?" Mac asked.

"We've got one DOA. Security for one of the delegates," Agent Fitzkirk said as he fell into step with Agent MacClellan.

"Salizar's man."

"Yes."

"Is he our only casualty?"

"Yes, sir. We've got other injuries, but nothing too serious. There's also--"

Mac stopped. "Great. Start pulling camera footage." He pointed to several of the cameras that were placed around the entire hotel. "This place is covered top to bottom, save for inside the rooms. We'll get a good timeline document of events."

"Already on it. There is something else," Fitz started.

Mac held up a finger, cutting him off. "Follow up on the APB. My guess is the shooter got away, but keep on state and local LEOs. We need to keep moving on this."

"You got it. There's one more thing."

"What is it, Fitz?"

Agent Fitzkirk pointed toward a small gathering of people near the bridge to the elevator. "Simonson's here and he's looking for you."

"That didn't take long," Mac said with a shake of his head. "You get on those cameras and APB. I'll brief Arthur."

"Who is Simonson?" Snow asked once they were on the move.

"Special Agent in Charge Arthur Simonson," Mac said. "He runs the local office. This probably won't be pleasant."

"There you are," Simonson said when he saw Mac approach. Snow immediately sized him up as a career bureaucrat. He knew the type and had crossed swords with more than one in his career. If he were to get hold of the man's file it would no doubt say that he was intelligent, probably top of his class at whatever Ivy League college his scholarship named after someone in his family tree paid for in full. Snow would be surprised if he was anything other than a lawyer. What he lacked in actual field work experience, he made up for in having memorized the FBI rule book backward and forward.

Snow immediately took a dislike to the man.

Special Agent in Charge Arthur Simonson spread his hands out to take in the damage all around him. "I'm guessing you've got a good explanation for this screw up, Agent MacClellan," he said. From his tone, he was looking for someone to place the blame on and Mac was the lucky winner.

Mac cleared his throat. "Well, I've got an explanation, but I wouldn't call it a good one."

"This is no time for jokes, agent. A man was killed right here."

"I am aware of that, sir," Mac said, going on the defensive. He pointed a few feet away. "I was standing right *there* when the bullets started flying."

"Watch your tone, agent," Simonson said through grit teeth.

"Yes, sir," Mac said, clearly biting back the words he really wanted to say. Snow had known Mac since they were kids. His mouth had gotten them into quite a bit of trouble back then, not to mention a few fights as well. Young Mac wouldn't have reined in the comment the way his mature older self did when confronted by his boss. Snow wasn't sure whether to be impressed or sad.

As Mac explained that he was pulling camera footage and had engaged local law enforcement to help in the search for the sniper, a voice whispered from beside Snow. "Are you okay?" He had seen his grandfather approaching, concern etched on his face.

"I'm fine."

"Now who's a bad liar," Archer said, keeping his voice low. "You look like you're ready to pass out."

"I'll be fine. How's everyone?"

"They're okay. Douglas is sticking close to Samantha. She's good."

"Thank God," Snow said.

Before Snow could say anything more, SAC Simonson noticed him. He pointed in Snow's direction. "And who are you?"

"Abraham Snow." He stuck out a hand, but the FBI agent did not shake it.

"Would you care to tell me what you're doing at my crime scene, Mr. Snow? I've been told that you're responsible for a lot of this mess."

"I just happened to be in the right place at the right time to help," Snow said.

"I see we've got another jokester here. Unless you want me to have you arrested, Mr. Snow, I suggest you stow your poor attempt at humor."

"Now you wait just a minute," Archer said, leaping to his grandson's defense. "I suggest you watch your tone, son. We're all on the same team here."

Simonson shook his head. "And you are?"

"Archer Snow. Snow Security. This man is my grandson."

"You must be so proud," Simonson muttered.

"You got a business card?" Snow asked his grandfather before the old man could say anything more.

"Sure." Biting back a retort, he handed one over from his shirt pocket.

Snow took out an ink pen and scribbled a name and number on the back of the card then stepped forward and offered it to Agent Simonson.

"What's this?"

"Call the number on the card and ask for General Henry Pinkwell," Snow said. "Ask him about me."

"Why would I do that?"

"Because I can help you. Plus, I have a feeling Homeland's going to show up and try to take this case away from you shortly. Hell, I'm surprised they aren't here yet. Having me here will help smooth that transition."

"I think I can handle Homeland Security, Mr. Snow."

"I highly doubt it," Snow said. "Call the number."

Simonson let out an exasperated breath then pulled out his phone and dialed.

"What the hell are you doing?" Mac asked.

"Trust me," Snow said.

"Yeah. Like that never gets me in trouble."

A few seconds later, Agent Simonson walked back over to them. There was a definite change in his demeanor. Instead of an angry man throwing his weight around, his expression now resembled that of a chastised child. He held out the phone for Snow.

"He would like to talk to you," Simonson said.

"Thank you." Snow took the phone. "Snow," he said plainly into the phone, trying hard not to smile in front of the humbled FBI SAC.

"Still making friends I see," General Pinkwell said. He had been one of Snow's superiors in his former profession.

"Yes, sir. You know me."

"This Simonson guy wants to string you up by your entrails, son. I've got him toeing the line for the moment, but you watch your step around him."

"Of course."

"I've set him straight. Had POTUS give you an endorsement since he's here in the office."

"I hope I didn't interrupt an important meeting, sir."

"Nonsense, son. You feel free to call anytime. I'm never too busy to talk to you," the general said. "I take it you saw Salizar."

"I did indeed."

"Tread carefully, Abraham. You know what's at stake here."

"Kid gloves, yes, sir. All I want to do is have a conversation. I need intel on the shooter and I can't think of a better source, can you?"

"Not at all. Just watch your six."

"Always," Snow said.

"You think he's involved?"

"Not sure, sir. He was clearly the target, but beyond that I'm uncertain."

"Our lives might have been a bit simpler if you hadn't intervened and let the shooter take out his sorry ass," the general reminded him.

"You know me, sir. Always leaping before I look."

"That's why you're one of the good guys," Pinkwell said. "It also makes you a giant pain in my ass."

"Well, you did tell me to get a hobby, sir."

The general laughed. "I guess I did at that."

"Sorry to interrupt your meeting. Please give Traveler my regards."

"I will. He asked me to send along his regards for your recovery as well."

"Tell him I appreciated the fruit basket."

"I will," Pinkwell said. "Agent Simonson shouldn't give you any more trouble, but if he does..."

"You'll be my first call," Snow said, smiling for the first time since he took the phone from the frustrated FBI agent, who was staring daggers at him. "I appreciate the help, General."

"Listen, I've got to get back in there. There's a package headed your way, something I think might help speed matters along. It should be there any minute now." The normally hard-bitten military commander's voice softened. "How are you feeling, Abraham?"

"Five by five, sir," Snow said, choosing his words carefully as all eyes were on him.

"After you finish up there, give me a call when you've got time to talk. I want to make sure you're okay."

"Thank you, sir. I appreciate that."

The general ended the call and Snow passed the phone back to Agent Simonson.

"You've got some influential friends, Mr. Snow," Simonson said. "I've been *asked* to turn over control of this investigation to you."

"I don't think that will be necessary, Agent Simonson," Snow said. "You should continue doing what you're doing. I'm only here to help." He looked toward the entrance and saw someone approach.

"And what will you be doing?" Mac asked.

He pointed to the approaching agent. "First off, I'm going to confer with Homeland Security. Then I'm going to have a little chat with Owen Salizar. I'd like Agent MacClellan to accompany me, if that's okay with you, Agent Simonson."

"Fine," Simonson said.

"Mr. Snow?" the new arrival asked.

"You got him."

"Agent Redding, Homeland Security." They shook hands. "General Pinkwell sends his regards. At this time, I'm turning operational control of the scene over to you."

"Thank you," Snow said. "But you don't need me telling you how to do your jobs. Do what you need to do and we'll debrief after I talk with the sniper's target. I will need a full dossier on Salizar, his security team, friends, family, the whole nine. I'll also need use of your van."

"You got it," Redding said. He handed over a small box. "I'll have everything ready for you in the van. Anything you need, call me. These are for you."

Snow took the box. "Thank you."

Without a word to any of the various law enforcement officers standing nearby, Agent Redding did an about face and headed back the way he'd come.

"What the hell just happened?" Agent Simonson said.

Snow pulled a gun, radio, and wallet from the box. He slipped the hard plastic holster onto his belt and slipped the two extra clips into his pocket. The radio went onto the opposite side. He flipped open the wallet. Inside was a freshly minted ID card identifying him as an agent of Homeland Security. A badge accompanied the card.

"I think you've just been promoted," Archer Snow said when he saw it.

"Looks like," Snow said. He turned to Mac. "What say you and I go talk to Salizar?"

"Sounds like a plan to me," Mac said.

7.

A quick elevator ride whisked Snow and Mac to the top floor of the hotel, the forty-third. The level contained only suites, including one currently occupied by Owen Salizar and his party.

"I don't think you won any points with Simonson," Mac warned once they were alone inside the elevator car.

"I can't tell you how not worried I am about that man," Snow said.

"Yeah, well, I love sticking it to the brass as much as the next guy," Mac said. "But I still have to work for this guy after all of this is wrapped up and you're out of the picture. The last thing I need is to be reassigned to some shithole gig because you pissed in his Cheerios."

"Don't worry. I won't let anything blow back on you," Snow assured him.

"If you say so."

Snow smiled. "Trust me."

"Okay," Mac said, rolling his eyes. "*Now* I'm worried."

Snow knocked on the door. He was about to repeat the gesture when the door opened and the angry security guard he had exchanged words with earlier filled the doorframe. It was the same guard who had refused to give him a weapon downstairs while they were taking fire.

"What do you want?" the guard said.

Snow flipped open the wallet to show the badge and ID. "Homeland Security. I need to talk to your boss."

The guard seemed to expand, leaning forward and flexing his position, a clear show of strength. Before he could say anything more, a voice called out from inside.

"It's okay, Erich," Owen Salizar called from inside. "Let them in."

Reluctantly, the guard stepped aside and ushered Snow and Mac inside. His frown deepened as they passed. Owen Salizar was sitting at a table at the far end of the room eating a bowl of soup. Next to him, on the end, sat his brother, Jamal. Snow offered the ID wallet again for the man to see, but he barely paid it any attention. Despite that, Mac also showed his credentials.

"I'm Agent Snow. Homeland Security. This is Agent MacClellan. He's with the FBI. We would like to ask you a few questions about the incident downstairs if you have a few minutes."

Salizar looked up from his soup.

"Incident?" Salizar's aide said. He stood from the chair he was sitting in nearby, defiant in the face of the agent's insult to his employer. "Is that what you are calling the attempted assassination of Mr. Salizar… an incident?"

"An unfortunate incident," Snow amended. "And you are…?" he prodded.

"Daniel Keihall. I'm Mr. Salizar's executive aide."

"Well, right now you can aide him by sitting down and staying out of the way while your boss and I chat."

Properly chastised, Keihall sat down, but only after a small nod from his boss gave him permission to do so.

"Once again I am astounded by the propensity for rudeness you Americans seem to have in abundance," Salizar said. "Daniel was merely inquiring, in his own way, if you have succeeded in catching the perpetrator who killed one of my men and tried to kill me and my brother."

"I'm afraid the shooter has temporarily eluded us," Snow said. "Don't worry. We'll catch her."

Salizar looked as though he had been slapped. "Her? You are certain it was a woman?"

"Very."

"How odd," Salizar said.

"Very odd," Jamal Salizar said.

"You don't think women are capable of handling a rifle?" Snow asked. He motioned toward the chair opposite Salizar. "Do you mind?"

Salizar shrugged them gave him a *go ahead and sit* gesture.

"Thank you." Snow sat and leaned back comfortably, lifting the front two legs of the wooden chair off the floor. He didn't say anything and for several long seconds, the room grew eerily silent, as if everyone in attendance was holding his breath. Snow smiled at the awkwardness that didn't seem to faze the man sitting across from him.

He decided to shift tactics. "So, who wants you dead, Owen?"

Salizar chuckled. "When you reach the level of success I've achieved, Agent Snow, there are many who would love to see me toppled from my position of authority, both in my own country as well as yours it would seem."

"And how many of those people do you think would want to kill you?"

"A great many I would assume."

"Maybe if you'd stop pissing people off," Snow said, egging him on.

"My brother is not--" Jamal Salizar started, but his brother held up a hand to silence him. Angry, but obedient, he complied and backed down.

"I do not know what you think you know about me, but I am the victim in this entire ordeal," Salizar said. "One of my men is dead. I have to explain to his family why their husband, their father, their brother, is not coming home from his visit to the United States of America. Your country is a dangerous place, Agent Snow."

"You'll get no argument from me there," Snow said. Seeing the momentary befuddlement on the man's face brought a smile to Snow's own. "What, did you think I was going to get into a cultural debate with you? I don't think so."

Snow leaned forward, returning the chair back to all fours. He rested his elbows on the table. "Our job is to keep you alive for the remainder of the deliberations, Mr. Salizar. I intend to see that happens. It's important."

"Thank you," Salizar said, although the words seemed to pain him.

"To that end, I need you to join me downstairs to go over some footage to see if you can identify anyone."

"I'm afraid I cannot allow that," the security man said. "This area is secure. I cannot say the same for the rest of this building."

"Is it not possible to bring the footage here?" Salizar said.

"I'm afraid not," Snow said. "We cannot remove it from our secure van downstairs."

"Then I'm afraid I cannot help you. I'm sorry."

Snow pursed his lips as he thought it over. "How about this?" he said with a snap of his fingers. He twirled a finger around. "Are any of these guys up to date on the people you come in contact with on a day to day basis? Perhaps one of your security detail… or maybe your brother or aide could take a look. That way you won't have to leave this secure location?"

Snow cast a look at Erich then to Daniel Keihall and back to Salizar.

"Well?"

Keihall leaned forward. "With your permission, sir, I can accompany the agent," he said. "If they have video of the attacker, I should be able to identify her if she is someone known to us."

"Are you certain, Daniel?" Salizar said. "You do not have to go."

The aide smiled nervously. "I am sure, sir. Your safety is of paramount importance. If I can help keep you secure, I am happy to take the risk."

"We'll take good care of your man," Snow said. "I give you my word."

Salizar nodded. "Very well."

Keihall walked over to stand next to Mac.

"His safety is in your hands, Agent Snow," Salizar said. "Keep him safe." He leaned forward. "And do try to stay on focus. I assume I'm understood?"

"I'm really not interested in anything except finding the shooter and putting an end to the danger to the deliberations. Whatever else you're into isn't my concern. I will keep your man safe and return him to you as soon as possible."

"Very well."

Snow nodded. He joined Mac and their guest. "After you, gentlemen," he said.

They left the suite in silence. As Snow pushed the elevator call button, he could see that Mac had questions, but he shook his head, letting his friend know that now was not the time to ask.

When the elevator arrived, they rode down to ground level in silence. It wasn't until they stepped inside the secure van parked in the luggage loading and unloading zone that any of them spoke.

"How you been, Brad?" Snow said, shaking the aide's hand with a smile.

###

"Brad?" Mac asked, clearly confused. "Who the hell's Brad?"

Snow smiled. "Tom MacClellan, FBI, allow me to introduce Brad Crosby. We… uh… worked for the same people. It's okay, Brad. Mac's one of the good guys."

"Nice to meet you, Mac," the man they had been introduced to as Daniel Keihall said, offering his hand.

Mac shook it, but still looked lost.

"Brad has been undercover with Salizar the past two years," Snow explained. "Remember, I told you earlier that he'd been on our radar for awhile now. Brad was tapped to go in and earn the man's trust. Looks like you've succeeded."

"It hasn't been easy," Agent Crosby said. "Salizar is a cautious man. I moved into the aide position about ten months ago when his previous aide fell ill. It's been tough getting close, but a month or so ago he stopped shooing me out of the office when one of his business partners comes in."

"Are you close to making your case?"

"Getting there. We've got some good intel. He's into some dirty shit, but we still can't prove his connection to terrorism."

"Looks like he's made himself at least one enemy," Mac said. "People don't generally contract a hit man to take you out if they like you."

"True enough," Snow said. "This shooter, she's a pro through and through. European based on her accent. She's worked to lose it, but it's there if you listen for it. You got any ideas who might have hired her, Brad?"

"None, but I'll see what I can dig up. Salizar has been looking to expand his company's global reach, including migrating into countries that don't generally like outsiders. He's bought a number of government officials in nearly every corner of the world."

"And now he's here," Snow said.

"These negotiations are the first step toward Salizar Biotechnix getting a toehold in the US," Crosby said. "So far it's legit, but until we can confirm whether he's working with terrorists or not, we've got to keep an eye on him. I hate to say it, Abe, but we would probably all be better off if you just let the shooter take him out."

"So I've been told," Snow said. "It's too late to second guess that now, though. It's done."

"There are rumors that Owen is looking to take the company legit, but he's facing stiff opposition from certain parties in his country, but also from his brother, who is definitely anti-American."

"It's all the rage these days, isn't it?" Snow quipped.

"It is. Jamal has been quite vocal with his comments. He's not a fan."

Crosby pointed toward the badge wallet in Snow's shirt pocket. "You really working with Homeland or you working this one for Mother?"

Snow shrugged. "I just happened to be here when the bullets started flying. The General pulled some strings to get me on the case in an official capacity, especially once I saw you were here. Why do you ask?"

"Even under as deep as I am, I hear things," Crosby said.

"What things?" Snow asked, suddenly on the defensive.

"I heard you took three to the chest, for starters. Not a lot of folks get to walk away from something like that. Then I see you here so soon after. Well, you can imagine my surprise."

Snow winced at the memory. "Well, truth be told, I only took one to the chest. One to the arm too. The third one missed. I think."

"You've always been a lucky S.O.B.," Crosby reminded him. "What are you doing here? You should be recuperating… either laying low on a beach somewhere with a beer in your hand and your toes in the sand or sitting around watching cure videos on-line. I saw this one last week with this juggling chicken. It was hilarious."

Snow laughed. "Believe it or not, that's how I ended up here. Came home to visit family and friends." He shrugged. "Go figure. I don't know how to juggle."

Crosby fished a thumb drive from his pocket. "Can you get this to Mother for me?"

"Anything good?" Snow asked, rolling it between his fingers.

"Not good enough to get me back home," Crosby said. "Not yet."

"I'll make sure he gets it."

"Thanks, brother. So, what do you need from me?"

Snow pushed a button on the computer and a still from the security camera opened. "Just what I said upstairs. You recognize her?"

Crosby leaned in close. "She doesn't look familiar, sorry. She a pro or one of the true believers?"

"True believers?" Mac asked.

"Salizar has been expanding his corporation for some time now," Crosby explained. "He's paid off the right people to take land from some of the locals who had the misfortune of owning land he wanted. It's like 'imminent domain' only at gunpoint."

Mac couldn't believe what he was hearing. "And he can get away with that?"

"Pretty much," Snow said.

"You'd be amazed what you can get when you pay off the right people," Crosby added. "As much as we hate it, it's not illegal back in his home country. Immoral, yes, but not illegal."

"That's not right."

"You'll get no argument from me, Agent McClellan," Crosby said. "Sorry I couldn't help with the ID, Abe."

"No worries, Brad," Snow said. "I assumed as much. Just wanted to make sure. Plus, it's damn good to see you man."

"You too. Can you do me a favor?"

"Anything."

"Check in on my family."

"I can do that," Snow said. "Where do they think you are?"

"They don't know. I told them it was classified. They understand."

The two men exchanged a manly hug. "Consider it done. You be careful, brother."

"You too." Crosby offered a hand to Mac. "Keep an eye on this guy, okay?"

"You got it. Watch your back, Agent Crosby."

"Thanks. I better get back before Salizar gets nervous and sends someone looking for me."

"I'll have Agent Redding escort you back upstairs," Snow said. "Stay frosty."

After Agent Crosby left the van, with Redding and two other agents in tow, Snow turned to Mac. "What are you thinking?"

"I haven't dealt with too many professional assassins, but something tells me that just because your new girlfriend missed doesn't mean she's going to pack it in and head home. My guess is she'll try to hit Salizar again."

"You're right," Snow said. "This isn't over."

8.

Abraham Snow was exhausted by the time he returned home.

After spending the rest of the afternoon with Homeland Security and the FBI, Snow finally left the scene around midnight and headed back to his grandfather's place. The clock was only minutes away from announcing one o'clock by the time he arrived. He wasn't surprised to see his grandfather waiting for him when he walked into the main house.

"Long day, huh?" Archer Snow said when his grandson walked into the kitchen.

Exhausted, Snow dropped into a chair and blew out a breath. "Long enough. This wasn't exactly the kind of R and R I had in mind when I came here."

"I'm sorry, kid," Archer said. "I just wanted to surprise you with Samantha being in town. You know I wouldn't have knowingly put any of you in harm's way."

"I know, Grandpa," Snow said. "It's not your fault. Sometimes shit just happens."

"Don't I know it. Why don't you get some sleep. We can talk again in the morning."

"Good idea," Snow said as he pushed himself away from the table. "You know what the worst part is?"

"What?"

"I missed dinner with you, Sam, and Doug," Snow said. "I was really looking forward to that."

"There's always tomorrow, kiddo. We're not going anywhere."

Snow waved his hand. "Yeah. Yeah. That's what they all say."

Before archer Snow could respond, his grandson was out the door. He watched as he slowly crossed the drive and climbed the steps to the loft apartment over the garage. He was breathing heavy by the time he reached the top step.

###

Abraham Snow's dreams were chaotic that night.

They were filled with violent images of running and fighting with gunshots and explosions galore. He was running down the tunnel that separated the hotel from the mall's food court, much as he had done earlier that day. This time though, the tunnel seemed to stretch on and on without end. He stopped, looked back the way he came. It too stretched off into infinity. He was trapped in a stark white tube, unable to make out anything beyond the curvature of the windows.

"Hello," he called and it echoed down the tube only to come back from the opposite direction moments later. *Am I running around in circles*? he wondered. *How did I get here*? *Am I trapped*?

He picked a direction and ran for all he was worth, his hearth thundering in his chest. The sound was so loud that it reminded him of the propellers on a twin engine cargo plane.

There! In the distance, he saw a speck, growing larger the closer he got to it. *Is that a door*? Hoping beyond hope that freedom was finally close at hand, Snow ran faster.

It wasn't a door.

Standing in the middle of the tube was a familiar figure. In contrast to the stark white of the tunnel, he was dressed all in back, with only white shirt cuss and a white tie punctuating the inky blackness. His suit all but shone against the brightness around them.

Snow, of course, recognized him immediately.

Ortega!

The dark one help up his hand and pointed a gun toward him, but Snow couldn't slow down, couldn't control his forward momentum. It was as if his legs had decided to work independently of the rest of his body.

The gun exploded in a flash of gold and orange, the discharge echoing along the tube like a signal to some far off place.

Suddenly, Snow was no longer running.

He lay on the stark white floor, a crimson stain flowing outward from beneath him. The blood pool continued to expand, flowing both directions within the tube until the floor was red in every direction. The blood flowed up the legs of the man who had freed it from the body of Abraham Snow. The black suit became red and it fit perfectly.

Ortega laughed.

Hie voice echoed in the tube.

Snow tried to move, but he was spent, done for. All around him, the white light was being replaced. He could see through the windows now. There was a jungle beyond, dark and foreboding. Something evil waited for him out there.

It would not wait for long.

The jungle pushed against the glass until cracks appeared. The glass shattered and the wilderness reclaimed the tunnel as its own until he was lying atop a grassy field, surrounded by nature at its finest.

Here, in this place, there was no need for snow.

Snow killed plants.

The jungle moved in for the kill.

Vines wrapped around his body, pulling him in varying directions.

The grip was so tight he feared his limbs might shatter under their pull.

He gasped for breath as the green leafy vines filled his mouth, nose, ears, and eyes. The jungle was swallowing him whole and there was nothing he could do about it.

Abraham Snow tried to scream--

--and woke up.

When he sat up in the bed, he was sweating. As in the dream, his heart was thundering in his chest. For the first time since he'd been shot, he felt like he was going to die.

Once he calmed himself, sleep eluded him. He checked the time on his phone. It had only been three hours since he fell into the bed. He was so tired that he dropped into bed fully clothed. Since getting back sleep did not look like it was going to happen, he got up. He booted up his laptop and checked his email. As part of his agreement with the FBI and Homeland, all of the reports that had been generated regarding the shooting had been forwarded to him. He read for the next hour, going through all of the official statements until his head hurt. Sadly, despite the massive amount of information at his fingertips, he was no closer to solving this mystery than he had before.

Snow understood that a good investigation takes time, but patience was not one of his virtues. He fired off a quick text message to his grandfather, letting him know where to find him when he awoke in the morning, changed clothes quickly, then hopped in his borrowed car for an early morning drive.

He'd always found comfort in the open road.

This morning, however, he felt anything but comfortable.

He hadn't planned to head back to the hotel, but that's where he ended up nonetheless. The crime scene barricades were gone and the hotel was once again open for business despite the heavy law enforcement presence. Sunrise was still a couple hours away. Snow showed his badge to the guard at the entrance and parked in the loading area near Homeland Security's surveillance van. He rapped his knuckles against the door and asked for a report when the night shift agent on duty answered. He wasn't surprised to hear that nothing new had popped up since he'd left the apartment.

He headed for the entrance, nodding to the agents standing post as he crossed into the air-conditioned lobby. The place was a hive of activity. Crime scene techs continued their work and several of the delegates on hand for the negotiations milled about in small groups, most of them holding a drink in their hands. The biggest change was that the debris had been cleaned up from the area and a new glass barrier had already replaced the shattered one that ran the length of the bridge where a man had died only hours earlier.

"Life goes on," Snow muttered.

"Indeed it does," a familiar voice said.

Snow did not turn to greet the man standing beside him. "Mr. Salizar."

"Is it not amazing how easily we humans are able to push past tragedy and continue on about our lives, Agent Snow? I mean, a man lost his life on this very spot yesterday and yet they…" He pointed toward the men and women sipping their drinks, laughing, and telling stories. "They move about as though nothing out of the ordinary has happened."

"As you said, it's human nature. We have this uncanny ability to move beyond tragedy and get on with our lives. It'' kind of heroic when you think about it."

"Have you had any luck tracking down the person who tried to kill me?" Salizar asked.

"Not yet. I have my people working on it."

"I'm sure you do."

Snow finally turned to look at the suspected terrorist. "So, knowing that the person who wants you dead is still at large, you thought it would be a good idea to take a little stroll? That doesn't seem very smart."

"I refuse to live my life in fear, Agent Snow. I will not become a prisoner in my room because a coward is unhappy with me."

"I cannot guarantee your safety down here."

"And I have not asked you to do so," Salizar said. "My security has been taken care of already, as you can see." He pointed to his guards nearby. "There is no need for you to worry about me."

"Oh, I can't help but worry about you, Salizar," Snow said. He grimaced the second the words passed his lips. He did not want to let this man push his buttons. "It's my job," he added.

"So you say. It is strange you phrased it like that."

"Oh? Why is that?"

"I am a man of resource. I had my people run a security check on you, Agent Snow."

"Very thorough of you. I take it you found something you'd care to discuss."

Salizar laughed. "Something like that, yes. It seems that there is no record of you working for Homeland Security prior to yesterday. How can that be?"

"Clerical error, maybe?" Snow smiled.

"Yes. I'm sure that must be it. How fortunate am I that your transfer happed just in time to thwart an attack on my life."

"You must have been born under a lucky star," Snow said.

"Perhaps you are right," Salizar said with a laugh. "Good night, Mr. Snow."

"Good night."

Snow watched as Salizar and his bodyguards loaded into an elevator, stopping the woman who had been waiting for a car to wait for the next car. He followed their progress until the glass enclosed elevator car entered the tube for the higher levels and was out of sight.

"Still making friends, I see," Brad Crosby said.

"Always," Snow said. He looked at his friend. "It's Daniel, right?"

"Yes. Daniel Keihall."

"Not too smart him coming out like this," Snow said.

"Don't think we didn't all tell him. He's a stubborn bastard, I'll give you that."

"We'll see how much that helps when someone starts shooting at him."

The second elevator that serviced the upper floors came into view. "That's my ride. I'm calling it a night. Have to be up in a few hours. The boss starts his meeting at ten."

"You'd better grab some shuteye then," Snow said. "I'll see you in the morning."

Snow watched his friend enter the next available elevator. Unlike Salizar, he motioned for the lady to go first. At least he was still a gentleman.

The car started upward when the woman turned to look out the glass windows. He caught only a glimpse of her profile, but it was enough. She had changed her clothes, her hair, and her skin tone, but he recognized her as the shooter he had faced off against earlier.

Snow pulled the radio from his belt and thumbed the switch even as he ran to catch the elevator. It was too late to recall it. Only two elevator cars ferried passengers to the uppermost levels of the hotel. The other banks only serviced specific blocks of floors, with the tenth floor being the only common floor above the lobby where each car could stop.

"This is Snow to all units. I have possible eyes on our target. Elevators. North bank. Ascending to the forty-third floor. Do we have anyone on forty-three?"

Nearby, an elevator door opened and he took it, pressing the button for the tenth floor. He knew it was an area with meeting rooms, open spaces for parties and presentations, which is why it was open to all elevator cars. As it started climbing, he wondered what his next move would be. He was in no shape to hoof it up three flights of stairs, much less trying to climb thirty-three of them. That would have been tough for him before getting shot. Now, it was impossible. His chest ached at the thought of it.

A flurry of chatter filled his ear as agents on duty reported in. As a precaution, Agents Snow, Simonson, and Redding had agreed to station a small contingent of agents in key areas of the hotel in the event of a second attempt on Salizar's life. Since the target was staying in a suite on the forty-third floor, they had focused on that are as their primary. However, the FBI was concerned that Salizar could have possibly been a target of convenience. Snow had disagreed, but on the off chance he was wrong, he agreed that all delegates should be offered an extra layer of protection so they stationed agents along most of the floors. They did not have enough personnel on hand to cover every floor.

"I've got eyes on the elevator," an agent said. "Two occupants. One male and one female."

"The male is not-- I repeat-- is not a suspect," Snow said into the radio.

He arrived at the tenth floor. It was empty, save for the cleaning staff straightening up after one of the many after hours parties hosted for the trade delegates.

"This is Parker on forty-three. Salizar has arrived at his room. We have secured the hallway and elevator bay."

"Target is to be considered armed and dangerous," Snow said. "Watch yourself, Agent Parker."

"Copy that."

Snow bit back a curse. He needed to get up there.

"Is something wrong, sir?" one of the cleaning staff asked. He was pushing a cart and collecting bags from the trash receptacles.

"How did you get that up here?" Snow asked. "Freight elevator?"

"Yes, sir. We use it so we don't interrupt the guests."

Snow flashed his badge. "Show me."

He followed the man to the far end of the hall. He pushed the call button and the doors opened.

"Does this go all the way to forty-three?" Snow asked.

"Yes, sir. Goes all the way from the top to the bottom."

"Bless you, sir." Snow pushed the button and the car started its upward climb. He wasn't going to beat her there, but at least he was still in the race.

"This is Snow. Be advised, I'm arriving at forty-three via the service elevator." He clipped the radio to his belt and pulled his gun before the door opened.

Snow stepped out slowly, leading with his service weapon. The coast was clear so he moved on. The freight elevator was at the far end of the hall, closed off by a door that led into the hallway to keep guests from being tempted to use the elevator instead of the guest cars. Snow pulled open the door and peered out carefully.

The hallway was empty.

"This is Snow. Anyone on forty-three? Please state your position."

No answer.

He moved forward.

"Somebody talk to me, dammit," Snow said.

Still nothing.

Now he was beginning to worry.

The lights were dimmer on the uppermost floors as opposed to the levels closer to the lobby. Moonlight through the skylight cast an eerie glow on everything, but Snow paid it no heed. The alcove where the elevators dropped off their passengers was empty. The cars remained in place and he pressed the button. The door to the first car opened. He flipped the switch that had the elevator in emergency shut down back to active and pressed the lobby button, sending it back down for his back up to use to join him. She had been smart to lock down the cars. It would take several minutes for back up to arrive now that they were moving again.

He repeated the process with the second car, sending it down as well.

He toggled the radio. "This is Snow. Elevators coming down."

"Copy that," Agent Redding's voice answered in his ear piece. "FBI has a helicopter inbound with a tact team on board. They'll be on the roof in ten minutes."

"Copy that," Snow said. "I'm moving to check Salizar's room."

"Wait for reinforcements," Redding called back.

"No time."

Leaving the alcove, Snow stepped back into the corridor. As with the floors below, one side had doors into the suites. The other had a four-foot high wall that overlooked the lower levels. It was a long way down. There was no sign of anyone in the hall so he double-timed it toward Salizar's suite.

The door was closed. He tried the handle.

Locked.

And he was short a key.

Of course.

Snow made a command decision. He braced himself and slammed his foot into the door. It took three kicks before the heavy doorframe cracked. Two more kicks were needed before he pushed the door open. If he was wrong, the hotel could bill him.

He wasn't wrong.

The shooter was waiting for him inside. She stood along the far wall, which sported floor to ceiling windows. The curtains were open and the lights of the city twinkled behind her, topped off by stars in a black, cloudless night. She blended into the darkness, a silhouette against the blackness. If not for the fact that she held Owen Salizar in front of her with an arm around his neck, she would have been all but invisible. Her hostage's white shirt stood out like a beacon in the gloom.

Snow did not see Agent Crosby, Salizar's guards, his brother, or the Homeland Security team that had been tasked with securing this floor anywhere nearby. He did see the lights of the FBI helicopter heading toward them through the window.

"We meet again, Mr. Snow," the assassin said.

"I told you we would," Snow countered, buying time for back up to arrive. "By the way, I never caught your name," he said.

"Do you really think I'm going to make it that easy for you?"

"Hey, I told you mine…"

"Rather foolish of you, wasn't it?" she said.

"Not at all. I'm rather a fun guy when you get to know me."

"I did enjoy our first date," she said.

Salizar grunted something that Snow couldn't understand with her arm digging into his neck.

"Shut up," she told her hostage.

"You heard the lady," Snow told Salizar. When the hostage fell silent, he turned his full attention back to her. "It's not too late to end this."

"My employer wouldn't see it that way. This only ends with either me or this piece of garbage dead."

"There might be a third option," Snow said.

"Do tell."

"We can arrest him."

The shooter laughed. "If you had any evidence against him you would have done that already," she said. "As he's strutting around right in front of you, it's a good bet you've got nothing tying him to anything."

"But I'm guessing you do. Come on, we can help each other and all walk out of here alive," Snow said. "Nobody has to die here."

"Would you please just shoot this bitch?" Salizar croaked.

"Shut up!" Snow said even as the shooter tightened her grip on the man's throat.

"You make a tempting offer, but like I told you, I'm a professional," she said. "I've got a reputation to uphold. Letting people live after I've taken the contract isn't good business."

"I can protect you."

"No. You can't."

The gun bucked slightly as she pulled the trigger.

Snow threw himself to the side and her shot missed, but only by centimeters, smacking the wall behind where his face had been seconds earlier.

Salizar struggled against her grip, breaking free with a shove.

The shooter regained her composure quickly, turned, and fired at the fleeing figure. Salizar screamed in pain and crashed into the couch, falling over the back before rolling to the floor.

Before the shooter could take a second shot, Snow popped back up and fired twice. The first shot caught her shoulder. The second hit her center mass, slamming her backward into the thick glass of the window, cracking it slightly on impact.

She dropped to the carpet, leaving a trail of blood behind her on the glass.

Snow ran to her side, kicked away the gun, then knelt next to her to check for a pulse. It was weak. She was unconscious, but alive, although barely. She tried to speak, but the words came out as barely a whisper. He toggled the radio mic.

"All clear," he called into the radio. "We're going to need medics up here a.s.a.p. I've got two people down."

"Copy that, Snowman," Mac's voice filtered back to him. "FBI chopper touching down on the roof now. We'll be on site in one minute."

"Roger that, Mac."

Snow got up and fumbled for a switch on a nearby lamp. The room came into full view as the light replaced the darkness.

"Salizar? You alive?"

"Yes," a pained voice called out.

Snow walked over to the couch. The businessman lay bleeding on the floor from a wound in his shoulder. Based on the blood leaking into the carpet, it looked bad, but it wasn't a fatal wound.

"It hurt?"

"Yes."

"Good. Where are your guards, your aide?"

Salizar tried to point toward the bedroom, winced, and tried to bite back a scream of pain.

Snow went to the door. A chair had been wedged under the handle. It made for crude, but effective doorstop. "Is everyone okay in there?" he called.

"Yes. We're okay."

He recognized Brad Crosby's voice.

"Stand back," Snow said then opened the door. "If you've got a weapon, I suggest you leave it in there. You come out armed and you're going out of here in cuffs."

Erich, the angry bodyguard was the first one through the door. He ran to his employer's side to tend to his wound. He sported a bruise to the side of his head that was beginning to purple. Snow would have been surprised if the man had gone down without a fight.

Crosby was the third one out the door. He was uninjured. Snow had been worried that the shooter would have taken him out after using him to gain entry into the suite. He was happy to see she hadn't.

"Medics are inbound," Snow informed him. ETA is…"

"FBI! Agent Snow?" The call came from outside the door.

"All clear," Snow said.

The lead agent stepped in, fitted head to toe in body armor, weapon at the ready. "We're secure," he said once he was inside. Lock down the corridor."

Snow pointed to the bleeding Salizar and shooter.

"We've got two bodies down, both require medical attention." He listened as the response came through his ear piece. He looked at Snow. "Medics are thirty seconds out."

"Thank you," Snow said.

"My pleasure, Agent Snow. Agent MacClellan would like a word with you outside, please."

"Understood. It's all yours."

Snow stepped out into the hallway and let out a breath.

"You okay?" Mac asked once they were alone.

"Peachy."

"Was it our friend from earlier?"

"Yeah," Snow said. "It's her."

"I guess she didn't take your warning to heart, huh?"

"I guess not." He looked back toward the suite.

"You kill her?"

"No," snow said, shaking his head. "Came close though. Any idea who she was or who hired her yet?"

Mac shook his head. "Not yet. She's good so we may never know. At least now we can get her prints. That will help."

"It's a good bet that whoever hired her will just hire someone else," Snow noted.

"Yeah, but he's on a plane back home today," Mac said. "That's someone else's problem."

"We've still got a man inside," Snow whispered. "I don't like the idea of leaving my friend in the line of fire."

"Maybe your friend, the general can help."

Snow chuckled. "Maybe. I'll brief him shortly."

"Good thing you were here," Mac said. "Why were you here this time of the morning?"

"Couldn't sleep."

"So, is this what life was like for you undercover the last few years?" Mac asked.

Snow smiled. "Nah. It was never this quiet."

9.

Abraham Snow shook hands with Agents Redding and Simonson.

After the debriefing, he excused himself from the investigation, returning full authority to both men. He also returned the badge, gun, and radio back to Homeland Security.

"So, this mean you're a civilian again?" Archer Snow asked as they watched the proceedings wrap up. There was still a lot of work to do, reports to file, and other odds and ends. He would probably have to go by the local office to sign a few things later in the week.

He laughed. "Maybe so."

"I have to admit, I'm proud of ya, kiddo. You handled yourself quite well."

"Thanks, grandpa."

"Kind of reminded me of me when I was your age."

"You can remember back that far?" Snow joked.

"Keep it up, smartass," Archer crowed. "I know where you live."

"Yeah. You do." Snow stretched. He was exhausted, but also invigorated. "I don't know about you, but I'm starving. Would you care to join me for lunch?"

"Sounds great. Just one condition," Archer said.

"There's always something with you."

"I just thought we might invite a few more folks."

Archer motioned toward the exhibition hall as the negotiations reached their end. The doors open and men and women exited en masse.

"It's over?"

"Yes," Archer said.

"Good." Snow smiled as he saw Doug and Samantha approach.

"How did it go?" Snow asked his sister.

"A tentative agreement was reached," she said. "We'll see what comes of it as we move forward. I've still got a lot of work ahead of me, but that can wait until tomorrow. Tonight, I'm thinking I need a drink. A very big one."

"First rounds on me," Snow said. "Doug, care to join us?"

"I'm still on the clock," Doug said as Dominic Snow walked over to them.

"Go ahead," he told his son. "You're on your sister's detail. Wherever she goes, you go."

"Thanks, Dad."

"You're welcome to join us," Snow said, offering an olive branch. For a moment, he thought his dad might accept.

"Maybe another time, Abraham," he said instead. "There's still a lot to do around here. Plus, I've got an after-action report to write. You kids go and have fun."

"We will," Archer said.

"Is it my imagination, or was he being nice?" Snow said.

"You behave," Sam said. "You two need to work out your issues. After all this time, you'd think you two would have grown out of it."

"I'll work on it," Snow said. "How's that?"

"It's a start."

###

The evening went better than expected.

It had been so long since Snow was able to sit back, relax, and enjoy a meal with family. He didn't have to be on constant guard, had no fear of letting a detail slip, and there were no lies to keep track of while spinning new ones. It was a refreshing change to be himself for awhile.

He didn't want the night to end, but like all good things, it did.

Snow hugged his sister tight. "It was so good to see you, Sammy," he said.

"Let's not wait so long to do it again," she replied.

"Promise."

"Dougie," Snow said, hugging his brother as well. "I'll see you soon."

Archer left with them, leaving Snow alone with his thoughts. Since he'd driven in alone, he would drive himself back the same way. The car was still parked out front of the hotel, where it had been since early that morning. He said a few good-byes to some of the agents milling about. He was about to pull out of the parking lot when he caught a glimpse of Owen Salizar getting into a limousine. His faithful bodyguard, Erich, joined him.

He didn't see Brad Crosby or any of the others with him so Snow assumed they were taking a different mode of transportation to the airport. As before, he couldn't shake the feeling that something was wrong.

"You still here?" Mac said, walking across the lot. "I thought you left hours ago?"

"Dinner with the family," Snow said. "It was nice."

"I bet. Can you believe this guy?" he said, indicating Salizar. "I'll be glad when he's on a plane and far away from here."

"Me too."

"Good riddance if you ask me," Mac said.

"You see Crosby anywhere?"

"Nope. The car was for Salizar and his bodyguard only. I guess his brother and the lackeys are on their own," Mac said as they watched the limo pull away.

"I guess so."

"Speak of the devil."

Snow turned back toward the entrance as Jamal Salizar walked out just in time to see his brother's limo pull out into traffic. The younger Salizar had hardly said more than two words in his presence that Snow began to wonder if he ever did anything but scowl.

Then Snow saw Jamal smile and all of the pieces fell into place.

"Son of a bitch."

"What?" Mac asked.

"It's not over."

"What?"

"We forgot about the second shooter."

"What second shooter?" Mac said.

"She wasn't alone, remember. There was someone driving the getaway car. I just realized what she said. *It's not over*. Her partner was her back up plan."

"Shit!"

"I think he hired them," Snow said, pointing at the younger Salizar.

"Another hunch?"

"Something like that."

"That's good enough for me." Mac toggled his radio. "This is MacClellan. I need Jamal Salizar held for questioning. Don't let him leave the hotel."

Snow started the engine. "Get in!"

Mac climbed in and Snow peeled out of the loading zone before he could buckle in. "You're not going to catch him," Mac said.

"Hang on!" Snow turned a hard left into oncoming traffic, tires squealing as they hit pavement.

"You do realize this is a one way street and you're going the wrong way, right?"

"You want to catch him, right?" Snow shouted.

"I'd like to be alive when we get there, Ham!"

Snow swerved around the oncoming cars, horn blaring at the oncoming crush of cars as they swerved to get out of his way. With Atlanta's one-way streets, the limo would have had to go a block in the opposite direction before heading back in the direction that would take it toward the airport. By taking the direct route he hoped to get ahead of the target.

He put the car into a hard turn, sliding into the road leading toward the interstate.

"There!" He could see the limo turning onto the ramp for the interstate.

"Doesn't look like anyone is following them," Mac said. "You think there's another sniper?"

"Maybe, but hitting the target through the limo's windows is tricky at best," Snow explained. "My guess is a bomb."

"You think Junior is going to bomb his older brother's car?"

Snow dodged a car, driving up on the curb and bouncing over it and onto the grass embankment next to the ramp. "Yes. With him out of the way, Jamal inherits the family business."

The car jumped back onto pavement and Snow poured on the speed. He could see Salizar's limo just ahead. He pulled up behind it, flashing his lights and blowing the horn to get their attention. When that didn't slow them down, he pulled alongside so Mac could flash his badge.

The driver wisely pulled the car to the side of the road.

Snow hit the brakes and his grandfather's car skidded to a stop in front of the limo. He and Mac were on the move as soon as he put it in park.

"Get out of there!" Mac shouted as he ran up to the limo. The driver rolled down his window. "Now! There's a bomb in the car!"

Snow ran to the back and yanked open the door.

"What is the meaning of this?" Salizar shouted.

"Time to go!" he told the two men inside.

"I have had about enough of you, little man," Erich snarled.

Snow pulled a gun from his waistband and pointed it at them. "Get out. Now."

They did as they were told and they moved quickly away from the limo.

Salizar was furious. "I will have your head on a silver platter for this, Agent Snow! How dare you pull a gun on me! How dare--"

The limo exploded.

###

"I think I've reached my fill of crime scenes," Abraham Snow joked.

He and Tom McClellan watched as the fire department extinguished the last of the burning wreckage of the limousine. All that remained was the charred husk that looked like the rotting carcass of a giant beast that had been picked clean by the carrion eaters.

"All done, Agent McClellan," the fire chief reported.

"Thanks, Chief. I'll have someone from the FBI lab pick it up for testing. I'll make sure you're forwarded a copy of the findings for your report."

"Appreciate that."

"You know, Snowman, my life used to be a lot less exciting before you came back to town," Mac said.

"Really?" Snow laughed. "You mean this isn't your usual night on the town?"

"Not even close. There were a lot fewer explosions for one thing."

"There was only one explosion," Snow countered.

"And two gun fights."

"Aw, that was kid's stuff. I could tell you stories that would curl your hair," Snow joked. "Come on. I'll give you a ride back to the hotel."

"I guess now you can get back to that resting thing you were talking about doing," Mac said once he was in the car and buckled in.

Snow started the car. "You mean this isn't restful?" he said before speeding off into the night.

10.

That night, Snow slept like a baby.

No nightmares woke him at all hours as it had the night before. He was troubled by the fact that they had not yet located the shooter's partner in crime or had even learned her name. Whoever she was, she was good. Her prints were not on file and neither the FBI, CIA, nor Homeland Security could place a name to the face, although each agency assured him they would keep trying.

After a long shower the next morning, he headed downstairs to share coffee and a donut with Big John before heading over to the main house to visit with his grandpa before he hit the road. He liked staying there, but he also wanted to get out and see how much his home state had changed while he was away. A drive tot he mountains seemed like a good way to start.

He froze when he stepped into the kitchen.

"What are you doing here?"

General Henry Pinkwell was sitting at his grandfather's kitchen table, the two men sharing old war stories over coffee.

"Is that any way to speak to a guest?" Archer Snow chastised him. "Where are your manners?"

"I'm sorry," Snow said. "I just didn't expect to see you here, sir."

"I told you we would talk soon. I figured, why wait? There's no time like the present, eh?"

"No, sir. Perhaps, you'd care to take a walk?"

"Sounds like a plan." Pinkwell stood. "Archer, it was damned good to see you again. It's been too long."

The two old soldiers shook hands.

"Be back in a bit," Snow said as he walked out the door. "I didn't realize you two knew one another," he said once he and the general were alone.

"Oh, yeah. Your grandfather and I go way back. A lot longer than either one of us cares to admit. He's a tough old bird. And a damn good man."

"You don't have to sell me, sir," snow said like a proud grandson.

"You handled yourself pretty well last night," Pinkwell said. "Agent Redding wrote a glowing evaluation of your performance, despite a propensity-- his word-- for leaping in head first."

"Yeah. That sounds like me."

"Did Jamal flip on Owen?"

"He did. Once we had him on the attempted murder of his brother, he started singing like there was no tomorrow. It's enough to arrest Salizar and hold him over."

"That's great. I guess that means Brad Crosby gets to come home?" Snow said.

"Soon. He's still undercover, working to find whatever he can while *cleaning up* Salizar's accounts. If all goes well, he'll be headed back to his family in a week or two."

"That's great."

"I thought you might appreciate that."

Snow's demeanor darkened. "Has there been any word on Miguel Ortega? Have you found him?"

"Not yet, but we haven't given up," Pinkwell said. "We'll find him."

"And when you do?"

"When I do you can expect a call from me. That's a promise."

"One I'll hold you to," Snow said.

"So, what's next for you, son?" the general said, changing the subject.

"I don't know," Snow said, kicking a pine comb. "I'm still nowhere near a hundred percent. A couple times these last two days I thought I was going to have a heart attack. I'm not so sure how good I'd be to you in the field, General."

"Nonsense. These past two days have told me all I need to know. Your job will be waiting for you as soon as you're ready for it."

"I appreciate that, sir. It might be awhile. I think I'd like to try being Abraham Snow for awhile. It's been a long time. I think it will be fun just being me for awhile."

"I understand. Doesn't mean I won't try to change your mind every once in awhile," General Pinkwell said playfully. "I wouldn't be doing my job if I let a valuable asset like you walk away, now would I?"

"I'd be worried if you didn't try, sir."

###

Archer and Abraham Snow watched as General Pinkwell's car disappeared into the distance.

"What did Hank want?" Archer asked.

"The same thing you do," Snow said.

"What's that?"

"He offered me a job."

Archer smiled. "I asked first."

"I gave him the same answer I gave you."

"If and when you're ready, all you have to do is say the word," Archer said.

"Funny, he said the same thing."

"He learned from the best, kiddo."

"Who?" Snow asked jokingly, although he knew the answer.

"Me."

The two men laughed as they headed back inside for another cup of coffee. Snow was ready to start his long overdue rest, but there was still one last piece of unfinished business he had to do.

There would be no true rest until Miguel Ortega was found.

Epilogue

Samson Brooks liked being his own boss.

As a freelance investigator (a term he hated, apt though it may be), he had the luxury of picking and choosing which clients he dealt with and which ones he turned away. He had moved to Hawaii after retiring from the service, mostly because he always wanted to be Magnum p.i., but also because he hated the cold.

And winters in Boston were very cold.

Brooks loved the water. There was something peaceful about hearing the waves crash against the shore. It was the closest he had ever come to knowing true peace. There was also something wildly intoxicating about watching beautiful women in tiny bathing suits run up and down the beach. For those reasons, and many more, he loved living on the island.

He sat on the terrace of his favorite watering hole, his bare feet dangling over the edge and digging in the soft sand. He lit up a cigar, one of his favorite guilty pleasures. It wasn't his only one by any stretch of the imagination, but it was his favorite. Drinking came in a close second, but he had promised a friend that he would keep that under control so these days he tried to stick to beer only.

Most days it worked.

Some, it did not.

"You got mail, Brooks," the bartender said, handing over a thick envelope. Phil was nice enough to let him use the bar's P.O. Box as a mailing address since he rarely stayed in any one place too long.

Brooks slipped the man a twenty, partly for the mail, and partly to put toward his tab. Once he was alone, he opened the envelope and read the file inside.

"Bad news?" Phil asked.

"Friend of mine's got a problem, Phil," Brooks said, his voice deep and intimidating. "I've been trying to help him out."

"What's he looking for, your friend?"

"Not a what," Brooks said. "A who?"

"Anybody we know?"

"Not this time."

"Too bad."

Brooks blew out a cloud of smoke. "Say, Phil, your buddy still making cargo runs to South America?"

"Yeah. Sometimes," Phil said.

"Do me a favor and call him. See if he's got room on his next run. The sooner the better."

"What's the cargo?"

"No cargo. Just me."

As Phil made the call, Samson Brooks looked at the photo of Miguel Ortega one more time. He flipped through the notes written by a friend of his in the South American intelligence community. He pulled a cell phone from the pocket of his Hawaiian shirt and dialed the number by heart. It was answered on the third ring.

"Snowman," he said. "I may have a lead for you, brother."

Keep reading. Abraham Snow returns in Snow Storm.

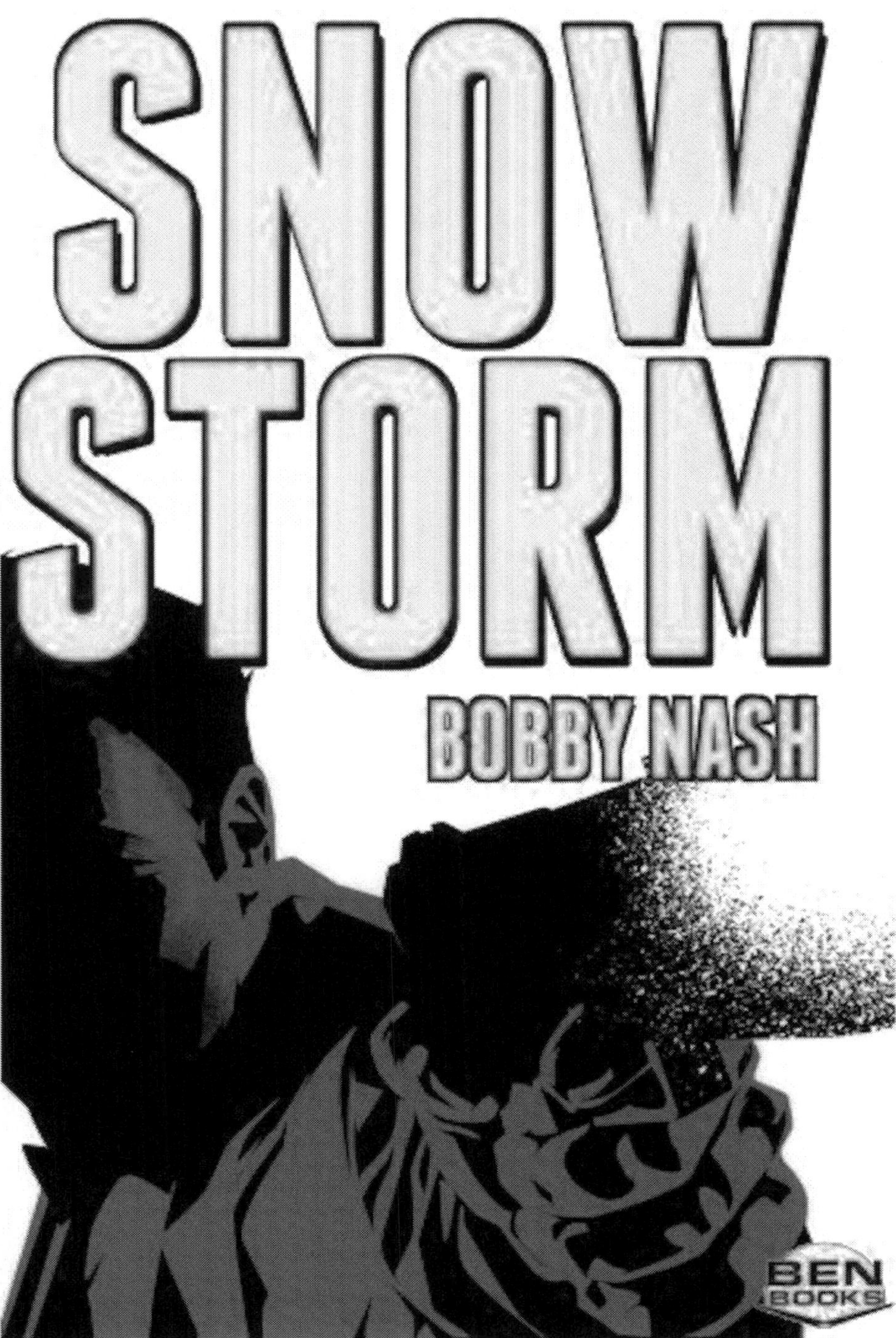
SNOW
STORM
BOBBY NASH
BEN
BOOKS

Getting in was easy.

Getting out was an entirely different matter.

This was, of course, by design. Much like those old cardboard roach motels he remembered as a kid-- the ones where roaches checked in, but they didn't check out-- the house looked ordinary and inviting on the outside. Snow crashed through the window as sounds of gunfire echoed behind him. He hit the ground hard, tucked into a roll, and came up already on the run.

Bullets smacked the ground nearby, but he knew better than to turn back to look. The only thing he could do was keep going and pray that the aim of the hired thugs chasing him did not miraculously improve before he made it to the road. He had considered firing back blind as he ran, but all that would amount to was a waste of bullets. He might need those before this was over.

A few seconds later the guns fell silent.

Snow breathed a sigh of relief, but didn't slow down. He wasn't out of the woods yet, both literally and figuratively.

The sound of flying bullets was soon replaced by a new, more primal sound.

Oh, great! Dogs!

His brain screamed a warning and suddenly he missed the men who were trying to shoot him. Not that he imagined they had gone far. No. He was quite certain they were on his trail and it was a damn good bet the dogs could run faster than those gun thugs.

Snow tore through the brush, felt the branches and brambles grab at him, scratching and clawing like a thing alive. There was no choice. He couldn't slow down now. If he slowed up, even just a little bit, the dogs would be on him and that would certainly ruin his day.

I need a favor, Snow thought, repeating back the words that had gotten him into this mess to begin with. When his brother, Douglas had asked him for a little "*off the books favor*" Snow should have suspected it would end up exactly like this, but when it came to his brother, he ignored little things like common sense and self-preservation instincts.

You should have known better, Snow, that inner voice reminded him now as he *huffed* and *puffed*, trying to catch his breath. A pinched pain jabbed at his chest where the scar from the bullet wound now lived.

The car was closer now, not far.

Even over the racket his chase through the woods was making, he could hear the engine idling. The car was a thing of beauty-- at least under the hood. The outside was as unremarkable as you could get, kind of an eyesore, really. Big John Salmon had been working on this beast off and on for a couple of weeks, starting with the engine and working his way out. Bodywork was next, but until he gave it the magic touch, the car was a bondo and primer colored mess. That made it the perfect vehicle for a covert operation.

Surprisingly, it hadn't taken all that much prodding to get Big John on board to help him. Big John was working hard to keep his life on the straight and narrow since returning to the world after a short stint behind bars. Snow hated putting his friend in a bad situation, but there was no one else he trusted to drive the getaway car. He had expected to have to wheel and deal, but his childhood friend had agreed as soon as he asked.

"Sounds like fun, the big man had said around a goofy looking grin.

Snow leapt from the short incline down to the gravel of the old country dirt road, slipping as he lost traction on the loose rock.

The car was ten feet away. He stumbled, regained his balance, and poured on the speed, kicking up small puffs of dust with each slap of sneaker on hard-packed red Georgia clay.

"Go! Go! Go!" he shouted before he was fully inside the car.

Big John didn't have to be told twice. Before Snow could close the door behind him, Big John had the old Chevy Camaro fishtailing down the dirt road, a plume of loose dirt filling the air behind it like a smokescreen. The engine roared beneath them, but even over the deep thrumming of the engine, Snow had no trouble hearing gunshots as the bad guys made it to the road.

There was no chance they would hit anything, not the way Big John was driving, but he ducked into the seat anyway.

"I think we're clear," Snow said.

He regretted it instantly when a bullet smacked into the doorframe, just inches away from where he sat.

"Or not," Big John deadpanned.

Snow spun around and could just make out the car in hot pursuit. From the passenger window, another gunshot rang out. Snow realized that the first hit was luck, but he also knew better than to press his own.

"They're firing blind," he said, to which Big John simply grunted.

"Can you lose them?"

Big John turned to look at his friend and smiled.

"Right," Snow said, eyes rolling as if to say, *Of course. What was I thinking?*

"Do your thing, brother," he said instead.

Snow wasn't a man unaccustomed to taking risks, clearly, but his friend and that smile behind the wheel were a lethal combination that made him just a little bit nervous. Big John Salmon was an artist behind the wheel. Even when they were kids, he managed moves with a big wheel, a bicycle, or a go-cart that Snow could scarcely fathom. Or, as his grandfather so succinctly put it, "*that boy can drive the shit out of anything.*"

He wasn't wrong. Snow, himself, had even joked that Big John could drive a brick if someone slapped some wheels on it. He could have gone pro and used his gifts on the racetrack, which, granted, he tried for a time, but eventually he took a wrong turn and ended up in the company of some very bad people. By that time, Snow was already gone, having run off to enlist right after high school-- the day after, to be exact. With Snow gone, Big John had found some new friends and they taught him a few new skills, most notably, how to steal cars. Apparently, he was as skilled at boosting them as he was at driving them.

It was the fencing of them where he got busted.

John served his time and when he got out, Snow's grandfather gave him a job and a purpose. He'd been on the straight and narrow ever since.

Until today.

Snow had hoped the job would be a simple snatch and grab. Doug's client, or was it his friend, he couldn't remember, had lost a very important package when his car was broken into at a hotel in Atlanta a few days earlier. The man had his reasons for not calling the cops. High on that list was an interest in keeping his job, which involved protecting company property. His losing the package outright would have been frowned upon by his employers, no doubt.

He had offered Doug a rather hefty finder's fee, which Doug then offered to split with Snow in exchange for his help. There were only two conditions: they had to get the package back fast and they had to keep it quiet. That meant off the books and off the radars of both Dominic and Archer Snow. Doug was adamant that neither their father nor grandfather find out what had happened.

Not the easiest of tasks, but Snow agreed.

"I should have stayed in bed," Snow muttered as Big John took the Camaro into a slide as they took a steep curve. Despite the pressure pushing him deep into the seat, the car was never out of Big John's control. *Like the man said, an artist behind the wheel.*

Crosscut Lane was a long, winding path through the middle of nowhere. Once upon a time Crosscut Lane had been used by lumber trucks to pick up cut timber for transport to the mill, but those days were long gone since the mill had burned to the ground decades earlier under suspicious circumstances. Nowadays, the road was mostly used by teenagers looking for an out of the way place to drink or get high because there were only a handful of houses accessible by the dirt and gravel road. Most of the houses in the area connected to another road that ran parallel to this one so the dirt road was pretty much abandoned, which also made it the perfect spot for racing thanks to its sharp turns and gravel that offered plenty of sliding challenges.

Good drivers could have a lot of fun taking the curves sideways out there-- as long as there wasn't another car coming the opposite direction. Those of lesser skill generally ended up either in a ditch or upside down in the Ocachobee River that ran parallel to the Crosscut Lane.

Snow had studied the atlas before heading out for the job, but Big John told him he had it covered. No surprise there. This was exactly the kind of road he would love to practice on and most likely knew it so well he could drive it blindfold. It was out of the way, quiet, secluded, and usually empty.

Of course, if there was one time that would not be the case…

Big John swerved hard when he saw the car coming right at them as he rounded a steep curve sideways, the wheels threatening to slip off the road as they kicked up massive plums of dirt. Without slowing, John shifted gears and took two wheels of the Camaro off the road onto the embankment, lifting the passenger's side into the air.

Snow grabbed hold of the door and held on tight, wishing he had buckled his seatbelt and thankful that it was embankment instead of a ditch. On this road, the odds were better than even, which you'd find around any given turn. Behind him, he heard the sound of blaring horns and wondered if the guys chasing them knew how to handle their ride the way Big John Salmon did. Somehow he doubted it, but there was no time to worry about that now. They weren't turning around and he could see the intersection ahead.

Snow braced himself.

The Camaro slide sideways from the dirt road onto asphalt, kicking and jerking as the tires fought for purchase on the two-lane blacktop. The rubber grabbed the asphalt like glue and jerked the car into position. Another shift of the gears and the car sped off without losing any time.

"Did we lose 'em?" Big John asked.

Snow turned to look.

"Coast is clear," he said and blew out a breath. "I just hope they didn't get a good look at your license plate number. Don't want them tracking you back to yours or my grandpa's place."

Without taking his eyes off the road, Big John reached up and pulled a thin sheet of aluminum from above his sun visor and handed it over to his passenger.

"You mean this license plate?" he said with a knowing smirk.

Snow barked a laugh. "When did you…?" he started.

"What?" Big John joked. "Did you think I sat in the car twiddling my thumbs the whole time you were inside playing secret agent man?"

"You are full of surprises, brother," Snow said.

"Aren't you glad I talked you into bringing me along?"

"Oh, yeah," Snow said. "I couldn't have done it without you, pal."

He dialed his cell. The person on the other side answered on the first ring. Snow dispensed with pleasantries and got straight to the point. “I got it,” he said instead.

After he ended the call, Big John gave him a questioning look. “Where to now?”

“Now,” Snow said, letting out a breath. “Now, I could use a drink.

SNOW STORM

1.

Angelo's Bar and Grill had become one of Snow's favorite hangouts since returning to Atlanta. The food was delicious and reasonably priced, two things which, in his experience, rarely went together, especially in a major metropolitan city. Angelo's had a wonderfully shaded outdoor patio that looked out on the always-bustling Peachtree Street, offering a halfway decent glimpse of the FOX Theatre marquee an easy walk away. About the only thing Snow could figure the place was missing was an actual Angelo. Neither the owner nor any of the employees were named Angelo, which he found rather amusing.

Whenever he came into the city to hang out with Mac or Doug, he made it a point to meet them at Angelo's. This trip was no different.

Snow and Big John had been the first to arrive and they started off with some appetizers and drinks. Big John ordered a soda while his friend ordered up a beer in a bottle. Big John was driving, but that wasn't his only reason for abstaining. He had given up the sauce in prison. It was a painful detox and not an experience he ever cared to repeat so drinking became one of those habits he chose not to pick back up once he was on the outside. Snow knew that he occasionally attended Alcoholics Anonymous meetings and had even offered to pass on the booze when they were out together, but Big John wouldn't hear of it. He explained that it didn't bother him and for Snow to enjoy a drink if he wanted one. Big John told him he would be his designated driver any time he needed one and that was the last time they talked about it.

Tom McClellan, who they had called "Mac" since they were kids growing up in the same neighborhood, joined them shortly after they sat down. Like Big John, Snow's friend Mac had changed a lot in the decade he was away. Surprisingly, he had gone to work for the FBI as a field agent, a revelation that had surprised Snow to no end when he first heard the news. Growing up, he would have put even money on Mac being the one with a criminal record instead of Big John. Funny how that worked out, huh? From everything he had heard since he got back, Mac was damned good at his job. He joined them on the patio and ordered a beer of his own while loosening his tie, a sure-fire signal that his work day was done.

Snow's older brother, Douglas was the last to arrive. He looked tired and Snow told him as much, but he assumed much of that was from stress. Douglas worked for their father at Snow Security Consulting, which was more stress than Snow cared to handle. Then again, Douglas and their father got a long a lot better than Dominic and Abraham Snow ever had. Sometimes Snow envied that relationship.

"Were you able to take care of that *little job* for me, baby brother?" Douglas asked after the server walked away with his order of a double bourbon.

"Little job?" Snow wanted to laugh. "You and I really need to talk about your definition of little."

"Come on, Abraham."

Snow pushed a padded envelope across the table to him. "It's here. No worries."

"Any trouble?"

"You mean besides the fresh bullet holes in John's car?" Snow deadpanned.

"Wait? What?" Mac said, suddenly interested in the conversation.

Snow waved it off. "Nothing you need to worry about, Mac. Just a minor domestic disturbance."

"Yeah, right," Mac said, taking a pull off his beer.

"Trust me," Snow said.

"Whatever you say, Hambone," Mac said.

"I assume you have something for me," Snow inquired.

Douglas smiled. "Of course." He tossed an envelope across the table to his brother. "My client thanks you."

Snow pulled out a crisp one hundred dollar bill then a second one. He tossed the remainder of the envelope across the table to Big John.

"What's this for?" the driver asked.

"Your cut."

"A bit uneven, don't you think?" he said as he counted the cash inside.

"Consider it bondo expenses," Snow said. "There's at least two bullet holes you're going to have to patch up."

"You sure?" John asked.

"Yep." Snow dropped the hundred on the table and sat the salt shaker on top of it. "These two should cover dinner and drinks. Speaking of which, where is the server? I'm starved. Let's order."

And order they did. For the next couple of hours, the guys laughed, talked, cheered, joked, told tall tales, and enjoyed themselves. It felt like something normal people would do, which is exactly what Snow had been hoping for. Spending the last ten years moving from one deep cover assignment to another had been an escape from the problems he had left behind him at home, but it meant being in control all the time. There were very few moments in the past decade where he could let his guard down and relax. One slip of the tongue, one wrong word and it was all over. Now that he was home he wanted to catch up on all of the normal things he had missed.

Things like just hanging out with the guys.

"Hey, did you guys see this?" Mac asked as he dropped a postcard onto the table.

Snow picked it up and glanced at the images. The postcard was for a local sci-fi and pop culture convention held in the area. Snow and his mother had attended a few times when he was a kid. "I didn't realize they still did these here?'

"Every Labor Day," Mac said. "Lots of traffic in the city that weekend. This place is a mad house."

"I can imagine."

"Did you see who'll be there?" Mac said, motioning with his finger for Snow to flip over the postcard.

Snow's face broke into a wide smile. "Well, I'll be," he said.

"Who is it?" Big John wanted to know.

He held up the card for all to see. "Miranda Shake."

"Isn't that the woman from that TV show?" Douglas asked. "Oh, what's it called?"

"Amazing Woman," the others said in unison.

"The New Adventures of Amazing Woman to be exact," Mac said.

"That's the chick you guys went to high school with, isn't it?" Douglas said. "I kind of remember her. Didn't she have purple hair for a while?"

"That's her. Although, back then her last name was Shaw, not Shake," Mac said. "She was pretty as a peach back then, but boy did she blossom after high school. She also had the biggest crush on your baby brother over there." Mac pointed at Snow, who ignored the jab.

"That was a long time ago," Snow said. "None of you seen her since then?"

"Nope. She didn't come home for any reunions, not that too many folks did," Mac said, casting a glance at Big John then to Snow.

"Some of us were otherwise engaged," Big John muttered.

"Yeah," Snow said with a shrug. "What he said."

Snow fell silent and stared at the promotional image of his friend on the card. He couldn't tell the guys, but he had run into Miranda a couple years earlier in a little bar in South America while he was undercover. It had been a chance encounter, but also a nice one. She had been having a rough time of it and they had been able to talk and catch up, though they had to do so on the sly since he was working undercover. They made it look like he picked her up at the bar and they went back to his hotel room. That had made him a big hit with the crew he was undercover with as they were all fans of her TV show.

Snow wondered how things were for Miranda now. He made a mental note to give her a call.

"I think we should go to this," Snow said to the group. "I think it would be nice to surprise her."

"If she even remembers us," Big John said. "High school was a long time ago, Ham and she rubs elbows with the rich and famous these days. I'm sure she forgot about us and high school a long time ago."

Before Snow could say anything else, a stranger stepped up next to the table and plucked the postcard from Snow's hand. He whistled as he looked at the photo.

"You know this girl?" the man asked.

"I do," Snow said as he turned to face the newcomer, a tall man easily six foot three with solid arms poking out the side of a sleeveless Hawaiian shirt. He was older, but had obviously been a weightlifter in his youth. His bald brown head sparkled in the sunlight.

It was a tense moment.

Until Snow laughed.

"Brooks!" Snow shouted and jumped to his feet. He and the stranger clasped hands and pulled into a big bear hug like the two old friends they were.

Brooks was older than Snow, easily by a decade or more and easily a few inches taller. The height difference would have been even more pronounced, Mac noted, if Snow's hair would comb flat like a normal person's hair instead of like a wild man.

"You do run in some interesting circles, brother," Brooks said once they parted. He pronounced it "bruddah" and dragged out the syllables.

"Don't I know it," Snow said. "Pull up a chair!"

As the man named Samson Brooks took space at the table, Snow made the introductions around the table.

"Brooks and I used to work together," Snow said. "He was my… handler, I guess is as good a term as any."

"Personally, I would have said *babysitter*, but handler works," Brooks joked.

Snow snerked.

"So, you really know this lady?" Brooks asked, tapping a finger on the postcard of Miranda Shake in her amazing Woman costume, effectively changing the subject.

"Absolutely," Snow said. "Our high school produced some of this country's greatest assets."

"Go, Panthers!" Mac added for emphasis.

They laughed.

"You look like a man who could use a drink," Snow told the newcomer.

"Now that sounds like a marvelous idea," Brooks agreed. "Set 'em up. Next round is on me."

Another couple of rounds and a few laughs later and Mac was the first to put the brakes on the festivities. "Well, as much fun as this has been, boys," he said, pushing away from the table. "I've still got to head back to the office for a bit before calling it a day."

"Look at you," Snow joked. "When do you become the respectable one?"

"Oh, that stinging Snow wit," Mac joked, a hand to his heart. "I'll see you guys later."

"Yeah, I should be taking off too," Douglas said, standing. "It was great meeting you, Mr. Brooks." Snow was actually surprised his brother had hung out as long as he had. He had never quite jelled with Snow's friends.

"Just Brooks, please," the older man said, his pearly white flashing as they shook hands. "It was a pleasure to meet all of you."

Mac nudged Big John's chair. "What about you? Don't you have something you should be doing?"

"Like what?" the driver asked, but he caught a look from Mac that spurred him into action. "Oh, right. That."

Mac shook his head.

"How are you getting back?" Big John asked Snow.

Snow looked to Brooks.

"OH, yeah. I'll get him there. No worries."

"We're out of here, then," Mac said, all smiles. "Give me a call later, Ham."

"You got it, Mac."

And then there were two.

"Nice group of friends you got there, Snowman."

"Yeah. They are." He leaned back. "So, you going to tell me?"

Brooks smiled. "Tell you what?"

"Don't play that with me, pal. You're obviously here to ask me something so you'd better just go ahead and ask."

"Sometimes you're too smart for your own good, kid. I've told you that before."

"You know how hardheaded I can be," Snow deadpanned. He tapped the side of his head and the wild mane of hair that sat atop it. "It takes a lot to get through the hair."

Brooks laughed. "I can't believe you haven't cut that rug off yet." He rubbed a callused hand across his freshly shaved dome.

"Something tells me I can't pull off that look like you do."

"Well, it helps to be this handsome."

"So, I've been told."

"How you feeling, brother?" Brooks asked, tapping a finger against his own chest.

Snow gave a halfhearted grin. "Getting by," he said, unconsciously running a hand across the wound beneath his shirt. It had hurt earlier, after his unexpected mad dash through the woods, but once he got his breathing back under control, the pain subsided.

"Most days it's fine," Snow said. "Sometimes I even forget that they had to pull two slugs out of me. Other days, it hurts like hell so I won't forget. You know how it goes."

He tried to wave it off, but his friend wouldn't let him off the hook so easily.

"It's not easy, brother," Brooks said. "And you know it. It's hard because it has to be, but you're hard too. Didn't I teach you that? You're stronger than the bullet."

"Whatever doesn't kill me, right?" Snow joked.

Brooks raised his beer bottle.

"To what makes us stronger."

Snow clinked his bottle against his friend's bottle.

"I'll drink to that."

2.

"How long you in town?"

Brooks was staying at a hotel a short walk from Angelo's so he and Snow paid the tab and walked the rest of the way. It was too nice of an evening to worry about a cab and the pleasant, calm weather, a rarity in Georgia, helped him ward off the effects of the several beers he had knocked back.

"Open ended," Brooks said. "I'm here on business, but I also picked up a case while I'm here on the Mainland so I'll dive back into that tomorrow."

"I didn't figure you'd ever want to get off that beach in Hawaii. What brings you stateside?"

"Daniella Cordoza."

And suddenly the world spun crazily around Abraham Snow. He reached out and found a wall for balance.

"You okay, brother?"

"Yeah. Just… just give me a second," he said as he tried to catch his breath, a finger unconsciously rubbing the bullet wound in his chest. After a moment, he regained his composure.

"Is she here?"

"Who? Cordoza? Nah."

"Level with me, Brooks," Snow said. All trace of joviality had been replaced by anger. "Is Daniella Cordoza here? In Georgia?"

"I swear, brother, she is not in this time zone as far as I know. I tracked her to South America based on the notes you sent me. I tracked her for a couple weeks, but I lost her trail. She's gone to ground. So has Ortega as far as I can tell. I guess the word got out that he shot a government contractor and figured laying low for awhile was his best bet."

"That doesn't sound like the Miguel Ortega I dealt with," Snow said. "Then again, it might not be. The name is just an alias after all."

"So, you said in your email. How's that work anyway?"

"It's a long story," Snow said.

"I got nothing but time."

On the move again, Snow relayed the details as he knew them.

Before his retirement a few months earlier, Snow was a deep cover operative. He had spent eighteen months worming his way into the organization of a criminal kingpin named Miguel Ortega. Ortega, for all intents and purposes was a ghost. No one could ever pin down any details about him. Even descriptions of the man were as varied as the stories surrounding him. Eventually, Snow figured out why. Miguel Ortega was not one man.

Miguel Ortega was an alias shared by several men.

And one of those men had shot him and left him for dead on a makeshift airfield in the middle of the jungle.

Daniella Cordoza was the liaison to Miguel Ortega. Snow thought he had played her perfectly, but in the months since being shot he was beginning to wonder if he had ever fooled her at all. Whatever else was going on with the investigation, which he had been told remained open and ongoing, Cordoza was the key to finding the man who shot him.

Snow had been ordered to let it go by his former employer, but he couldn't. He had been running his own investigation off the books for the past few months, although with limited success. He had even called in some old favors, including one from his former partner, Samson Brooks.

"And you're sure about the alias part?" Brooks said.

"That's about the only part I am sure of," Snow said. "Ortega is more than just one guy. It's brilliant if you think about it. No two people are likely to give the same description of the guy. There's no way to accurately pin him down as he could be in more than one corner of the world at the same time. Lots of room for reasonable doubt.

"Kinda smart," Brooks said.

"If anyone knows who the *they* are that makes up Ortega, it's Daniella Cordoza. She's the lynchpin that ties them all together."

"That's some heavy shit, man," Brooks said. "I knew this chick was bad news, but I didn't realize how much. You sure she's not an alias too?"

"Pretty sure. Cordoza's a snake. You corner her, don't take any chances."

"I've got some good people on her trail, brother," Brooks said. "Don't worry. We'll find her."

"And this case you picked up here?"

Brooks waved him off. "Nothing I can't handle. Doing some digging on a corporate gig. Mostly background. You know, cake walk stuff. I'm supposed to meet with the client in the morning."

"You need any help?" Snow asked. He already suspected the answer.

"I don't know, man. I can probably handle it, but you know how much I enjoy your company. Besides, you know the area better than I do."

"I'm going to regret this, aren't I?" Snow said.

"Probably."

"Sounds like fun."

###

Samson Brooks was staying at a rundown pay-by-the-week motel off Interstate 85 just outside of the city. It was close enough to walk, but far enough out that only those not worried about walking would be brave enough to try it.

Brooks definitely fit into that category.

The man was built like a linebacker, or at least someone who had been a linebacker when he was younger. As his forties moved closer to fifty, Brooks' frame was leaner, but still muscular. The bald head and goatee sealed the look and reminded Snow of a TV character from the 80's, especially if he put on sunglasses. Brooks' deep timbre had also been known to cause a man to back down, especially once they learned that Brooks' bite was just as loud as his bark.

The lobby reeked of a mix of industrial strength cleaner, urine, and something that could only have been tracked in on someone's shoe. Bake all of that under the brutal Georgia summer sun and it was potent. Oddly enough, it was not the worst place either man had spent time. Unlike the movies, going deep undercover in the real world more often than not meant dingy hotels, dives, and holes in the wall that required a mandatory tetanus shot afterward. Very rarely, did you end up in the lap of luxury, eating caviar in five-star hotels while beautiful women sunbathed topless nearby.

"You know, you don't have to live like this anymore, bubba," Snow joked as they climbed the concrete stairs to the second-floor landing. "An extra couple bucks could get you something that smells better."

"Says the man living rent free in his granddaddy's mansion."

"I do not live in my granddaddy's mansion," Snow said matter of fact. "I live in the guest house."

"Oh, well excuse me, Mr. Magnum," Brooks joked. "I stand corrected." He pointed to the room at the end of the walkway. "This is me."

They were a couple steps away when both men saw it.

They stopped, each one moving closer to the wall.

"I take it you didn't leave that open," Snow said, pointing to the door that stood open a crack.

"No, sir," Brooks said as he pulled a gun from the waistband of his pants where it had been hidden by his open Hawaiian shirt. Snow had noticed the gun earlier, but didn't give it a second thought. Brooks was not the kind of man who was never more than arm's reach of a weapon.

Snow had been that way himself not so long ago. He wasn't sure when exactly it changed, but the fact that he was not armed at that moment spoke volumes. "You got another one of those?" he asked.

"Not on me," Brooks said. He motioned for Snow to stay back as he maneuvered into position to take the door.

Snow just hoped they didn't spook the cleaning lady.

Since he wasn't armed and had his hands free, Snow pushed open the door. It creaked as it swung inward, bouncing against the concrete wall.

Brooks pushed through the doorway first, weapon at the ready. The room was small, consisting of little more than a main room with a bed, dresser, a table with two chairs, and a bathroom that was by the door and easily checked. A small kitchenette alcove did not provide enough cover for anyone to hide. The room was a shambles.

"Tidy," Snow noted.

"Not really." Brooks pointed toward the sliding door that led to the small balcony porch.

Snow nodded.

Before Snow had taken more than a couple of steps into the room, a man came through the open door behind him. He was quick, agile, and by the way he moved, definitely a trained professional.

Then again, so was Snow.

Snow swiveled and used the man's momentum against him, knocking him off balance into a toss that sent him soaring over the bed to the floor beyond where he crashed into the cheap pressboard nightstand that broke under his weight.

Brooks was almost to the balcony door when it happened. He turned at the sound, but then caught movement on the balcony from the corner of his eye.

He was already on the move when the glass shattered next to him.

The shooter was inside almost instantly.

Brooks was waiting for him with a solid left hook the face that dropped him like he had been hit by a prizefighter.

The shooter hit the floor hard, but there was no time to enjoy the moment.

The man Snow had flipped over the bed was on his feet and moving toward him, bobbing and weaving like an MMA fighter. Brooks was ready for him.

Snow wasn't sitting idly by watching as Brooks and the bad guy collided. He was busy with a third man that had followed his friend inside and the two men tussled in the kitchenette. Snow wasn't bad when it came to close quarters combat, but it wasn't his specialty. His opponent, on the other hand, was quite adept.

He hammered Snow's gut with blow after blow as he backed him up against the kitchen counter.

The newcomer had a weapon, but Snow relieved him of it quickly with a jab to the wrist followed by a painful, bone-wrenching twist. The gun clattered across the faded linoleum and he kicked it across the kitchenette and out of reach.

Snow pivoted as his body, which screamed in pain under each impact. He was still not fully recovered from being shot months earlier and had slowed a step. His doctor had warned him after another fight not too long ago that too much physical assertion before he had a chance to fully heal from being shot could trigger a heart attack… or worse. Snow wasn't really too keen on finding out what could possibly be worse than a massive coronary. Even as that thought flashed through his mind, he managed to get his arms around the assailant's head and twisted, bouncing him off the refrigerator and throwing him against wall.

Before the man could recover, Snow grabbed the freezer door and opened it hard, slamming the metal door into the man's face again and again until the fight went out of him and he slumped to the floor with a wet, pained moan.

Snow scooped up the man's gun and pointed it at him, but the fight had gone out of his attacker, who groaned painfully on the floor, blood pouring from his broken nose. Snow spun quickly, leading with the gun and hoping to help his friend.

He did need it.

Brooks shouted as he grabbed his attacker in a tackle that lifted him off the floor. The two men fell over the bed in a whirl of swinging arms and kicking legs before they slammed into the wall on the other side.

The attacker swung wildly, but missed his target. Instead, an old lamp with a dull, faded shade, the only lamp left upright in the room, caught the brunt of it and the bulb popped as it hit the floor.

Brooks didn't waste any time renewing his assault. Two quick left jabs to the man's solar plexus doubled him forward--

--straight into the path of Brooks' attack.

Brooks caught the man with a hard right to the face that dropped him like a rock. He landed face first on the bed, bounced softly, then laid there, not moving.

The third man lifted himself off the floor and reached for his gun.

With his back turned, Brooks didn't see him, but Snow did.

He made a clicking sound with his teeth to get his attention and the third man froze. Slowly, he turned to see the gun pointed right at him.

"Drop it."

The gun dropped to the floor.

"Get up," Snow said, motioning upward with the gun.

The third man did as he was told.

"Who are you and what do you want?" Snow asked.

"Ask your friend there," the man spat.

"I'd rather ask you." He leaned in closer. "And I really do hate to repeat myself."

The third man blew out a resigned breath. He knew he was beaten. He opened his mouth.

Brooks sucker punched him before he could say anything.

"Now what the hell did you do that for?" Snow demanded. "He was just about to tell us…"

"Whatever that man told you would have been a lie."

"How do you know that?"

"I just do," Brooks said, scooping up the guns belonging to the two attackers they had disarmed. "Now, come on. Let's get out of here before their friends arrive."

"What makes you think there's more of them?"

Brooks shot Snow a disapproving look. "Guys like these always have friends."

Brooks sprinted back toward the stairwell and Snow followed suit to keep up with his friend. At every corner, Brooks checked to make sure the coast was clear before moving on. They were also most to his rental car when they heard the first siren.

"Sounds like the cavalry is on the way," Snow said, standing next to the car and trying to catch his breath.

Brooks unlocked the rented Oldsmobile and slid in behind the wheel. When Snow didn't immediately follow, he rolled down the passenger side window. "You waiting on an engraved invitation or something?"

"Cops are on the way. You're the aggrieved party here, remember?" Snow said, relieved. He was very careful not to use the word *victim*. It was not a word that would sit well with Brooks.

"Cops can't help us, brother."

"Why not?" Snow leaned in front of the open window. "What are you into, Samson?"

"Get in the car and I promise I'll tell you everything."

"Brooks…"

"Get your ass in the car, Abraham."

It wasn't a threat, but Brooks' tone told Snow all he needed to know about the seriousness of the situation. The fact that the man had called him by his first name instead of "Snow" or "brother" hammered the seriousness of the moment home. He saw a side of Brooks he had only seen a couple of times before.

He was afraid.

But of what? Certainly, not those goons back at the hotel.

"Okay, so who the hell were those guys?" Snow asked once he was inside the car and they had pulled out of the motel parking lot.

"I don't know."

"Don't bullshit me, brother," Snow said. "They certainly knew who you were. That little ambush back there was for you, not me. Nobody sets up something like that without a reason so talk."

"They were hired guns."

"Those three were amateur hour compared to us," Snow said. "You have to admit, despite all its faults, *Mother* knew how to train us. You probably could have taken them even if I wasn't there."

"Probably?" Brooks shot him a crooked grin.

"Well, let's face it, you aren't getting any younger, you know?" Snow joked.

"I can still run circles around you, punk," Brooks said matter of fact.

"Will you at least let me call my friend, Mac? Maybe he can find out what's…"

“No,” Brooks said defiantly. “Just no, okay?”

Snow held up his hands in surrender. “Fine. You win. It’s your show. So, where too now, Kemosabe?”

Brooks took the next left. “I’ve got no idea. This is your city. You tell me.”

“Take the next right then get on the interstate. Head north.”

“Where we headed?”

“My place,” Snow said. “You can crash with me until we sort this mess out.” He turned to look at the driver. “That means you tell me everything. You got it? No bullshit, Brooks.”

“Scouts honor, brother.”

Snow grunted. “Like you were ever a Boy Scout.”

3.

"All clear."

Snow hadn't been expecting trouble when he got home, but he wasn't going to bet his life on it, and certainly not his friend's life. His grandfather's home, which he and his brother, sister, and cousins had taken to calling the farmhouse, sat well away from the road down a long, winding driveway. That made it difficult to check out the house from the road, especially now that the sun had started to set, but not impossible. After a few minutes, Snow was satisfied that whoever these guys were that had ambushed Brooks, they hadn't learned of his relationship to the man. That was good news. It meant that Brooks' hadn't gotten on the wrong side of spies or a foreign government.

"We good?" Brooks asked when Snow got back in the car.

"Yeah. Looks clear." He fished the cell phone from his pocket. "Just one quick call and we'll know for sure."

After three rings, a scruffy familiar voice answered.

"Hey, Pa-Pa," Snow said, adding an extra lilt to his voice. "Just wanted to call and tell you I got held up and might be a little late."

He smiled as he listed to the man on the other end. "See you in a sec," he finally said and disconnected the call. "We're clear."

The security gate started to slide open before they reached it and Brooks drove straight through, noticing that the gate began to ratchet back closed once the car was safely on the inside.

At the farmhouse, which in no way described the mansion owned by Archer Snow, an older man stood on a porch that wrapped around the side and back of the house. He had a shotgun leisurely resting against his shoulder. Brooks couldn't see his face because the cowboy hat he worse shadowed his face, thanks to the bright porch light he stood beneath.

He parked the car and Snow got out, motioning for him to do the same.

"You expecting company, kid?" the older man said.

"Nah," Snow said, waving off his grandfather's concerns. "Just cautious."

"Let me guess, some kind of safe word in the phone call?"

"Something like that," Snow said, smirking proudly.

"Ain't none o' my grandkids calls me Pa-Pa," Archer Snow said as he walked down the steps. "Not unless they want to get their asses kicked. Or there's trouble brewing."

Archer offered his hand and Brooks shook it.

"Archer Snow."

"Samson Brooks, Mr. Snow. I've heard a lot about you." He craned his head toward the younger Snow. "Our boy here says good things about you."

Archer's face broke into a wide grin, which only emphasized the familiar resemblance. "Does he now?"

"Complete hogwash, every word of it," Snow said playfully. 'You should know better than to listen to my friends, by now. They're liars and scoundrels, the lot of them."

"Well, you do know how to pick 'em, kiddo," Archer said, turning back toward the house. "You boys come on inside."

Brooks looked at Snow, who simply shrugged before falling into step with his grandfather. A quick shake of his head and Brooks followed. It wasn't like he had anywhere else to be.

After returning the shotgun to the cabinet near the door, Archer led them into the living room. Despite the mansion-like exterior, Archer Snow kept the inside of his home simple. The décor was not overly fancy, but warm and inviting. He motioned toward several chairs arranged around the room.

"So, what's going on?" the older Snow asked as he sat in a comfortable recliner.

"Just a little local trouble, Mr. Snow," Brooks said. "I don't want you to have to get involved. I was just giving junior here a ride home."

Snow shook his head. "He's going to crash with me for a day or two. His motel wasn't quite as safe as he would've liked."

"Sounds like you've had one hell of a day," Archer told his grandson."

Snow grimaced. "I take it you talked to John."

"I did indeed."

"It's not as bad as it seems," Snow started.

Archer cut him off. "You, me, and Douglas will get into that tomorrow. Right now, I'd like to know what's going on with you two."

"So do I, actually," Snow said.

With all eyes on him, Brooks sighed and settled back in his chair. "Well, I can see where he gets his stubborn streak from," he joked. "After I retired, I settled in Hawaii. There was just something about living in a place like that, always close to the beach, plenty of ladies in tiny bikinis to watch jog on the sand, and a never-ending supply of Mai Tai's to keep my manly thirst quenched."

"How long until you got bored?" archer asked.

Brooks smiled and waggled a finger toward his host. "He's a shrewd one, your grandpa," he said.

"Don't ever play checkers with him," Snow said. "He cheats."

"Oh, let's not start that again," Archer huffed. "I was with The Agency once upon a time, myself. I know how it feels to retire. It's great for a week, maybe two, but then…"

"Exactly. I was going stir crazy."

"So…" Snow prodded.

"So, I started taking cases, helping people out when they needed it. Nothing major, just enough to keep me occupied. You know."

Archer nodded.

Brooks cast a glance toward Snow.

He held up his hands. "Don't look at me. I'm retired."

"Uh huh," Brooks said as he stretched.

"R.E. Tired."

Archer interrupted. "Anyway, you were saying…"

"Right. Small jobs. Nothing too big. At least not at first. I got a call from a lawyer friend of mine. I helped him track down some folks a few times and whenever he could, he tossed some business my way. This one didn't seem like anything out of the ordinary. This lady split with her husband and then she up and moves away, taking their now teenage daughter with her. The dad, Anthony Mann needed someone to help find the kid so he could get in touch."

"Did you find her?"

"Sort of. I found the ex-wife." Brooks blew out a breath. "That's when things got weird."

Snow leaned forward in his chair, arms resting on his knees. "What happened?"

"I found the ex. She changed her name, which was weird and set off a few alarm bells. The daughter changed her last name as well. At first I assumed the mother had remarried and the daughter had taken the new guy's name, but she never remarried. Mom works for a manufacturing outfit based out of Texas and travels a lot for the job. She owns a small home in Florida, but also keeps an apartment in Atlanta. My guess is that's where the daughter's living these days. I found out she was accepted to Georgia Tech."

"That makes sense. Was she there?" Archer asked.

"I've not been there yet. Something about this whole thing didn't sit right with me so I did a little digging into both the lady and her ex-husband before I did anything else."

"Uh oh," snow muttered.

"You know it, brother. After I got back to the mainland, I headed to Florida and made a few discreet inquiries."

"And?"

"Well, turns out the ex-wife and daughter changed their names for a reason," Brooks said. The dude who hired me wasn't actually the girl's father. I met the real Anthony Mann in Florida. He hadn't seen his wife and daughter for some time, but he knew why. It was the same reason he had changed his last name."

"Oh, I don't like where this is going," Snow said.

"Turns out they went into witness protection after testifying against Mann's family. Mann's old man is… get this… Antonio Manelli."

"The mobster?"

"Right the first time, Snowman," Brooks said, tapping a finger against the side of his nose before pointing toward his former partner. "Mann washed his hands of the family business years ago, but he refused to testify out of some sense of family loyalty. Some crafty D.A. got to his ex-wife and got her to tell what she knew. It wasn't much, but it was enough to put them in the crosshairs. After they were gone, he changed his name to Mann and walked away from his family. My contacts pretty much agree he's cut all ties. I don't think he's involved in the family business."

"And now you think you've led them to the daughter?" Archer said bluntly, already dialing his cell.

"Maybe. When those guys showed up at my motel, I was pretty sure Manelli's goons had gotten wise to me."

Archer held up a hand to pause the conversation. "Hey. It's Archer Snow," he said into the phone. "I need you to track down a…" he turned to Brooks. "What was the mother's name?"

"Pamela Masters."

"Pamela Masters," Archer said. "She has a home in Florida and here in Atlanta. Find her and put a tail on her. Do not approach. Call me the minute you get eyes of her, you got it? She might already be under surveillance so no unnecessary risks, understood? Good. Call me as soon as you do." After a pause, he added, "Yes. We'll probably bring her in so go ahead and have a jet on standby."

He flipped the phone closed. "I've got one of my best guys on it," he said. "We'll find her."

"Damn," Brooks whistled. "And I thought Mother worked quick back in the day."

"Mother ain't got nothin' on him," Snow said. Normally, neither of them would talk about Mother, the code sign for their former intelligence operation, but like his grandson, Archer Snow had spent his fair share of time working covert operations before pulling the pin and settling into retirement. Mother wasn't an official title, of course, but it became accepted shorthand for operatives.

"What about the daughter?" Brooks asked. "It's a good bet they know she's here."

"What say you and I take a ride back downtown and see if we can find her before they do?" Snow said, already getting to his feet. "I can have my buddy Mac sit on her place until we get there."

Brooks was on his feet. "Sounds like a plan. Lead the way, brother."

"Good." Snow was glad that Brooks hadn't argued about getting Mac involved this time.

"Want me to tag along?" Archer asked.

"Can you stay here and keep tabs on your guys looking for Miss Masters. You have any contacts in Wit Sec?"

Archer snorted.

"Right," Snow said. "I forgot who I was talking to for a minute there. See if your contacts can help. If the Manelli Crime Family is looking for this woman, I doubt it's for a nice, friendly chat."

"Will do," Archer said. "Be careful."

"Aren't I always?" Snow joked and tossed his grandfather a playful wink.

"Don't make me answer that, kid."

"Just do me one favor, brother," Brooks said as they headed for the door.

"What's that?"

"This time bring your gun."

4.

It was dark by the time Snow and Brooks reached Atlanta.

The city sparkled against the deep purple night sky that was quickly on its way to a starry black night without a cloud in the sky. Despite the heat, humidity, and that oh so lethal combination of pollen and ragweed that played hell with his sinuses, Snow loved this city. He had grown up there and although it had changed a lot during the years he was away, some things never changed.

Atlanta's horrendous traffic was one of them.

Once they finally reached their exit, Snow took side roads until they were parked across the street from Katie Masters' apartment building.

"This is it," Brooks said with a whistle as he looked up at the high-rise building in the heart of downtown, just a few blocks from the Georgia Tech campus. "Great location. An easy walk to her classes."

"Or an easy bike ride," Snow said, pointing at a small group of four young ladies stopping in front of the building. They let themselves in with a keycard and carried their bicycles inside. From the backpacks each wore, it wasn't hard to peg them as college students.

"One of them your girl?" Snow asked.

Brooks scratched his salt and pepper bearded chin. "Hard to say. She's a lot younger in the photo I have." He pulled the image up on his phone and handed it over so Snow could get a good look.

"They didn't have anything more recent?" he asked, but then remembered Brooks' client was searching for someone he hadn't seen in years. "Guess not. It's possible she changed her hair color. If I was in hiding, I would."

"Not really something I would have to worry about," Brooks smiled and rubbed a hand across his bald scalp.

"Point taken. What's her apartment number?" Snow asked.

"I don't know."

"What do you mean you don't know? How can you not know?"

"Look, Snowman, these people have gotten pretty good at hiding, you know. It took a lot of digging to find the right building." He blew out a breath and looked out the window, suddenly interested in the sidewalk. "I was planning to check all this out tomorrow," he finally said.

"Oh, brother," Snow groaned. "Just once, I'd like for something to be easy."

Before Brooks could offer a rebuttal, Snow caught a glimpse of Mac approaching. He lowered the window and waved him over.

"That her?" the FBI Agent asked once he crouched next to the driver's side door.

"We think so," Snow said with just a hint of sarcasm. He pushed open the car door and stepped out into the humid Atlanta evening. "What say we go find out, huh?"

Brooks followed suit and the three men jogged across the street as drivers blasted their horns. Brooks flipped off a couple of the drivers, but none of the angry motorists was brave enough to take on the big guy so they inched along in peace.

At the door, Snow looked at the tenant list. "I don't see your girl's name listed," he said.

"Would you post your real name if you were hiding from the mob?" Brooks said.

"Good point." Snow reached out to press a button at random.

"Wait?" Mac grabbed his arm. "You don't know which apartment is hers?"

Snow pointed toward Brooks. "It's on his to do list."

Brooks was about to comment when someone walked up behind them. "Can I help you?" a new voice asked.

Together, the three men turned to see a young woman who was probably in her early twenties jogging with her dog on a leash. She was gorgeous and ran in place to keep her heart rate up, her long auburn hair bouncing from side to side in a ponytail. Her dog smartly seemed leery of the three strange men on their doorstep.

"Yes," Snow said. "Do you know…" He snapped his fingers. "What's her name again?"

"Katie Masters," Brooks said.

"Right. Sorry. Do you know Miss Masters?" Snow continued, realizing from the sideways look on her face that they must sound like a trio of weird stalkers or something. "Let me start over…" he said, putting on his best disarming smile.

"Excuse me, ma'am," Mac said, pushing forward to interrupt before things became even more awkward. "Agent Tom McClellan. I'm with the FBI. We just need to make sure Miss Masters is okay."

"I don't know," the jogger started.

"You're smart to be cautious," Snow said. "I tell you what, let's try this." He pulled a business card from his pocket, flipped it over, and wrote a phone number on the back, He handed the card to the woman. “Can you give this to her and have her call me. We’ll stay right here where she can see us from a window.”

She took the card. “Okay. Wait here.”

“Thank you,” Snow said.

The guys stepped away from the door and waited as the jogger let herself in and closed the door behind her, careful to make sure the electronic lock latched the door and kept the strangers locked outside.

“Oh, no, she doesn’t think we’re creepy at all,” Brooks joked.

“I wouldn’t be surprised if she’s calling the cops right now,” Mac added with a huff.

“She’s not gonna call, Snowman,” Brooks said.

“She’ll call,” Snow said with certainty.

“I wouldn’t be too sure, brother. We’re going to have to…”

Before he could finish, the cell phone in Snow’s hand came to life. He gave his friends an *I told you so* look then answered on the second ring. “Hello.”

“Are you really with the FBI?” a cautious voice asked.

“I’m not, but my friend here is. Look down and he’ll hold up his badge for you.” Snow nudged Mac, who opened up his credentials wallet and held them in the air so the woman looking out of an upper story window could see them.

“I see it,” she said. “What do you want?”

“First things first. Are you Katie Masters?”

“Yes.”

“Good. Thank you for calling me. My name’s Abraham Snow.” He pointed to his companions. “This is Mac… Agent McClellan… and that’s Brooks. We’re here because we think you might be in some trouble,” Snow said.

“What kind of trouble?”

“Someone claiming to be your father hired my friend here- he’s a private investigator- to find you,” Snow said. “When he found out the man was lying about his identity, he came to us and we’re here to make sure you’re okay.”

“So, what do you want with me?”

“We just want to talk, ask you a couple questions, and make sure you are okay.”

“I don’t know…”

"I know this must seem odd, Katie. Believe me, I get it," Snow said. "How about this?" He pointed toward a small sandwich shop across the street with patio seating. "How about we meet over at the sandwich shop so we can talk there. Bring some friends with you, if you'd like. There's plenty of people around. Crowds are always good."

"She's not going to go for it," Brooks mumbled.

Mac *shushed* him.

"We're going to head over there now, okay, Katie? We'll see you in a few minutes. Okay?"

A silent moment passed with only the sound of her breathing coming through the phone. Snow knew better than to push her. The last thing he wanted to do was spook her any more than she probably already was. All he could do was try to gain her trust, which wasn't going to be easy. He couldn't blame her. If three men had told him the story he just told her at her age, Snow would have thought he was crazy too.

"Fine," she relented. "Give me a few minutes."

"Okay. We'll see you there."

###

They had been sitting there for about ten minutes when she arrived.

Katie Masters looked younger than her reported age. Her long dark hair was streaked with multi-colored highlights that fell around her shoulders with a slight bouncy curl. She was wearing jeans, a T-shirt, and sneakers, probably in case she needed to run. She didn't carry a purse, only a smartphone clenched in her left hand.

"What's this all about?" she said as soon as she sat down across from Snow. She was all business and he respected that.

"A man claiming to be your father hired me to find you and your mother," Brooks said. "And now we're here."

"But it wasn't my father who hired you?"

"Not so much, no," Brooks muttered.

"Not much of a shocker there," she said. "My dad barely had time for me when we lived with him. I'm sure he doesn't miss me at all."

"I'm sure that's…" Snow started, but she cut him off.

"Don't," Katie said. "Just don't."

Snow held up his hands in surrender. "Hey, it's cool. I understand. My father and I don't exactly see eye to eye."

"Hardly the same thing," was her only retort.

"You're probably right," Snow said. He wanted to say more, but there was no point. Katie Masters had already made up her mind about her father, much like Snow had made up his mind about his own. Nothing he could say would change her mind any more than a few platitudes would change the way he looked at Dominic Snow.

"So, just to make sure I've got this straight, you told this guy pretending to be my father where to find me based only on his word?" She seemed angry and who could blame her. They had basically just dropped a massive bomb on her life.

"No. This guy had all of the appropriate documents, photos, and was recommended by a respected officer of the court," Brooks explained. "He had all the bases covered. By the time I realized he wasn't really your dad I called it quits, but he sent a few goons looking for me. I didn't tell them where you live, but from the preliminary work up I gave him… well, I just wanted to make sure you and your mom were okay."

"And is she?" Katie wanted to know. "I tried to call her and there was no answer."

"We have people checking on her as we speak," Snow said, already typing a text to his grandfather. "I'll check on it, okay?"

"Fine," Katie said. "And you think these guys, these… what did you call them… goons… have found me?"

"Maybe. A few of them jumped me back at my motel earlier today," Brooks said.

"What?" Mac said. Up to that point he had been listening quietly and staying out of it. "Why the hell didn't you call me?" he asked, looking straight at his friend.

Snow shrugged. "Talk to him, man," was all he said.

Katie interrupted. "Wait. Before you guys go into your full Three Stooges routine, let me see if I've got this right. The guys you wanted to keep away from me followed you here so your brilliant plan was to come to my door? Did it never occur to you they might follow you here too?"

"The thought crossed my mind," Brooks said. "We can protect you."

"Staying away from me would have been a good first step!" she started, pushing her chair away from the table with a loud screech of wood against concrete.

"We have your mother," Snow said, which took some of the fire out of her. "She'll be on a private plane heading to Atlanta within the hour."

"Can I talk to her?"

"Sure," Snow said. He shook his phone. "I'll have them call this number."

"Thank you."

"No problem." Snow sent the text then placed the phone on the table between himself and Katie Masters. He leaned forward. "Look. In our haste to make sure you were safe we may not have handled this as well as we could have."

"That's an understatement," she said.

"But, now that we're here, we want to make sure you stay safe," Snow said. "We think…" he took a breath, trying to figure out the best way to say what needed to be said. "It's our belief that your grandfather is the one trying to find you and your mother."

"My grandfather?"

"It's possible he holds a grudge against you and your mother," Brooks added. "You know, her testimony and your leaving."

Katie laughed, which was the last thing any of the guys expected.

They shared a look, each man shaking his head.

"Why is that funny?" Mac asked. "Who's her grandfather?"

"You ever hear of a guy named Antonio Manelli?" Snow said plainly.

"Sure. He's a…" That's when it dawned on Mac. "Oh!"

"Oh, indeed," Snow said.

Katie waved her hands to get their attention. "Look, you're barking up the wrong tree, fellas. My grandfather isn't holding a grudge against me, my mom, or my dad, and I know that for a fact."

"How's that?" Mac asked.

Katie blew out a breath. "My grandfather paid for all of this, my school tuition, rent, books, you name it. Whatever I need, or want, for that matter, all I have to do is ask."

"You're in contact with your grandfather?" Snow said.

"I am."

"You do know that's against the relocation arrangement your mother made with the State Department," Snow said. "Witness Protection means no contact. You could be placing yourself or your mother at risk."

"Oh, please," Katie said with a laugh. "I've been in touch with my grandfather for years now. If he was going to do something to any of us, don't you think it would have happened by now? He certainly wouldn't have to hire some p.i."

"You don't seem all that surprised that we think he might hurt someone," Mac added. "I take it you know what kind of business your family is in, don't you?"

She shook her head. "I do. He found me about five years ago. I was excited to see him. I mean, he is my grandfather after all. I missed him. We had a long talk and I convinced him to leave my mom alone in exchange for him having a relationship with me."

"And he agreed to that?" Brooks asked.

"Well, I am sitting here, aren't I?" she said with a smug grin.

"Indeed you are," Snow said. Before he could say more, his phone jangled on the table. He answered it on the second ring. After a quick conversation, he handed the phone to Katie. "Your mom would like to talk to you," he said.

She grabbed the phone, but Snow held firm. "After that, we're going to relocate you somewhere safe for a couple days until we get this sorted out. Agreed?"

She shook her head.

"Your grandfather may not be after you, but someone is," Snow said plainly. "I'd like to get you under wraps someplace they can't find you until we figure all this out. Okay?"

Katie grimaced, but finally conceded. "Fine," she said with a nod.

Snow released the phone and let Katie Masters talk to her mother.

5.

Snow wanted to order a beer.

It had been that kind of afternoon, but no matter how much he wanted a nice cold adult beverage he tried never to drink when on the job. Of course, the fact that he wasn't actually working for anyone didn't matter. His friend, not to mention Katie Masters, needed his help. That was good enough for him. Plus, the most potent drink on the sandwich shop's menu was Mountain Dew.

Katie said goodbye to her mother and handed the phone across the table.

"Snow," he said once the phone was back in his hand. On the other end was the familiar voice of Archer Snow, his own grandfather. Archer gave him a rundown on the details he had dug up since they left him and an ETA on the plane carrying Pamela Masters.

Snow ended the call without a lot of pleasantries.

"So, here's the plan," he said to Katie and the others. "I need you to pack a bag with enough clothes for a few days, maybe a week. Whatever you can get in one or two bags and carry in a single trip. We can always send someone by to get more if you need it. One of us can go up with you if you'd like."

She smiled as she stood. "I think I can manage. The building has a key card lock. I'll be okay."

"Fine. I'll walk you to the front door," Mac said, getting to his feet. "I'll be there when you come out. Will that work for you?"

"Fair enough," she agreed.

Snow held out the phone for her. "Take this." On her surprised look, he added, "in case your mom calls back."

She smiled and nodded. "Thanks."

"Don't mention it."

Mac motioned toward the exit. "Shall we?"

With another nod, Katie Masters turned on her heel and headed out, her FBI agent escort at her side.

Snow and Brooks watched them cross the streets, weaving their way through Atlanta's heavy evening traffic.

"She's handling this better than I expected," Brooks said.

"Impressed?" Snow asked playfully.

"Actually, yeah. A bit."

"Tough girl."

"Let's just make sure we keep her in one piece," Brooks added.

"Mac's good at what he does," Snow said, standing up for his oldest friend. "He's got her covered."

"And we've got him covered," Brooks continued.

Snow smiled. "Almost liked we've done this before, huh?"

Brooks snorted a response.

At the door to her apartment building across the street, Katie swiped her card and stepped inside while her FBI escort crossed his arms and leaned against the wall outside. He looked none too happy, but that was by design. The last thing he wanted was anyone to sidle up to him and try to start up a conversation.

"I take it you have a plan?" Brooks asked after a moment.

"More like the makings of a plan."

"That's reassuring," Brooks said, rolling his eyes.

"Weren't you the one who taught us the joy in learning to make things up on the go?"

"Doesn't sound like me?" Brooks said.

"Be prepared."

"That's the Boy Scouts."

Snow smiled. "How about improvise and use what's at hand?"

"Now that sounds like me," Brooks joked.

"I'll feel a lot better once we've got her tucked away somewhere safe," Snow said.

"I take it you have a place in mind?"

"I do. Snow Security keeps a few apartments around the city as safe houses. They're all set up under dummy corporations so they can't be traced back to Snow… at least not easily. We can set her up there and put a guard on her until we get this figured out."

"Good plan," Brooks said. "I guess I taught you better than I thought."

"You weren't too shabby," Snow deadpanned. "I did pick up a few additional tricks along the way too. I might surprise you."

"Brother, of that, I have little doubt."

Before Snow could respond, Brooks pointed toward the apartment building across the street where Katie Masters stood with Mac. "Looks like she's ready to go."

"Snow handed the keys to Brooks. "Grab the car."

"On it."

Instead of walking back through the restaurant to get back to the street, Brooks hopped over the three foot tall wrought iron fence and small bushes that ran the perimeter of the patio area and made a beeline for Snow's car.

Snow stood, dropped a couple of dollars on the table as a tip even though none of them had ordered anything. He leaned against the fence and watched. The raised patio offered him a fairly unobstructed view of things. From there he could keep an eye on everyone as Mac and Katie made their way toward the car where Brooks waited. Everything looked normal, or as normal as evening rush hour looked in downtown Atlanta.

A sea of slowly moving cars was between them, but he could still see everything.

That's when he noticed something out of place.

Panel vans were not uncommon sights in the city. This one was light blue with a sign on the side that marked it as Aces High Heating and Air Conditioning Services. On its own the van didn't look too out of place parked next to an apartment building across the side street that intersect Peachtree and ran next to Katie Masters' building.

It took a second or two before he realized that it wasn't the van itself that was bothering him, it was that he could make out movement inside. The bed of every working heating and air van he had ever seen was usually packed to the brim with spare parts and tools. That didn't leave much room for anything else.

A surveillance van on the other hand…

That's when he noticed the collection of discarded cigarette butts lying next to the driver's side door, dropped there by the driver who had been sitting in one place a very long time. Amateur move. That meant trouble.

Snow vaulted over the waist-high fence and bushes. He hit the sidewalk already running. Horns blared as he cut through the traffic, squeezing between cars and in one case, doing his best Dukes of Hazard impression as he slid across the hood of a shiny red imported sports car as the owner shouted at him through the windshield.

Snow shouted Mac's name, but over the noise of bumper to bumper traffic, he didn't hear him at first.

Brooks, on the other hand, noticed his friend's sprint through gridlock and he abandoned the car and started running toward them, gun in hand.

He shouted again and this time Mac and Katie turned to see Snow bounding over a car heading their way.

On alert, Mac's hand instantly went for the weapon he kept in a shoulder holster.

"What's going on?" Katie asked.

Before he could answer the heating and air conditioning van dropped into gear and with a bark of tired on asphalt, headed straight at them.

Mac grabbed Katie by the shoulders and pushed her out of the way as the van spun around in the middle of the side street. Spinning tires sent white pungent clouds of burnt rubber into the air. The strong odor stung the nose and eyes.

The side door slid open and two men leapt out. They were dressed in black and wore vests, helmets, and body armor. Both were armed. The first one out the door took a swing at Mac just as he pulled his weapon, catching him unawares with a hit to his wrist, which disarmed him. Mac's gun clattered across the concrete and out of his reach, but he wasn't out of the fight. Mac wasn't a big guy, which often meant he was often underestimated, much to the detriment of his opponents. Mac was scrappy. He didn't go down easy or without a fight and there was a lot of power in his punch. A quick jab at the attacker caught the man off guard. Mac caught him across the face with an arm blow that staggered him. Blood spattered from his nose.

A shove sent the man to the ground then Mac turned on the second man. He had advanced on Katie and held her tightly by the arm. She screamed and fought back, but he wasn't letting up.

"Hey!" Mac shouted and got the man's attention. Then he planted a fist into the man's face, but miscalculated and smacked the helmet instead. The impact was painful and Mac felt two fingers break on impact.

The attacker was quick. He snaked out with a backhand that caught Mac unprepared and took him off his feet and he landed hard against the sidewalk.

Momentarily dazed, Mac was unable to get back on his feet fast enough to stop the man who had hit him from tossing Katie Masters into the van. Her shouts of protest faded as the panel door slid shut behind her, cutting her off from freedom.

The attacker took another look at Mac and smiled, his teeth surprisingly white against the darkness of the body armor he wore. His assault rifle was trained squarely on its target.

"Tough luck, bub," the man said and pulled the trigger.

Which was when Snow made his entrance.

He dove for his friend and tackled him at the same moment the gunman pulled the trigger. Bullets zipped past them like angry bees, but miraculously, none of them hit their target, instead, chipping away at the brick wall behind them.

Snow and Mac hit the ground and rolled with the impact, stopping suddenly when they hit the short concrete wall that ran along the sidewalk to separate the apartment garden area from the street.

There was no time to rest or lick their wounds. Spinning tires spewed more noxious rubber into the air as the driver made for the side street. It was the only open getaway option open to them.

"You okay?" Snow asked Mac. A quick nod and a grunt from his friend and he was on the move. Gun in hand, snow ran for the van. In his periphery, he saw Brooks approaching from the other side of the street.

Brooks ran full out and inserted himself between the van and its escape route. He leveled his gun, the .45 was his weapon of choice, and fired twice, each shot hitting the front windshield, spider-webbing the glass.

The van veered left then right, popping up over the curb and sideswiping a parked car. As he ran to catch up to the van, Snow wondered if Brooks had clipped the driver.

The question was answered when the van lurched forward and, with the sound of rending metal, it pulled away and drove into the night before the could catch up. Not that they didn't try, but on foot they were no match for the van's horsepower.

At the bottom of the hill the van swerved, made a left, and disappeared from view.

"Dammit!" Brooks shouted after catching his breath.

"It's okay," Snow said.

"No. It's not! They got her, man" Brooks shouted. "They got her and it's my fault!"

"So, let's go get her back," Snow said.

6.

Katie Masters was scared, but even more than that she was mad.

Her abductor pushed her into the room. She didn't know his name, but had dubbed him *Hal* because he had breath so bad it could have knocked over buildings. The other man, the one who had been shot, she thought of as *The Screamer* for obvious reasons.

The office was immaculate, not to mention larger than her entire apartment. The floor was polished marble, the walls an off white color that clashed with the rest of the décor. There were two couches at one end that formed an L shape. From the couch you could watch the 70" flatscreen TV that hung from the wall above the fireplace or stare through the large windows at the swimming pool beyond.

At the other end of the office was a desk, flanked by bookshelves containing assorted odds and ends, statues, trophies, photographs, and even the occasional book or two amongst the assorted odds and ends and photographs. The room felt a lot like a trophy room to past glory more so than it did a place of business.

Once her captors had left her in such opulent surroundings, Katie Masters heard the door latch close behind her. Running was not an option, but she had figured that out the moment they pulled her out of the van and she there nothing but fields of grass and woods as far as the eye could see.

Whatever was going to happen was going to play out here.

"They didn't hurt you, did they?"

The voice came from the far end of the room and startled her, although she didn't do much to give that away. She hadn't noticed him there before, but the old man sat on a couch with thick pillow cushions that he seemed to sink into. It was only when he scooted forward to sit on the edge could he be seen.

"Who are you?" she asked.

"Didn't anyone ever tell you it's not polite to answer a question with a question?"

"You mean like you just did?" It was all she could do to contain a mischievous grin.

"Touche, Miss Masters. Well played. You are every bit as clever as I was told." With a soft grunt, the old man pushed himself into a standing position. He was rail thin, almost to the point of being underweight. She wondered if he might be sick or something, but kept the question to herself.

"So, who are you?"

He smiles and clucked his tongue against his teeth. "Ah, ah. You first."

Katie sighed. She detested games and that seemed to be exactly what this guy was doing, playing games. "No," she said in that tone that only a teenager could pull off. "They didn't hurt me."

"Excellent," he said. "I'm not going to hurt you either..." his voice trailed off as if searching for the next words. "That doesn't mean I won't have one of my boys do it if you get out of line though so don't get any bright ideas, okay?"

"Well, I've been told I'm clever so no promises."

"Fair enough. Do you know why you're here?"

This time she made the clucking noise. "I believe you owe me an answer. Rules are rules."

He laughed. "Indeed they are. Please forgive my rudeness. My name is Gerald Roarke. Perhaps you've heard my name before?" He offered his hand.

“Can't say I have." She looked at her surroundings from the locked door to her kidnapper's outstretched hand. "I'd love to say it's an honor to meet you, but under the circumstances I think we both know that would be a lie."

He let his hand drop. “Fair enough.”

“I'm guessing you and my grandfather are... I don't want to say friends, but...”

“Business associate will do,” Roarke said.

“Really? My first guess would have been rival.”

“Like I said, you're a clever girl.”

She nodded acceptance of the compliment.

He walked over a nearby sitting table that was flanked by four cushioned chairs and motioned toward one of the empty chairs. With no other options available to her, she accepted with a nod and made her way to the offered chair.

Once she sat, her host followed suite, choosing the chair opposite her. He crossed his legs and smiled, looking every bit the charming businessman she assumed he had been in his youth.

“Is it safe to assume that you were the one who hired a private detective to find me?”

“Straight to business, eh?” He said with a big smile, his voice carrying. “You're definitely Antonio Manelli's granddaughter, I'll give you that. He must be very proud of you.”

“You'd have to ask him.”

“I'll be sure to do that the next time I talk to him, which should be pretty soon, I'd reckon. I'll tell him you said hello.”

“Go right ahead.” She crossed her arms over her chest and waited for him to make the next move.

“I'm curious,” he said, changing the subject. “What made you seek out your grandfather after all your parents did to keep you away from him?”

“He's family.”

“Is that the only reason?”

“Isn't it enough?" She blew out a breath. “My Mom lost her Dad when she was too young to remember him so Anthony was the only grandparent I had left and all I had were vague memories. No matter what he's done, he's still my grandfather and I wanted to have a relationship with him so I made that happen.”

“That couldn't have made your parents very happy.”

“I imagine not. That's why I didn't tell them.” She shot him a mischievous grin.

“I'm starting to like you more and more, kiddo,” Roarke said. “I'm glad we got to meet and have a little chat.”

“Are you planning to hurt my mother?”

The question caught Roarke off guard. “Why would I want to hurt your mother, Katie? As far as I can tell she's a very nice lady whose only flaw seems to be that she works too much and doesn't spend enough time with her daughter.” He leaned forward in the chair, elbows resting on his knees. “Hurting your mother gets me nothing.”

Now it was his turn to flash a grin. His tooth grin was far more menacing than hers could ever be, but she suspected he had been perfecting that look for decades.

“Besides, it's not your mother who is the apple of ol' Antonio Manelli's eye...” the grin faded into a taut, serious line. “You are.”

Up until that moment, Katie Masters had been more angry than afraid.

Not any more.

###

Abraham Snow was frustrated.

It has been almost two after the shooting and they were still on sight as the local cops locked down the scene and took their statements. As soon as local law enforcement realized an FBI agent was involved, even though he was off duty at the time, a courtesy phone call had been made to the Atlanta field office to inform them that one of their own had been involved in '*an incident.*'

That call got the Feds involved, including Mac's boss, Special Agent in Charge Arthur Simonson, who did not like him one bit. This wasn't exactly news to him nor did it bother Snow in the least because he didn't think much of Simonson either.

As soon as he arrived on scene, SAC Simonson pulled Mac aside. Although he couldn't hear everything that was being said, the words "irresponsible" and "trouble" came though loud and clear. During the rant, Simonson pointed in Snow's direction more than a few times.

"Damn, brother, but that man does not like you a whole bunch," Brooks said as he sat down next to him on the retaining wall.

"Feelings mutual," Snow said.

"Your brother call back yet?"

"He'll call as soon as he gets something."

"Once Doug gets a lock on my phone's GPS, we'll know who took Katie. Then we an go get her back."

"No more mistakes on this one, Snowman," Brooks said, his voice like a hoarse trombone. "I've failed that little girl too much already."

"She's not a kid, man," Snow said. "That young woman's grandfather, the same grandfather she's gone out of her way to reconnect with, might I add, is the head of the Manelli Crime Family. Those family roots run deep, you know."

"I am aware."

"I'm not so sure you are," Snow said. "The Manelli family has been active since the end of World War II. Hell, probably even before that. You don't get that kind of longevity without getting your hands dirty."

Brooks held up his hands, palms out then flipped them around. "Had plenty o' dirt on these hands in my time, brother. I'm not naive. If I have to get dirty to get that girl back, you know I will."

Snow blew out a breath and waggled his own hands. "These have been in their share of dirt too, brother. As much as I might like to fool myself into thinking that I can keep them clean from here on out, I know it's a temporary solution at best. Especially with Ortega still breathing good air."

"Ain't no man wants you to be able to walk the straight and narrow more than me. I'm proud of what you're doing here, of the life you're trying to build," Brooks said before getting to his feet. "You can sit this one out. I'll take it from here."

Snow stood as well so he could keep his voice low. "You don't get to play that card with me, brother," he said, emphasizing the word to drive home his point. "There's more we've got in common than the dirt on our hands and that's the blood. I don't know about you, but I've bathed in enough blood to do me a lifetime."

"Then let me go it alone from here, Snowman."

"Not going to happen, son. We might not come from the same parents, but you and me, we're family. If you think I'm just going to let you waltz into the shit storm that's waiting for you by yourself then you don't know me as well as you think. Besides, I'm not quite ready to have to make your funeral arrangements."

Brooks knew better than to argue with Snow, especially when he made sense. "You're a right pain in the ass, you know that?" he said around a resigned smile.

"The very definition of a younger brother, huh?"

Brooks laughed. "You watch that age crap, punk. You ain't exactly no spring chicken yourself."

"So I keep being reminded," Snow said, absently rubbing at the scar on his chest.

"You two planning something stupid?" Mac asked as he joined them.

"Always," Brooks joked. "Some might call that our specialty."

"You in the doghouse with Simonson again?" Snow asked.

"No more than usual. I'm sure he'll think of more to say before I see him next."

"He's gone?"

"'Afraid so."

"Darn. I was hoping to say hello," Snow groused. "Did he ask about me?"

"You know, I think your name did come up once or twice," Mac said around a chuckle. "If it was up to him, I think he'd have had you arrested on site and shipped off to a black site somewhere."

Brooks and Snow snorted.

"Not that we have such things, of course," Mac deadpanned.

"Of course not," Snow and Brooks said in unison.

"You in trouble with the *sack*?" Snow asked Mac.

"No more than normal."

"Simonson bench you?"

Now it was Mac's turn to laugh. "Are you kidding? Once he found out whose granddaughter it was that got snatched, he was all too happy to let me run free. He seems to think we're going to go off half cocked and get ourselves killed or start some kind of bloody mob war. Either way, he comes out smelling like a rose."

"You've known me a long time, Mac. I never go off half cocked."

"Yeah," Brooks agreed. "Half is being generous. I'd say one quarter cocked. That sound about right to you?" He looked at Snow.

"Yeah. That sounds right."

"So, what's our next move?"

"Uh uh, Mac. No way," Snow said, waggling his fingers. "No way am I going to be the reason you lose your job."

"We can handle it, Agent McClellan," Brooks said.

"Tough," Mac said. Before his friend could protest, he added, "You're not the only one who gets to play the *we're brothers* card. Not with me."

Snow held up his hands in surrender. "You win."

"Good," Mac said with finality. "So, what's the plan?"

"In progress," Brooks interjected before Snow could say anything.

Snow shot the big man a look.

"It's coming together quite nicely, thank you," Snow told Mac.

Behind him, Brooks wiggled his hand to say it was a *so-so* plan and shrugged.

"When do we start?" Mac said.

Brooks' phone rang. "It's your brother," he said and handed it over to Snow.

Snow took it. "I'm guessing right now," he told the FBI agent before answering the phone with a simple "Snow."

Mac and Brooks watched as he stood, walked in slow, small circles while muttering into the phone. It was a short conversation.

"Doug's found my phone," he said. "We're good to go."

7.

Snow told Doug to meet them back at his place.

By the time he pulled up the drive, his brother and the man he'd met earlier, Mr. Brooks were already stocking up the same beat up old car that Abe and Big John had used to help him out earlier. John stood nearby. He looked nervous, but Doug assumed he was worried about the car.

Historically speaking, Snow was not known for being gentle with equipment. As a kid, he broke everything, including a couple of lawnmowers, which had irritated their father. That paled in comparison to the car he'd flipped over out on old Harry McCarty Road when he was sixteen. The car was a total loss, but flipping end over end would do that to any car.

Luckily, Snow had walked away with barely a scratch.

Their dad hit the roof.

Things had been tense between father and son before the wreck, but that was the moment, the inciting incident where things became strained. For the next two years, Douglas and Samantha walked a delicate tightrope around them both, even once they no longer lived under the same roof. The only safe harbor in those days was their grandfather's farm. Archer Snow made sure his home was a demilitarized zone, which was ironic considering the family history.

Then one day his brother was gone.

And now, ten years later, he was back. Douglas was happy to build a new relationship with Abe, but they were starting from scratch like two strangers recently introduced. Missing ten years had that effect.

Everyone acted as though Snow was unpredictable, but Douglas knew better. If there was one constant in his brother's life, this was it. He always returned to their grandfather's farm.

And this time he brought company with him.

While Snow and Mr. Brooks loaded weapons into the car, Big John Salmon watched quietly, keeping distance between him and the weapons. He was still on parole and had kept himself far away from trouble since his release, but the big guy had a hard time saying “no” to Snow. Douglas hoped his participation didn’t blow back on him or get him back into old, familiar patterns.

Grandpa Archer stood apart also, talking on the phone, and waving his hands erratically, passing the phone from one to the other as he gestured. Like most of the Snow family, Archer liked to 'talk' with his hands.

"Looks like you're preparing for war," Douglas told his brother once he stepped out of the car.

"I hope not," Snow said with a playful smile as he pushed an earwig into his ear. "But you never know."

"It's better to have it and not need it than to need it and not have it," Douglas recited.

"That's how you do it." He dropped a bag into the back seat of the car. "She still in the same place?"

"Tough to know for sure. The phone hasn't moved, but it's possible they took it from her. I can't think of any reason the kidnappers would have let her keep it."

"If they're smart then that's exactly what they did. Otherwise, we would have heard something by now."

"You'll be going in blind."

"Won't be the first time," Snow joked. "Comes with the territory, kid."

Douglas hated it when he was called 'kid' like he was twelve or something. He knew Abraham didn't mean anything by it, but it still grated nonetheless. "Is there anything else I can do to help?" he asked.

"I think we've got it covered, but you're welcome to join the party," Snow said. "It could get hairy. You ready for that?"

Douglas inflated a bit. "I've been wanting to get out in the field more often," he admitted. It was true. He loved his job, but it kept him mostly landlocked at the Snow Security building. The work was rewarding, but it was also safe, predictable... boring. Sometimes Douglas wanted to be more like his brother and grandfather. They were men if action, often leaping headfirst into trouble without giving it so much as a second thought.

Most days that was not Douglas Snow, but on occasion he dreamt that it was.

"Catch a ride with Mac," Snow said, pointing down the drive as a Plain Jane four door sedan pulled up. The unmarked cars were supposed to blend in without drawing attention, but they tried so hard to be ordinary that they stood out as much as if they actually painted FBI on the doors.

Snow handed his brother an earwig of his very own. “Keep this in your ear at all times. It’s not exactly comfortable, but you don’t take it out. Understood?”

“Not my first ear piece either,” Douglas said, masking his irritation.

Archer caught up with them once he finished the call.

“Good news?” snow asked.

“Pamela Masters’ plane lands in less than an hour.”

“I assume you’ve got someone meeting her?”

“Yeah,” Archer said. “Me. I’ve got a car and a couple of guys coming by to pick me up. We’ll get her secured at the office while you find her kid.”

“Works for me,” Snow said. “Thanks for your help. I know you get tired of hearing this, but I owe you one, Gramps.”

Archer laughed. “You’re wrong. I never get tired of hearing that.”

The Snow boys headed over to meet with the others.

“Nice car,” Brooks deadpanned as Agent McClellan stepped out of his unmarked monstrosity.

Mac shrugged off the comment as he joined them. “She gets me where I need to go. Sometimes that’s enough. Nice arsenal,” he said, trying hard not to smile.

“Best I could do on short notice,” was Brooks’ comeback.

“So, where we heading?”

Snow motioned toward his brother as he passed earwigs around to his companions. “Doug?”

He laid out the file and a map on the hood of the car. “GPS tracking puts your phone here,” he said, stabbing a finger onto the map.

“Looks big,” Mac said as he popped the microphone in his ear. “Horse farm?”

“Give that man a prize,” Douglas said. “The property is owned by a businessman named Gerald Roarke. He owns Roarke Construction and a few smaller businesses. The recession hit him hard. He had to sell off some of his assets when the construction market went in the toilet. He’s leveraged to the hilt, could lose it all.”

“Gerald Roarke,” Brooks repeated softly. “Why is that name familiar?”

Mac blew out a breath. “The Roarke’s are connected. If this Gerald Roarke is the same guy I think he is, then you’ll looking at mob ties.”

“Considering who the girl’s grandfather is, I’d say it’s a pretty good bet it’s the same guy,” Snow said. “Mob means muscle so we’re going to have to do this one clean and sneaky. These guys aren't going to care about a badge, FBI or no, Mac. We're going to have to go at them sideways."

"Clean and sneaky?" Mac asked.

"It's a thing," Snow said.

"Oh, I'm sure."

"Doug?" Snow prompted.

"Right. It looks like the property has been in the Roarke family for a few generations. I didn't trace it all the way back though because it didn't seem germane to the case."

Snow nodded in agreement.

"Horse farm means lots of grazing grounds and that means lots of wide open spaces," Archer said. "Sneaking in ain't going to be easy."

"No. Not easy," Douglas parroted. "From the house, you have a full field of view of the property. Not a lot of room to hide."

"Hence the *sneaky* part," Snow said.

"*Clean* and sneaky," Mac corrected him.

"I assume you have a plan," Archer asked before his grandson could form a retort.

"Working on it," Snow said.

Collectively, the group rolled their eyes, but he ignored them. If there was one thing that his brother had going for him, Douglas decided, it was his ability to adapt and roll with the punches. That was just another way that the Snow brothers were different. Douglas was a planner. He would never have considered moving on an objective without a plan in place and certainly would not react well if the plan fell apart, as they were prone to do.

It was in those moments, however, those tense moments when the shit hit the fan, that Abraham Snow thrived.

It was hard not to be envious.

"We good?" Snow asked, looking at each man in turn. "Go or no?"

"Whatever we have to do, let's go get that girl back," Douglas said, speaking for everyone.

"You heard the man," Snow said proudly. "Let's move out."

###

The Roarke horse farm was huge.

The property, which had been in the family for generations and covered one hundred and twenty acres suitable for handling many groups of horses at any given time. In addition to the main house, there were four stables, five barns, and two guest lodges on the premises. There were two ponds and plenty of fresh green grass for the horses to enjoy.

From a distance, it reminded Snow of his grandfather's farm. Just like Archer Snow's place the Roarke horse farm was no longer used for its original purpose. There were still horses on the property, but not, he suspected, for business reasons.

When Roarke's name came up in Doug's briefing, all the pieces fell into place concerning Katie Masters and her abduction.

If Katie's grandfather was a bad guy, then Roarke was worse. The Roarke family had been linked to a numbered of open-unsolved cases up and down the East Coast and as far west as Las Vegas. According to Mac, local, state, and federal agencies had even assembled a joint task force to take down the Roarke's and their ilk, but so far all of their efforts had resulted in a lot of knowledge, but very little proof. Papa Roarke had been playing this game a long time. He knew how to cover his tracks.

They split up and approached the property from opposite ends. Mac and Douglas took the East Side while Snow and Brooks came in from the west. After dropping off his passengers, Big John covered the north side, which was the backside of the property. They were under direct orders to sit tight and watch while Snow and Brooks went in. If they ran into trouble, the others would come in like the cavalry.

Ideally, Snow would have preferred more boots on the ground, but under the circumstances, he was happy to have as much help as he did. For minute there, he figured he and Brooks would have to go in on their own. It was doable with two, but would be messy. There had been a time when messy wouldn't have bothered him, but Snow was looking at things a lot differently these days. Taking a bullet to the chest tended to make a man re-evaluate his priorities.

And Snow had been doing that a lot since returning home.

Some things, however, he decided, could never be left behind.

"You ready?" Brooks asked, drawing him back to the present.

"Five by five, partner," he said. He tapped his earwig. "Moving in."

Security was a joke, which surprised Snow considering who owned the property. A ramshackle wooden fence guarded the perimeter, but it was in such disrepair that they easily stepped over the fallen posts.

He could see the house in the distance. It wasn't too much of a hike, but far enough that the bad guys wouldn't see them coming. At least that was the plan. He was beginning to wonder if Douglas had gotten it wrong. Was this place really deserted? Or was it all a facade to keep people like Snow and his friends away? Either way, there was one question that had to be answered. If the old horse farm was truly abandoned--

--how had his phone end up inside?

On the other side, he took a knee and scanned the area. “Clear,” he said softly.

Brooks joined him. “This seem too easy to you?”

“Yeah. Stay frosty.” Snow stood and sprinted to his next position where he repeated the process. If anyone had seen their approach, they did not seem concerned enough to do anything about it. There were two possibilities, he decided. Either the people inside were far less effective that they had assumed...

...or far more dangerous.

“What do you think?”

“I've got five bucks on trap,” Brooks said.

Snow smiled. “You always did like to hedge your bets, brother.”

Brooks shrugged. “What can I say, I don't like to lose.”

“Neither do I.” Snow moved in closer until the house was only a couple dozen feet away. The fact that they had gotten so close without so much as an alarm sounding bothered him, but turning back wasn't an option. Not as long as there was a chance that Katie Masters was being held inside.

Once Brooks moved in closer, Snow sprinted across the open space between his position and the side of the house. If it were a trap, this would be the most obvious place to spring it.

Snow was only a few steps from the wall when he heard the first hint that anyone was actually inside. A quick closed fist alerted Brooks to hold, which he did as soon as his partner raised the hand signal.

Snow eased forward to look through the window, but couldn't make out much on the other side through the pulled curtains. All he could see were shapes, blobs of gray moving on the other side. He held up a single finger to tell Brooks that there was only one guard on the other side of the window.

Brooks nodded then searched around until he saw what he was looking for. He hefted the rock. It had weight, but wasn't much bigger than a softball. From his spot by the tree, it was an easy enough throw for him to make. With a grunt, he sent the projectile flying toward the house. His aim was true.

The sound of breaking glass filled the air.

From inside, Snow heard the footfall of a single guard running toward the break point. He waited until he heard the crunch of glass beneath shoes before he made his move. He pulled the pin on a flash bang he had brought with him and tossed it through the now shattered window and braced for the POP!

He didn't have to wait long.

Smoke poured from the opening and he heard a man coughing inside. Snow was about to leap in front of the window, gun leveled and ready to find his target when the coughing got louder. Before he could move, the guard's head pushed through the smoke, gasping for air outside the broken window.

Snow wanted to laugh.

Had Katie Masters' life not been in immediate danger, he probably would have, but time was tight. He didn't have time to waste.

"Hi there," Snow said, smiling at the startled guard.

Snow punched him square in the face and knocked him back inside.

"Wow," he said, shaking his head in disbelief as he looked inside to the man sprawled on the floor coughing and rubbing his sore nose.

"Did that really just happen?" Brooks asked as he ran up beside him.

Snow shrugged.

"It's so hard to find good henchmen these days," Brooks deadpanned. He shook his head before climbing through the window. Once inside he looked down at the disoriented guard. "You should be ashamed of yourself," he told the man.

Brooks unlocked the door and Snow pushed inside. The smoke from the flash bang had already started to dissipate as Brooks used zip ties to bind the guard's hands behind his back. The guard mumbled something unintelligible.

Brooks pulled the man close and stared him down. "You keep your trap shut, brother."

"Or what?"

"You won't like the alternative," Brooks said with a sneer.

"Trust me," Snow said. "It's not pretty."

Once Brooks had secured the guard in a small pantry that barely gave him room to turn around, he and Snow pushed forward.

"We're in," Snow said, tapping his earwig to activate it.

"Copy that," Mac's voice sounded in his ear. "Any resistance?"

"No," Brooks said.

"Nothing major," Snow clarified.

"Stay frosty, boys."

Snow and Brooks exchanged a look and tried not to smile at Mac's comment.

They made their way down the hallway that ran the length of the house, stopping to sweep every room they passed. All of the rooms were empty and some looked like they had been that way for a very long time. The sweeps were quick, one of them going inside while the other stood watch in the hallway, alternating from one room to the next.

At the end of the hall they moved into a large open atrium in the center of the house.

"This seem right to you?" Snow asked as they walked into the empty room at the far end of the house. The room was spacious and was used as an office. Desk, chairs, a couch, and a pool table filled the room.

'Nothing about this has felt right from the moment I took this case," Brooks said plainly. "Did we miss them?"

"Looks like."

"Damn!"

Snow tapped his earwig again. "Hey, Doug?"

"Yeah?" his brother's voice sounded in his ear.

"My phone still here?"

Snow listened as his brother tapped at the tablet he used to track the mobile phone.

"Yeah. According to geo-location, your phone is in the house." Another tap-tap-tap on the glass display. "I'd say it's less than fifty feet from where you're standing."

"This place is empty man," Brooks said.

"Call my phone," Snow said.

"What?" both Doug and Brooks said simultaneously.

"If my phone is here, we'll hear it ring and then I can find it," Snow said, trying not to sound, as his brother liked to call it, *snippy*.

"Good call," Douglas said. "Dialing."

There was no ring, but Snow could hear the soft buzz of the phone on vibrate. "Keep ringing it."

"You got it," Doug said.

The phone buzzed again while Snow and Brooks looked through cushions trying to find the source.

"Got it," Snow said and held up the phone as though it were a prize in a scavenger hunt. He hit the button and the display screen lit up. "That's weird."

"What?"

"It's set to record," Snow said, holding the screen up for Brooks to see.

"Smart kid," Brooks said.

"Yes she is." Snow stopped the recording and hit play.

"Is it safe to assume that you were the one who hired a private detective to find me?" Katie Masters' voice said from the recording, only slightly muffled by the cushion where she had stashed the phone.

"Too smart," Snow said, tapping his ear-piece. "John, come pick us up!"

8.

Archer Snow was not a patient man.

Over the years he had learned how to fake it enough to succeed in business, especially in one such as his where he had to deal with clients who had no concept of time management or sticking to his schedule. Still, he learned how to keep his irritation hidden.

Sort of.

After twenty minutes standing around the Gwinnett County airfield, he was about ready to explode. The plane, which should have been on the ground fifteen minutes earlier, was running late. The last update he'd received had the aircraft at roughly ten minutes out. To most people, ten minutes wasn't much. To Archer Snow, ten minutes could have just as easily been an eternity.

He kept his frustration in check though and had somehow resisted the urge to shout or tear someone a new ass for the delays. It was no way to run a business. He blamed himself as much as anyone. He was the one who had chartered the private flight for the woman he was on site to meet. Things had spiraled quickly so there hadn't been time to dispatch one of the Snow Security Consulting jets to pick up the passenger and ferry her to the airfield so he had done the next best thing.

"She's on approach now, Mr. Archer," Randall Rook, the private field's operations manager told him.

In addition to being a man whose work ethic consisted on skating by on the least possible effort he could muster, Rook also had the unfortunate distinction of having a name that reminded Archer of a comic book character, or someone out of the old pulp magazines. The combination of his name and incompetent nature made it difficult for Archer to take him seriously.

"Thank you," he said simply.

"Five minutes," Rook added.

"Thank you," Archer said softly through grit teeth.

As the flight operations manager made his way back to his office, or wherever the hell he went when he wasn't getting on Archer Snow's nerves, the CEO of Snow Security Consulting walked over to the small security detail waiting next to the SUV they had arrived in twenty minutes earlier. Archer had arranged for two of his own security people to meet him there to greet the plane. He wasn't expecting trouble, but it was also his experience that trouble rarely showed up when you were looking for it. Trouble preferred to sneak up on you when you weren't looking and bite you on the ass.

"Ready?" he asked.

"Yes, sir," Daniel Sisko said as he pulled a duffel bag from the back seat and transferred it to the back to make room for their guest.

Sisko had been with the firm for years, as had his partner, Anson Tuck. While Sisko reorganized the gear, Tuck stood next to the open driver's door, ready to slide behind the wheel as soon as he was needed. They were seasoned professionals and good at their job, which was precisely why Archer had requested them.

"She's on approach now, sir," Tuck said, pointing as the small jet dropped below the clouds and headed their way.

"Well, it's about damn time," Archer groused. Okay, so maybe he still had some patience issues to work on, but that was a problem for another day.

It took another two minutes for the plane to touch down on the runway and then another four for the jet to taxi at interminably slow speed over to the hangar where they waited.

Once the plane stopped and the door opened, he got his first glimpse of the passenger. She was stunning and confident and made a beeline for him as soon as her feet touched asphalt. When she spoke, he realized that it was an act, a brave face she wore to keep from falling apart under the circumstances. He understood exactly how she felt.

"Mr. Snow?"

"Yes, ma'am. I'm Archer Snow. I'm sorry we had to meet under such circumstances, but if you'll come with me we can get you someplace safe until…"

"Where's my daughter?" Pamela Masters demanded as she fell into step next to him.

"I'm afraid I don't have a good answer for you yet," Archer said. "I've got a team working on it and expect an update any time now."

"That's not good enough," she said and stopped dead in her tracks.

He turned to face her, his voice firm and unwavering. "No. It's not. Right now, nothing will be, but you have to trust me," Archer said. "We're doing everything we can to get your daughter back safe and sound."

"It's not enough."

"I agree," a voice said from behind Archer before he could respond.

He spun around and came face to face with a man he had never met before, but definitely knew because his face had been plastered all over the news a few years earlier.

"Antonio Manelli," Archer said plainly.

"Good. You know who I am. That will make things easier," the newcomer said.

Antonio Manelli was the head of the Manelli Crime Family, one of the longest surviving organized crime empires currently operating inside the United States. In the case of the Manelli family, it really was a family business. Anton Manelli had been an East Coast mover and shaker in the early 30's and expanded to the West Coast in the late 30's, although he eventually consolidated his power base back to the East Coast when California players pushed back.

Like his great grandfather, Antonio Manelli was a powerful man on the East Coast and smart too. He had moved the family into more and more legitimate businesses, which made him one of the richest men in the country, which gave him new inroads to politicians and Twenty First Century movers and shakers.

Men like Manelli were dangerous.

Archer Snow understood the Manelli's of the world. He had been working against their kind for most of his life, but these days, as a private citizen, he wasn't as directly involved as he would like to be. He certainly did not do business with their kind if he could help it.

That decision had been taken out of his hands.

"What are you doing here?" Archer asked, stepping between the newcomer and Pamela Masters. One of Manelli's thugs had a gun on Archer's men, keeping them sidelined.

"I called him," Pamela said.

It took a moment for that to sink in. Archer spun to face her, certain he had misheard her. "You did?"

"Yes, she did," Manelli said.

"Why would you do that?" Archer asked her and ignoring the mobster.

"How can you ask me that?" Pamela Masters shouted. "Someone took my daughter!"

"And we're going to get her back."

"I don't know you," Pamela spat back. "I don't know anything about you. Until I stepped off that plane you were just a voice on the phone! How did I know I could trust you? For all I know, you're the ones who took my daughter and wanted me to complete the set!"

"Miss Masters, I…" Archer started, but let his words fade off. Even he could see the wisdom in what she was saying. "Better the devil you know, huh?" he said instead.

"Yes," Pamela said softly. "I've been running from these people and what they represent for so long, but if there's one thing I know about my former father-in-law, it's this-- he loves his granddaughter."

"She's right," Manelli said. "I do."

"If it were up to me, we'd never have to deal with him or his family again, but my daughter wanted a relationship with her grandfather. As much as it pains me, I can't stand in the way of that. I wasn't close with my grandparents and sometimes I regret that. I don't want my daughter growing up with those same kind of regrets. Can you understand that, Mr. Archer?"

"I can. Do you understand why I think this is a bad idea?"

"Oh, I know it's a bad idea," Pamela Masters said. "I just don't have any other options."

Before he could argue the point, Archer's phone jingled in his pocket, Elvis warbling out a classic tune. He cast a look at Antonio Manelli before reaching for it. He had the feeling that making sudden moves might not be the best course of action with this crowd.

After a nod from the crime boss, he fished the tiny device out of his pants pocket.

"Archer Snow," he answered, his tone all business even though he recognized the number. He hoped the call would bring welcome news.

"It's Abe," he heard his grandson say over the connection.

"Give me good news, Abraham."

"I wish I could. We were too late. Roarke and the girl are gone."

"That's too bad," Archer said, casting a sideways glance at Manelli, who stared daggers his direction.

The last thing he wanted was to cause the mobster to overreact. When men in his position overreact, someone got hurt, usually the bearer of the bad news. Archer had no interest in trying to take out Manelli and his three goons on his own.

"We've got a lead, though," Snow said. "The girl was able to leave us a clue."

"Oh?"

"Yeah. Smart kid. She set my phone to record then hid it. I guess she figured we'd track it."

"You get a destination?"

"Sorta."

"Care to elaborate?"

"Roarke snatched the girl to get to her grandfather like we suspected. He told Katie that her grandfather was coming here."

"I'd say that's pretty much on the money."

"You know something we don't?" Snow asked, suddenly concerned.

"You could say that. I'm at the airfield with Katie's mother…" he glanced once more at the criminal, who was talking softly with his daughter-in-law. "…and grandfather," Archer continued.

"Manelli's there?"

"In the flesh. Hang on a second."

Archer turned back toward Manelli. Unlike most men who came face to face with the crime boss, Archer Snow didn't cower before him. He looked the man straight in the eye.

"I'm warning you…" he started.

"Warning?" Manelli said, the start of a smile curling the edge of his lip.

"Yes. Warning," Archer said. "I won't have you turning this city into a war zone. If we do this… *if…* then we do it smart. I want your word on that."

"I'm not accustomed to being talked to like this, Mr. Snow," Manelli said, his voice even and unwavering. This was a man used to being in control. "I did my research on you. I know all about you and your business. You've earned a reputation for excellence and getting the job done. From what I hear you're damn good at what you do. That's the only reason we're having this friendly conversation. Were it not so, trust that I would not be so civil. Now, if you know me, and I'd be really disappointed if you hadn't done your homework too, then you know that I take care of my own and I'm damn good at what I do too."

"We work together then," Archer said plainly. "We get your granddaughter back. No cowboy nonsense."

"You have my word," Manelli said. "To a point."

"Fair enough." Before putting the phone back to his ear, Archer turned back toward Katie's mother. He saw the fear, the expectancy in her watering eyes. This was a woman on the brink of losing the most important thing in her life and she had no idea how to save her or who to trust. Archer could sympathize. Trust did not come easy to him under the best of circumstances. If their roles were reversed, he too would feel an icy fist around his heart as she must be feeling at that moment.

He opened the car door for her and motioned her inside.

"Let's go get your daughter back, Miss Masters," Archer said.

9.

"You did what?"

Of all the things he expected to hear his grandfather say when he got back on the phone, the words he heard the old man utter were the last ones that Abraham Snow would not have made the list. He listened carefully and managed not to interrupt as Archer Snow laid out the rest of his plan.

"You can't be serious?" he said once his grandfather finished.

"Dead serious."

"Do you trust Manelli?" It was the million dollar question.

Silence filled the air between them until Archer finally said, "I do. The only thing he's worried about is his granddaughter. Trust me, if the shoe were on the other foot and that bastard had Samantha, I'd be doing the same thing."

The thought of his sister in harm's way made Snow fist clench around the cell phone. If Manelli really cared for his granddaughter like Archer believed, then Snow was willing to look past the man's criminal deeds, call a temporary truce, and help him get her back. "Okay. What's the plan?" he asked.

"We're calling a meeting. See what Roarke wants in trade."

"It's risky," Snow said.

"When isn't it?" Archer said playfully, reminding his grandson that this was not his first time in the trenches. Archer Snow played the loveable old man routine too well, sometimes and Snow forgot that he had spent many a year working for the same black bag organization Snow had only retired from a few months earlier.

"We're coming to you," Snow started. "Where are you?"

"No need. We're about to head out. I'm taking this lot back to the office. We'll be safe there. My driver tells me that Highway 316 is shut down. We're taking 20 toward the Mall. We'll hit 85 South there."

"It's a good bet Roarke knows Manelli's in town." Snow warned.

"All the more reason to get him somewhere secure, wouldn't you say?"

"I'll call Dad and have him lock down the building. He'll be ready for you when you get there."

"Good idea," Archer said. "What else you got?"

"Not much. The horse farm's a bust. Just a couple guards. We missed them."

"Okay, stay on it."

"The guys have things in control here," Snow said. "John and I are coming to you."

"That's not nec--"

"No debate. You need back up if things go sideways. We're it."

With a sigh, Archer reluctantly agreed. "See you when I see you."

"We're on our way."

"Have Doug call me if they find out anything."

"Got it. Stay frosty, gramps."

Archer hated being called *gramps*, which was the main reason Snow did it. A little good natured ribbing never hurt anybody. Plus, it helped alleviate the tension Snow felt. He was used to jumping in front of bullets himself. It was a new experience seeing his grandfather do the same.

"Talk soon."

"Copy that," Snow said and silenced the phone.

"Bad news?" Brooks asked.

"Is there any other kind?"

"Not lately."

Snow couldn't disagree.

###

Big John met up with them just ahead of Mac and Doug.

"You heard?" Snow asked his brother and friends.

"I did," Mac said. "I pulled the file on Manelli. This guy's bad news. If he's here and Roarke knows about it…"

"He does," Brooks interjected.

"Oh, I think it's safe to say Roarke was counting on it," Snow said.

"Then it's a good bet things are about to get bloody," Mac said without hyperbole. "When these two go head to head, it usually ends with bloodshed. Lots of bloodshed. I've got to call this in, Ham."

"Agreed," Snow said. "We're probably going to need the backup, especially if Roarke and Manelli brought foot soldiers with them." He pointed to Brooks, Douglas, and Mac. You guys head toward the office. Mac, see if you can spare a couple of your FBI buddies to swing over and keep an eye on the place just in case Roarke plans a pre-emptive strike."

"Consider it done," Mac said. "Where will you be?"

Snow opened the car door. "John and I are going to head them off at the pass."

"I'm going with you," Brooks said.

Snow knew better than to argue and time was running shot so he simply shrugged and slid the seat forward so his one time mentor could get in the back. "Fine. You're in the back."

"They've got one helluva head start on you. How do you plan to catch them?" Douglas asked.

Snow smiled. "Spoken like a man who has never taken a ride through the countryside with him," he said, craning his head toward the driver. "Catching them won't be a problem."

"Let's go," Big John said from the driver's seat.

"Be careful," Snow told Mac and Douglas. "Call me as soon as you're in place."

"We've got it," Mac said, pointing to the car. "Go!"

"We're gone!"

As soon as Snow was in his seat, he turned to the driver. "Know any shortcuts?"

Big John Salmon smiled and Snow decided that would be a good time to put on his seat belt. The driver dropped the car into gear and took off, although Snow decided that *launched* might have been a better way to phrase it. They were already pushing eighty miles per hour by the time the tires touched the asphalt of the old country road at the end of the driveway. The car took the turn from the dirt road that serviced the horse farm onto the single lane flat top sideways, leaving only black skid marks on the asphalt to mark their passing. With deft precision, John changed gears and picked up speed.

From the backseat, Brooks held on in silence.

"You okay?" Snow asked, trying not to grin.

"You kidding? I love a good roller coaster ride," Brooks said. He was kind of convincing. Almost. It was his eyes wide open that betrayed his words.

"I'm going to remember you said that," Snow said.

With a small smile, Big John Salmon pushed the gas pedal to the floor and held it there.

"Exactly, how do you plan on catching up to them?" Brooks asked as he held on tight. "This beast may be fast, but they've got a big damn head start on us."

"Shortcut," was all Big John said.

Before Brooks could ask, "What shortcut?" the driver took the car into a steep turn and they were no longer on anything resembling a road.

The car jerked and bounced across the rough-hewn path that ran through a pasture of some kind. It wasn't until Snow yelled "Cow!" That Brooks realized what type of pasture it was they were tearing across at top speed. The driver easily avoided the bovine roadblock, taking the Camaro into a slide that looked like something Brooks had last seen in a Fast and Furious movie. The poor old cow stared at the passing car with a blank expression, as if cars came tear-assing past him on a daily basis and this was just another day at the office. Then again, maybe they did. Brooks knew very little about what country boys did for fun.

Up ahead, the wide-open spaces were coming to an end. Laughing softly, Big John tugged the wheel hard, sliding across the mud and grass, cutting rough troughs to mark their passage. Shifting gears, the car leapt forward and down an embankment that was steep enough the Brooks had to push against the back of the seat in front of him to keep from flying forward. It did satisfy him to see that Snow was also having trouble holding on as the stunt driver took them through a labyrinth of trees, rocks, and stumps until they crossed the small creek and started up the embankment on the other side.

"Where the fuck are you going, man?" he finally shouted.

"Shortcut," the driver repeated, never taking his eyes off the… well, road wasn't the right word. The car bounced over washed out holes, slid across damp grass and slick mud, but Big John took each sideways slide or unexpected bump in stride. Brooks could have sworn the big man was enjoying himself.

He was right.

"There's 85!" Snow shouted as the car ended its off-road adventure and jerked onto a small two lane road that ran parallel to Interstate 85 South. The road ran through a subdivision so now there was traffic to contend with, not that such a thing hindered Big John. He driver passed a couple of slow motorists without losing any speed.

"We need to get off this," Brooks said.

"No argument," Salmon said. "Hold on. We're almost there."

"Almost where?"

Before the driver could answer, he took the car into a hard left turn, leaving the hardtop road and taking them off-road once more. This time it was a short trip, but less smooth than their foray through cow country.

A small, dilapidated fence was all that separated the community of homes from the busy expressway. The Camaro cut through the rusty chain link fence like a knife through butter with only a soft *PLINK!* to mark the moment.

On the other side of the fence, the ground dropped several feet down a steep incline. The driver picked up speed and launched the getaway car over the embankment, just barely missing the edge of the ditch that ran next to the highway.

The car hit grass and skidded sideways, but Big John quickly regained control and pulled them smoothly onto the expressway. Thankfully, at that time of the day, the traffic wasn't bad so Big John changed gears and put the petal to the metal as they used to say in movies.

"Time?"

"Ten minutes," Snow said.

"That's got to be some kind of record," Salmon said, proud of the accomplishment.

"Next tune up's on me," Brooks deadpanned from the backseat.

Snow smiled.

"Think we'll catch them?"

Snow looked back at his friend. He tried to hide the worry in his face, but couldn't. Even though he could take care of himself, Snow couldn't help but be concerned that his grandfather was once again in harm's way because of him.

"I hope so," was all Snow said as they sped toward the city.

10.

Archer Snow was the first to catch sight of their tail.

He didn't want to say anything that would ramp up the anxiety in the SUV, which was already thick enough to cut with a butter knife. Pamela Masters was holding tightly to her emotions, keeping them locked down tight for the moment. He suspected it would not take much to break her concentration though. She was wound pretty tight. Thankfully, she had stopped staring daggers at her estranged father-in-law and was now silently watching the world pass by out her window.

Sitting in the roomy back seat between Archer and Pamela, Manelli had given up his attempts to talk to her and he too sat quietly, no doubt pondering his next move. Antonio Manelli was not a man accustomed to sitting back and letting others do for him. He was a hands on kind of man. Archer could respect that, if not the man's profession.

Archer leaned closer and kept his voice low.

"We've got company," he said.

Obviously, subtlety was another area where the mob boss was lacking because he jerked around in his seat so suddenly that it disrupted people in cars the next lane over. "Where?" he said loudly.

"Three cars behind us. Silver Oldsmobile."

"Are you sure?" Manelli asked.

"It got on the expressway with us, but didn't take the opportunity to speed past like all of the other cars," Archer said. "You may not know this, not being from around these parts, but anytime a Georgia driver is doing less than the speed limit, they're either avoiding one of our many speed traps or they're up to something."

"And you think these men are the latter?"

"I do."

"What's going on?" Pamela asked.

"We're going to make a slight detour, ma'am," Archer said, trying to keep them all calm. "Driver, in about one mile there's a turnoff to the right. It's an abandoned rest area. The state uses it for storage now. It'll be empty. Pull off there, would you?"

The driver looked in the rearview mirror and made eye contact with his boss.

Manelli nodded his approval.

Archer hit redial.

###

"Snow!"

"Slight change of plans," he heard his grandfather say on the other end of the phone.

"Where are you?"

Archer filled him in on their current whereabouts and plan.

"Perfect. We're just a couple minutes behind you," Snow said. "They're pulling off at the old rest area just past the Mall of Georgia exit," he told Big John.

"Got it."

"Find a shady spot until we get there."

"No promises," Archer said before ending the call.

"There!"

Snow pointed to the exit just ahead, but Big John was already ahead of him. He swerved around a slow moving pick-up truck that was hauling a load of scrap metal and then took the closed off ramp into the abandoned rest area. Before the car stopped, both Snow and Brooks were chambering a round in their guns.

"Stay here," Snow told Big John, although he suspected that directive to fall on deaf ears. He was right.

"Not a chance." Salmon pulled a manual load Smith and Wesson from the glove box before sliding out the passenger door.

Brooks followed right on his heels. He was shaky, but happy to be back on solid ground.

The rest area was an older model, a throwback to the rest areas of the 70's and 80's, not the large centers that dotted the interstates these days with their museums, free wi-fi, and hiking trails. In its heyday, this place had been a quick stop off to use the restroom or stretch your legs before continuing the long, lonely drive to Atlanta. Of course, that was long before the Mall of Georgia was a gleam in some designer's eye or the area had grown up and filled out with businesses, homes, restaurants, and shopping centers. Shutting it down saved the state a great deal of money and the place had outlived its usefulness.

Then they found a new use for it. The main building had seen better days, having succumbed to the ravages of age and brutal Georgia Summers, but the state had set up pre-fab metal sheds used as garages where they parked their snowplows and salt trucks, something only used once or twice a year. It was out of the way and safe. There were two sheds visible from the entrance, but there were probably others behind it. Snow wasn't sure. The last time he had been there, he was a little kid on a family trip when they made a pit stop long enough for him to run into the restroom and pee while his father complained about how much time the unscheduled stop were wasting. That was a long time ago.

Two SUVs were parked near one of the garages. The one in the back's doors were open. Snow and Brooks approached from opposite sides, weapons trained on the vehicle. The back was cot occupied and they stared at one another across the empty seat through the open doors.

The car wasn't completely abandoned though. The driver remained behind the wheel, though not by choice. He was dead. A small caliber shot had pierced the driver's side window, catching the driver in the side of the head and splattering blood and brain matter all across the front windshield.

"Is he…?" Brooks asked even though he knew the answer.

Snow shook his head.

"Your grandpa?"

Snow shrugged then pulled his phone from his pocket. He sent Archer a text. He didn't want to risk calling him in case the bad guys were there as well. The message was simple. *I'm here. Where R U?*

A text came back almost immediately. *Around back. Ambushed. Had to run.*

Snow pointed in the direction and they ran to the front edge of the shed. Brooks held back as Snow chanced a quick look. If he took fire, Brooks would be able to get a bead on the shooter. Thankfully, no one took a shot. Whoever the bad guys were, they were chasing them on foot.

Snow pointed and then eased around the corner, leading the way with gun raised and ready to fire. It was slower than barreling in with wild abandon, but being smart in tense situations like these almost always trumped leading with your emotions.

Snow and Big John stayed next to the wall of the shed as they made their way forward. An Oldsmobile was parked up ahead and they each took a side to verify it was empty. Not too far ahead of the car was a familiar vehicle, a light blue panel van with Aces High Heating and Air Conditioning Services stenciled on the sides. The van was beat up from its first run in with Snow and Brooks when Gerald Roarke sent his men in it to kidnap the granddaughter of his chief rival.

The van was also empty.

Brooks was across the cracked asphalt driveway that was losing its battle with nature as grass and weeds pushed their way through the breaks, threatening to reclaim their piece of the Earth. If there was trouble, not being all bunched up together would work in their favor. It was a tested tactic he and Snow had used on previous occasions. It worked.

After confirming that the car was empty, the three of them continued onward, checking the obvious ambush points and coming up empty each time.

"Where are they?" Salmon asked.

Snow shrugged. "There's only so far they can go. The woods offer cover, but you can only go a short distance before you hit 985. This place sits in the triangle where Interstates 985 and 85 intersect. There's not a whole lot of space to hide."

Brooks shrugged, silently asking the obvious question. *What now?*

Snow pointed toward the woods and Brooks moved in that direction. He then pointed Big John toward the second shed. "Check it again, then come around the far side, just in case," he whispered.

With a nod, Salmon moved off as well.

Snow walked up the center, staying on the path.

He didn't have to go far before he heard a commotion.

It was his grandfather.

And he was shouting.

11.

Archer Snow stared at the barrel of a 12 gauge shotgun.

"Now you hold on just a damn minute, son!" he shouted as the man wielding the weapon approached.

"Shut your mouth, old man," the gunman said. He was easily twenty, maybe thirty, years Archer's junior and clearly did not think of a man Archer's age as a threat. That was his mistake to make.

His boss, on the other hand, was just a few years younger than the elder Snow and he had a little more respect for a fellow warrior. Archer had done his homework on Roarke and he assumed that, given the situation, the mobster had probably checked him out as well. Roarke's family might have been on the losing side of their mob war, but he was not a stupid man.

Antonio Manelli was simply smarter than his rival.

Manelli's remaining guard stepped between his boss and the shooter.

Archer tried to stop what he knew was going to happen next, but he wasn't fast enough. Manelli's man went for the gun in the shoulder holster concealed beneath his jacket. Before he could pull his weapon free, another of Roarke's men dropped him with a shot to the head. He was dead before his body crumpled to the ground.

Archer spread his arms wide to keep his own men at bay. Neither Daniel Sisko nor Anson Tuck reached for their weapons, but like Manelli's man, they had positioned themselves between Pamela Masters and the men who had kidnapped her daughter. Their job was to keep her safe. They knew their boss could take care of himself.

"No one else needs to die here today," Archer said plainly, trying to reign in the chaos. "We all want a peaceful end to this, Mr. Roarke. Isn't that right, Mr. Manelli?" He didn't turn to face the man behind him so he hoped like hell he was nodding.

"That defeats the purpose of my coming here, Mr. Snow," Roarke said as he stepped forward, a gun in one hand, the other holding tightly to Katie Masters' arm. "Or did you forget that my aim here is to kill the man you've elected to protect?"

"Katie?" Pamela Masters started, but Archer's men held her back.

"Mom!"

"It's going to be okay, Katie," Manelli told his granddaughter, finally finding his voice. "Just stay calm."

"Calm is a very good idea," Archer said. "This doesn't have to get bloody."

"It's a little late for that," Manelli said. Archer hadn't seen him pull his gun, but now he noticed it in Manelli's hand, although it was held at his side. That was a relief. At least the mobster was willing to listen.

"No it's not. There's a way to end this where we all walk away healthy," Archer said. "What do you say, gentlemen? Let's chat." He nodded to a small clearing away from the assembled crowd.

Archer took two steps in the direction he indicated and Manelli fell into step next to him. Slowly, Roarke released the grip on his hostage and passed her to one of his men. Then, once he was certain it wasn't a trick, he walked over to join the other two men.

"Good," Archer said when the three of them were together. "That's a step in the right direction."

"What's your interest in this, Snow?" Roarke said. "How can you protect scum like this?" He flicked an angry glance at his rival.

Before Manelli could respond, Archer cut in. "My only interest here is getting the girl safely back to her mother," he said.

"What is she to you?"

"An innocent bystander, Roarke. That girl has done nothing to you. She's not part of your war."

"What do you know about any of this?" Roarke demanded.

"More than you might think. You've both made the news a time or two."

Manelli shrugged.

"Plus, I hear things."

"What do you want, Roarke?" Manelli finally asked.

"I want what's due me?"

"And what, pray tell, do you think you're due, huh?" He took a step forward, anger reddening his features.

"Easy now," Archer warned.

"You… your family has taken so much from me and mine," Roarke said. I just want back what I had."

"You know how this game works, Gary," Manelli said. "You win, you lose, then you do it again. You lost your fire. Your head wasn't in the game and you lost. You have to live with that."

"See, that's where you're wrong. I got back in the game," Roarke said, pointing toward Manelli's granddaughter. "And I grabbed myself some leverage."

"What do you want, Roarke?" Manelli asked. "Specifically. I can't give you *back in the game* or whatever past glory you think you need to relive. I don't care how far you've fallen, no one can give you those things. What I can give you is something substantial. Name your price."

"You think this is all about money?" Roarke croaked.

"What else? You forget, I know you, Gary," Manelli said. "I know what you've done and who you did it to. The fact that one of your own hasn't put a bullet in your brain yet is, in fact, surprising to me. The only interest you've ever had is in what you can get for yourself. Well, here's your chance. I can't give you a golden parachute, but I can make walking away worth your while."

The two men stared across the few feet that separated them, Manelli's offer hanging between them like a living thing.

Archer held his tongue, afraid to say anything that might toss a match on this tinderbox of a situation. One wrong move and the shooting started.

"Well, what's it going to be, Gary?" Manelli asked again, louder this time. "You tell me what it's going to cost to get my granddaughter back!"

Oh, crap, Archer thought.

Roarke, who had seemed to at least be considering a peaceful end to the situation, blanched. His features twisted as the rage of losing everything he had to Manelli and his people bubbled back to the surface.

"Come on, man," Archer said, trying to keep the situation calm. "You're so close to getting what you came here for. Don't throw that away because Manelli's an asshole. Whatever history you guys have is just that… history. This isn't about you." He pointed toward Katie Masters. "It's about her. It's about keeping her safe."

"Whose side are you on?" Manelli sneered.

"Don't you listen?" Archer said. "I'm on your granddaughter's side. Always have been. You two can kill each other for all I care, but she doesn't need to see that, does she?"

"You want to know what I want?" Roarke asked. "You want to know what I really want?"

"Yes!"

"Fine! I'll tell you!" Roarke lowered his voice to just above a gravelly whisper. "I've wanted you dead for so long that the thought of killing you made me hard. Now, I realize that killing you isn't the answer. Killing you won't make me feel better." He shrugged. "In fact, I'm pretty sure that killing you would just get me killed."

"You're smarter than I gave you credit for, Gary."

"And no matter how far I've fallen, I'm not ready to die. Not yet."

"Then that brings us back to the only question that really matters," Roarke said. "What do you want?"

"A new start."

Archer and Manelli looked at one another, both of them surprised by the answer.

"Beg pardon?"

Roarke lowered his voice again. "A new start. I want to work for you."

Manelli laughed. "What possible reason would I have to do that? I don't trust you. I can't trust you. Hell, even your own people don't trust you."

"Easy, gentlemen," Archer said.

"Tell me why I should trust you."

"Because I've got no one left. This… this handful of guys, that's all I've got left. It's not about trust, it's about loyalty. And my loyalty can be bought."

"What does that get me?" Manelli asked.

Roarke smiled because he knew that he'd hooked Manelli. "I might be down and no longer on top of the game, but I do know where a lot of the bodies are buried and I know many secrets… secrets I'm willing to share with you… for a price. Is that worth upgrading to the golden parachute package?"

"And if he agrees, Katie goes back to her mother?" Archer asked.

"Yes."

Archer turned to Manelli. "Well?"

"I would need to see this intel you claim to have, but yes, if it's useful, we have a deal. I won't let you work for me, but I'll help you disappear, start over somewhere fresh where you can enjoy your retirement."

"I can live with that," Roarke said.

Archer clapped his hands together. "Excellent. What say you two shake hands and we holster the weapons, what do you say?"

Roarke lowered his weapon and Archer let out a breath.

A shot exploded around them, blood flying from the newly formed hole in Roarke's forehead. The force of the impact pitched him forward and instinctively, both Archer and Manelli sidestepped the lifeless sack of blood and bone as if fell to the ground between them.

Archer pulled his weapon and Manelli raised his, both men spinning in the direction from which the shot originated. Archer expected to see his grandson standing there, having put down the bad man.

Unfortunately, Abraham Snow was nowhere to be seen.

Roarke's man, the one who Roarke had left in charge of Katie Masters, stood firm, his weapon smoking. He had since handed off their captive to one of the two other man with him. The third man stood back a few steps and had his weapon, a Browning Bolt-Action Rifle pointed at them as well.

Archer tried to calm the situation. He lowered his gun slightly, but did not holster it. His trust only went so far. Roarke had been willing to talk, but something told the elder Snow that this man whose name he did not even know, was not interested in discussing things rationally.

"Save your breath, old man," the new head of the Roarke clan said. "It won't work on me."

"All we want is the girl," Archer said. "That hasn't changed."

The new boss smiled. "Actually, something has changed," he said.

"What?"

Archer recognized the look in the younger man's eyes and he knew what was going to happen next, as surely as if they were following a playbook.

"No!" Archer shouted, already moving.

The new boss smiled--

--then pulled the trigger.

12.

Abraham Snow ran.

Gravel crunched underfoot as he made his way down the makeshift road that cut through the former rest area. He had picked up the pace when he heard his grandfather's voice shout and was at a full run by the time he heard the gunshot.

The sound echoed off the trees and metal building the Georgia Department of Transportation had erected in the spot to store their infrequently used vehicles and even more infrequently used winter weather equipment. Since GDOT had taken over the space, grounds keeping duties had fallen by the wayside as tufts of tall grass sprang up all over the site, the Earth attempting to retake its space from the concrete, gravel, and other man-made inventions designed to keep Mother Nature out.

None of that concerned Snow as he ran around the corner, gun in hand.

Two men lay bleeding on the ground, one not moving, the other clutching at his wounded arm. Snow assumed the bleeder was Antonio Manelli. Archer was kneeling next to the man, trying to stop the bleeding. Two men approached with weapons pointed at them, Katie Masters' mother, and two men Snow recognized from his grandfather's company. Although they outnumbered the bad guys, Snow understood that they had leverage.

They still held Katie Masters hostage.

Snow looked for Brooks, whose path would have brought him out behind the man holding Katie. He kept her far enough away from the others that, even if they were able to make a move on his partners, they would not be able to rescue the girl before he killed her. It was a smart plan, but one doomed to failure.

Snow saw Brooks emerge from the trees. His friend spotted the kidnapper and his hostage and made his way toward them in relative silence. The noise of two connecting interstates on either side of the rest stop created a kind of white noise effect that drowned out almost everything else.

It was the only cover they were going to have.

Snow tucked the gun in his belt behind his back, blew out a breath to steady himself, then walked out of his hiding place into the clearing, hands held out from his body in as non-threatening a manner as possible.

"Hi, guys."

The lead gunman did not take his gun or eyes off Archer and Manelli, but his partner turned toward Snow.

"Drop it!" the man shouted.

"Okay. Okay," Snow said. He showed the man his empty hands. "No gun. I just want to talk."

"I think there's been more than enough talking today," the leader said.

"How can you say that?" Snow joked. "You haven't talked to me yet. I've been told I'm a fascinating conversationalist."

"I don't have time for you." He waved the gun to the side. "Get over there with the others."

"All right," Snow said casually. "We're all good. Just one question though?"

"What?"

"Where's Katie Masters?"

"Not really something you should be concerned about at the moment, pal," the leader said.

"Oh, I'm not concerned," Snow said as matter-of-fact as he could. "I was just curious if you know where she'd gotten off to?"

"What?" This time he did turn, looking toward where he had left his leverage.

The girl was gone.

The man who had been holding her lay in a heap on the ground. He was out cold, but at least Brooks had left him alive when he rescued Katie.

With the two men's attention diverted, Snow pulled the gun from his waistband and fired. His aim was good, nailing the closest gunman in the shoulder and dropping him, the weapon falling from his now useless fingers. He would live, but it would not be a pain free life.

Before Snow could turn toward the leader, Archer was already in motion. Scooping up Manelli's dropped handgun, he pointed it at the man who had shot both Roarke and Manelli.

This time they stared down the barrel of each other's guns.

"Stand down," Archer ordered. "You've lost."

"Not yet. I'm still the head of this family."

"No," Archer said. "You're the man who murdered the head of your family then tried to kill a rival head. Son, I may not know everything, but all you've done today is paint multiple targets on your back."

"I…" he started, but nothing he could say would change the facts. "I didn't think…"

"No. No you didn't. I can still help you get out of this."

"How?"

"You can make Roarke's deal. I'll help you disappear."

The leader lowered his gun. "Doesn't sound like much of a deal."

"It beats the alternative," Snow said as he walked over and plucked the gun from his hand.

As soon as the leader was unarmed, Archer lowered his weapon. "You okay?" he asked Snow.

Snow barked a laugh. "I was about to ask you the same thing."

"Where's my daughter?" Pamela Masters asked, her eyes wide as panic once again threatened to overwhelm her.

"I'm here, Mom," Katie said as she and Brooks walked back into the clearing. Big John Salmon was a few steps behind them.

Katie ran to her mother and they threw their arms around each other, hugging one another tight.

Brooks smiled as he and Daniel Sisko took the three gunmen into custody, zip tying their hands behind their backs while Anson Tuck took over treating Manelli.

Big John called 911 and an ambulance was ten minutes out. He relayed the information.

Snow clapped his friend on the back. "Thanks, pal."

"Anytime, man. You know that."

"He going to be okay?" Snow asked Sisko of the wounded mobster.

"He'll live."

"Good." He turned to the rescued kidnap victim. "How about you?"

"I guess I will too."

"Smart thinking with the phone." He held it up and wiggled it back and forth. "It was a big help."

"I'm glad you got here in time," Pamela Masters said.

Snow looked over at his grandfather. "So am I. Sit tight. We'll have you out of here soon."

"Is he… is my grandfather all right?"

Snow nodded.

"Can I?"

"Go ahead," Snow said, motioning for her to go. "I think he would like that."

"Thank you again," Pamela Masters said before following her daughter.

"My pleasure."

Snow rejoined his grandfather and they walked over to the three gunmen now sat.

"So, what now?" the leader asked.

"Just what I promised. I'm a man of my word."

"We'll see."

"Just one question," Archer asked.

"What's that?"

"What's your name? Roarke didn't exactly introduce everyone."

The leader smiled. "No. Why would he, huh? I'm Jason. Jason Roarke."

"His son?" Snow said.

"Nephew. Not that he treated me like family, mind you. I was just another nobody on the payroll."

"Well, Jason Roarke, you better thinking about what new name you'd like," Archer said. "You're not a nobody anymore."

Roarke laughed. "Just my luck. I finally make my bones and then lose it all the same day."

"My father used to always tell me something that fits moments like this," Archer said. "Some days life's a bitch. Today is your someday."

13.

The next couple of days were a blur.

As happens anytime weapons are discharged, there are reports to be written, paperwork to be filed, and depositions to deliver. Snow and his friends had arrived at the FBI field office in Atlanta together and did their debriefing one at a time then met up again at Snow Securities in the building next door.

Antonio Manelli was recovering nicely from his wounds in a nearby private medical facility. Since he had committed no crimes while in the area and had no outstanding warrants against him, there was nothing the local authorities could do but post a round the clock watch on him and escort him out of Georgia as soon as he was medically sound to leave.

Likewise, the FBI had no reason to hold him either. Sure, they all knew he was connected to the mob, but what they lacked was proof, a fact that drove Mac's supervisors at the Bureau nuts.

Archer Snow was proving to be of little help in that regard also. He told the FBI that he had not witnessed Manelli commit any illegal acts in his presence, which was technically true.

Once Manelli was discharged, Mac and a few of his comrades, escorted the mobster to the airport, watched him board his private jet, and waited until it was in the air before they returned to the office.

Snow and Brooks met with Katie and her mom at the same restaurant where he had first met Katie when all of this started. It seemed fitting.

"Will you be staying here?" Snow asked when the subject shifted to Katie's college career.

"I still haven't decided," she said. "We're coming up on the end of the semester and I'm going to take a bit of time off and spend a little of it with my mom and some with my grandfather."

All eyes turned toward Pamela.

"I'm not crazy about the idea," she said. "But, if she wants to spend time with him, I'd rather know about it."

"Good plan," Brooks said. He handed both of them a card. "If you ever need anything. You give me a call and I'll drop what I'm doing and be on the first plane."

"Thank you," Pamela said as she accepted the cards.

"Same here," Snow said. "You know how to find me."

###

After saying their good-byes to Katie and her mom, Snow returned to his loft apartment above his grandfather's garage with Brooks in tow. Since his friend's hotel room was technically still a crime scene, Snow had offered to let him crash on the sofa for as long as he wanted.

Besides, they had things to discuss-- business that Snow preferred they keep between themselves. That was the main reason Brooks had ventured back to the mainland from the paradise he called home.

"I love what you've done with the place, brother," Brooks said after tossing his duffel on the couch.

"You not a fan of the '*lived in*' look?"

"Depends on who's doing the living, I suppose," Brooks snarked.

"Touché."

The apartment was clean, but cluttered. There were several dozen boxes of various sizes stacked unceremoniously around the room. With the apartment's open floor plan, there was plenty of room for the stuff, even in its current state of disarray.

"You moving in or out?" Brooks asked as he strummed on an old guitar leaning against the wall.

"In, I think," Snow chuckled. "I pulled all this stuff out of storage last week. I haven't seen most of this stuff in ten years or more. It's taking longer to sort through it than I thought."

Snow picked up a stack of books from the sofa and moved them to the table so his friend would have a place to sit. Brooks kept standing, walking around the room looking at the odds and ends lying about.

"I didn't think I'd kept so much," Snow said with a chuckle.

"Hard to put down roots doing the kind of work we do," Brooks admitted. "Although, it looks like you're making an effort. You're certainly doing better than most."

"I don't know about all that," Snow said.

Brooks shrugged.

"Maybe. I don't know. It's not easy trying to remember the guy I was before... well, before."

"Getting out doesn't mean you have to go back to being the same guy you were a decade ago. Sure, you aren't your aliases, but that doesn't mean they weren't part of you."

“I did some things while I was under that I'm not proud of,” Snow said as he pulled two beers from the refrigerator and offered one to his guest before he plopped down on the sofa.

Brooks took the offered beer and leaned against the wall. “You think you're the only one?”

“No. I guess not.”

“Definitely not,” Brooks said pointedly. “It ain't easy doing what we do... or what we did. There are things I did to maintain my cover that will stay with me to the day I die, brother, but you know what-- and this is the part that lets me sleep at night-- is that it was all for the greater good and I can live with that. I can live with it.”

Off Snow's blank stare, he added, “And so can you.”

“Sounds good in theory,” Snow said softly. “Not so easy in reality.”

Brooks chuffed a laugh. “What’s reality?” He started walk around the room again. “We’ve all got regrets, brother. Doing what we do… what we did… it ain’t easy and it sure as hell ain’t for everybody. You have to lock away the real you in a dark hole inside yourself. Sometimes, if you’re under long enough, you have to lose the key. The trick is finding it later.”

“I know all this,” Snow said.

“I know this ain’t your first rodeo, kid,” Brooks said. “I’m the last one who’ll try to tell you how to build your life, but I’ve seen you with your family, your friends. Like it or not, my brother, you’ve got a good thing going here. Don’t you know how lucky you are? There’s a lot of our kindred out there who would kill for the post game life you’ve built here.”

“Yeah. Maybe.”

“No maybe about it.” Brooks tapped the side of his head next to his eyes. “These puppies see all, remember?”

“How could I forget, Columbo?” Snow joked.

Brooks laughed.

“Speaking of which,” Snow said, leading the conversation away from his personal life. “You said you had some information for me.”

“I do. Sorry it’s taken so long to get here.”

“Tell me you’ve found Ortega and it’s all good.”

“Well…” “Not exactly.” Brooks began pacing back and forth.

“Spill it, Brooks. Did you find him or not?”

“Sorta.”

"That's not an answer, Samson," Snow said, irritated at his friend trying to tap dance around the answer. "Just tell me what you found on Ortega."

"Okay. I tracked down some of Ortega's hired guns, hoping I could at least trace back the money to their boss. No joy there though."

"No. The money is run through a series of wire transfers in and out of banks in the U.S., Switzerland, and the Grand Caymans. So far, the DOJ has had little luck tracing it."

"And we all know how thorough those Department of Justice bloodhounds can be."

"While I was under, I suggested putting the IRS on the trail, but my request was denied."

"Smart idea," Brooks said. "Who better to sniff out hidden money?"

"That's what I said. Guess the boys at Justice didn't want to share the finder's fee."

"How sure are you that Ortega isn't actually this guy's name?"

"Very," Snow said. "There are way too many varying descriptions of the man, not to mention times he is recorded in multiple places at the same time. No, Ortega is like a code name used by several men."

Snow resumed pacing.

"I'm fairly certain there's a real person at the head of the Ortega organization. I don't know if it's the bastard that shot me or not, but finding him is a good first step toward me putting this to bed."

"Your old bosses know you're still working this?" Brooks asked.

"They'd be stupid to think I'd let it go," Snow said, grabbing another beer for each of them and handing over another cold one to Brooks. "You know we've all t=got that one case… that one we just can't let go of. This is mine."

"Oh, I get it, brother," Brook said, popping the cap off his beer.

"So, you mentioned Daniella Cordoza before. You think she knows who sits at the head of the Ortega table?"

"If anybody does, I bet it's her," Brooks said. "You spent time with her while you were under, right?"

"I did," Snow said, once again absent-mindedly rubbing fingers across the wound in his chest. "Getting close to her helped get me in good with Ortega."

"And just how close did you get?"

"As close as I had to," Snow said. "You know the job."

"I do indeed."

"You telling me you've never bedding an asset while under cover?"

"Oh, I never said that," Brooks joked. "You'll get no judgement here, brother. You do whatever it is you have to do to get the job done."

"Yes," Snow said, suddenly very interested in a spot on the floor.

"Do you know where Daniella Cordoza is right now?" Brooks asked.

"No. I lost track of her after I got shot. I tried to find her after I got out, but my resources are a bit more limited than they used to be. I didn't have much luck."

"I think we should focus on finding her."

"I don't want to take my eyes off Ortega though," Snow said. I need to keep pulling intel on him."

"And I'm not telling you to stop." Brooks stood, stretched, then walked over to the porch overlooking the lake. "All I'm saying is we put the focus on Cordoza."

"Where would you like to start?"

"Tell me everything," Brooks said. "Let's start with an easy one. Is Daniella Cordoza her real name?"

That brought Snow up short. It was not a question he had even pondered before.

"I… I don't know," he said.

"Well, I think it's time you an' me did some digging and found out," Brooks said.

Epilogue.

Daniella Cordoza walked in out of the sun.

Dressed in a dress and shoes that cost more than some middle-class Americans brought home from the day jobs in a year, Cordoza looked like a million bucks. She had super-model looks and an intellect great enough to keep her highly in demand.

She was the total package, beauty and brains in one very expensive package.

This wasn't her first trip to the Dubai and probably not her last. She loved everything about this place except the heat, although she was growing accustomed to that as well. It seemed that her work took her from one hot and/or humid region to another. Perhaps next time, she told herself, she would schedule a meeting to take place in the Caribbean or some other nice place where she could tack on a little vacation afterward.

Ah, it was good to dream.

Cordoza signed in at the front desk and was greeted by the aide of the mediator she was there to meet. Her employers were looking to move their business into the Dubai market, but that meant jumping through multiple hoops with not only local government, but also some very influential men who were the real power in the city.

Having a third party act as a mediator was the usual course of action in cases such as these. It had pleased Cordoza to offer up a recommendation for her host to vet for the position.

The aide opened the door on the thirty-ninth floor and ushered her inside an air conditioned meeting room with a breathtaking view overlooking the ocean. Her new potential business partners sat on one side, their demeanor serious and business-like.

She took a seat opposite them.

The mediator sat at the head of the table, essentially between both sides.

She made her introductions across the table, meeting each of the men there in turn. None of them offered to shake hands.

"And may I present our mediator for these negotiations…"

"Hi,' the perky young woman said as she took the new arrival's hand and shook it. "I'm Samantha Dean from Hanson and Diamond. A pleasure to meet you."

And you as well, Mrs. Dean. American, yes?"

“Yes, ma’am. That’s part of the reason I was surprised when we received the invitation to join your negotiations. We’re usually the last ones on Dubai’s speed dial.”

“Oh, I wouldn’t worry about that,” she said. “I heard you are the best and my employer is always looking to hire the best.”

“Then let’s hope this is the beginning of a fruitful partnership,” Dean said as she took her seat.

“Oh, I believe it will be,” Daniella Cordoza said as she sat down and smiled at Abraham Snow’s sister across the table.

“So, let’s get started, shall we? Who would like to go first?”

Keep reading. Abraham Snow Returns in Snow Drive.

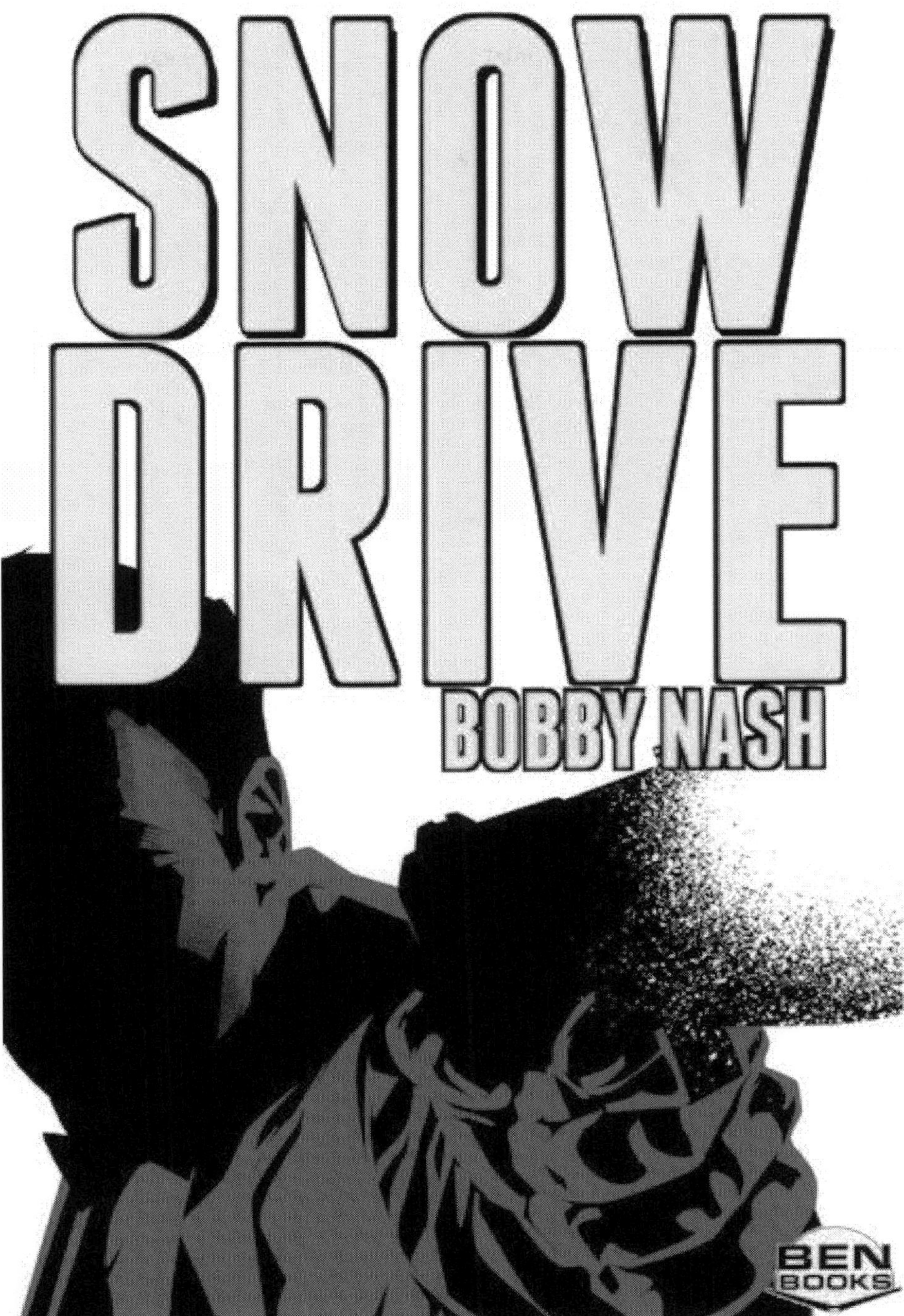
SNOW
DRIVE
BOBBY NASH
BEN BOOKS

Heat rose off the pavement in waves.

A cool winter chill hung in the still southern air in direct contrast to the eerie, ghosted view rising off the track. There was no snow or precipitation in the forecast save for a slight chance of rain and no one really expected that to happen. The stands surrounding the one and a half mile Atlanta Motor Speedway racetrack stood empty, devoid of screaming fans. The crowds would come later. The pits, on the other hand, were a bustle of activity as crews readied their pit garage for Sunday's race.

None of that mattered to the man taking the steep turns at one hundred and eighty miles per hour, however. His only thoughts were focused on marking the best time he could on his final lap.

The number fifty-seven car was purring like a dream as it hugged the turns.

The stock car screamed across the start/finish line at top speed and the driver let out a *WA-HOOO*!!! of excitement.

In the pits, Grant Chambers clicked the stopwatch he grasped tight. To say he was pleased with the time would be an understatement. It wasn't the driver's best time, but it wasn't his worst either. Grant

Chambers was a legend in NASCAR. He was a nine-time Cup Champion and three time Daytona Five Hundred Winner. Currently enjoying a great season, Chambers was rumored to retire at the end of the following season after a farewell tour and run his family racing empire from pit row.

Although neither he, his partners, or his family had made any public announcement about the retirement, word somehow leaked and the rumor mill has been running rampant since. The more he tried to deny the rumors, the more people seemed to believe them.

He was tempted to confirm it, but they had all decided that it would be better to announce after the current season was done so it did not distract from this season's cup chase.

He also didn't want to do anything to take attention off the incredible season his son has been having. Grant checked the time again and whistled. It was impressive. His son, Chase Chambers, was the man behind the wheel of good ol' number fifty-seven. He was an up and comer, a whiz on the circuit, having just won his fifth consecutive race of the season. Sports insiders were already starting to follow his career with interest, comparing his driving style with that of his famous father. There was already talk of him being an odds on favorite to win the cup.

Grant was proud of his son, proud to know that the Chambers racing team would still have a Chambers behind the wheel when he retired.

Speaking of whom…

Grant looked around for his son. After crossing the finish line, he knew that Chase would do one last lap before pulling the car into the garage. He was surprised he hadn't made it in already.

He toggled the microphone on his headset.

"Chase, you bringing her in or what?"

"On my way," his son's voice called back in his ear. "There's a problem. Injectors are locked open. I can't throttle her down."

"What's that?"

"I'm coming in hot," Chase said. "Clear me some space!"

Grant shouted for everyone to get clear and everyone scattered, putting distance between them and the thick concrete wall that ran the length of pit row. If a car was coming in hot and unable to stop using conventional means, the driver could use the wall for deceleration by hitting it at just the right angle and using friction to slow the car.

It was a solid plan, in theory.

Part science and part gut feeling, there were a hundred things that could go wrong with the maneuver. Not the least of which was the amount of damage that could be done to both car and driver.

The vehicle came off the turn low, another tactic for keeping a car's speed down. Chase drove through the grassy area leading to the pits, using the soft earth for resistance. Leaving the pavement was a good way to burn off speed.

The car bounced back onto the asphalt at the entrance to pit row. Number fifty-seven shimmied as the tires grabbed the surface.

Chase tried throttling down once more.

Nothing happened.

The car hit the wall hard, sparks flying as metal scraped against concrete and steel.

Grant Chambers ducked as a piece of sheet metal tore off of the car and flew into the pit area, just barely missing his head by inches.

The car slowed.

It was not enough to do any good.

A tire burst, the sound echoing up and down pit row like a cannon being fired.

Grant watched in horror as his son's car flipped end over end into a rolling mass of twisted metal and ruptured hoses. Fluids sprayed in all directions before it came to rest in the center of pit row.

That's when the number fifty-seven car burst into flames.

Fire and rescue were dispatched to the scene as drivers, mechanics, and crew all ran to help with the damage and to see to the wounded driver.

Grant Chambers ran to the burning wreck that had once been his car. He shouted his son's name as he approached.

The car exploded before he could reach it.

"Chase!!!"

Grant Chambers' world fell apart as he watched the car burn. His legs turned to rubber and he dropped to his knees.

"Chase…"

"Dad?"

He spun around to see his son lying on the ground nearby, a couple of guys from a rival crew having reached him first and pulled him from the wreckage before the fuel tank ignited.

"Oh, thank God," Grant said. He forced his quivering muscles to work and ran to check on his son.

Rescue and EMS were on the scene seconds later and examined Chase Chambers. Although he appeared to be fine, track rules required a visit to the track's medical facility.

As they loaded his son into the ambulance, Grant Chambers stared in disbelief at the flaming pile of rubble that had been a finely tuned state of the art piece of high tech equipment only moments before. He was thankful that his son had survived the crash, but he was also worried. This was not the first accident to have befallen Chambers Racing in recent weeks. He had chalked it up to bad luck at first, but that excuse no longer flew. Someone was trying to destroy his company. Grant was certain of that fact. What he did not know was who or why, but he had a suspicion. What he needed was proof.

For that, he would need help.

And he knew exactly who to call.

SNOW DRIVE

1

Abraham Snow was excited.

He hadn't been to the racetrack in years. The last time he had visited the Atlanta Motor Speedway, his dad had surprised him, Douglas, and Samantha with tickets. He had agreed to take the kids to the races to give their mom a much-needed day off.

Or so they had been told at the time. Snow would later learn that his mother had stopped taking her medication and was having issues dealing with things. When this happened, Snow's grandfather, Archer would step in to help. Like everyone else, Laura Snow loved the old man and listened to his soothing words. It was the exact opposite reaction she had to her husband, Dominic.

Snow and his dad rarely saw eye to eye, even when Snow was a kid. He couldn't put his finger on the reason their relationship was strained, but it had been as long as he could remember. No matter who was at fault, and Snow admitted that there was enough blame to go around, there was one thing that he and his dad had in common.

They both loved the races.

Since he had returned to Georgia after retiring from his previous profession, Abraham and Dominic Snow had given one another a wide berth. They were civil when they saw one another, but there was definitely a chill in the air. Not surprising as things had been chilly between them for a couple of decades.

When Archer Snow, who was not only Abraham's grandfather and Dominic's father, but also the owner of Snow Security Consulting, ergo, their boss, asked them both to accompany him to the Atlanta Motor Speedway to meet with one of their clients, they both agreed to be on their best behavior.

Dominic was always in business mode. He was straight-laced, stern, and in serious business mode all of the time. Those attributes made him the perfect Senior Vice President of Snow Security, but when it came to being a Dad, he was lacking.

At least as far as Abraham was concerned.

Snow's brother and sister had much better relationships with the old man than he did so he begrudgingly admitted that some of the reason for the distance between them was on him. Douglas and Samantha were still on great terms with their father, but rarely talked to their mother. Laura Snow was a free spirit, eager to follow the whims of her heart wherever they might take her. One day, the wind blew her out of their lives and she never looked back.

Snow always felt close to his Mom, even after she left. He had looked her up after he was released from the hospital and moved into the spare apartment over his grandpa's garage for his recovery. They spoke on the phone and exchanged the odd email, but he had yet to see her in person. Each time he brought up getting together for lunch or coffee, she always had a convenient scheduling conflict and a promise that they would get together soon.

He was beginning to think he would believe it when he saw it.

Of course, he saw his Dad more often than his Mom, but they talked less, which worked in their favor and kept the peace.

At least he had his grandpa.

Archer Snow was the best. He was equal parts best friend and co-conspirator. Growing up, Archer was just like the other kids and Snow always loved spending time at his farm. He had grown up near his grandfather so they spent a lot of time together.

Years later, when Snow learned that he had gone into the same line of work that his grandfather had retired from, they only became closer. As the vast bulk of Snow's work was either highly classified or off book, as they called it, having someone to talk to about his former life was a blessing.

Archer had arranged for a company van to shuttle them from their office in Century Center to the speedway. The drive would take an hour or so, given traffic. Unfortunately, with Atlanta traffic, all bets were off. At least the interstate was open. The past few months had been a traffic nightmare since a fire beneath Interstate 85 burned so hot that the elevated freeway collapsed. Traffic, which was already bad before, became a nightmare while repairs were made.

Thankfully, that was behind them now.

"Thank you all for clearing your schedule for this," Archer Snow said from his seat in the van. In the interest of time, he had decided to hold the briefing enroute to the track.

In addition to Archer and Daniel Sisko, the driver and Archer's personal security, the passengers were Abraham, Dominic, and John Salmon.

Abraham and John were not actually full-time employees of Snow Security, but they did work for Archer either as consultants or outside contractors. Archer wanted his grandson to be part of the family business, but the only way he and Dominic would ever be able to work together was with this type of arrangement.

"Our client has been having some issues and asked us for help," Archer said.

"Who's the client?" Snow asked.

"Grant Chambers," Dominic said.

"Chamber Racing," Snow said. "They're having a helluva year."

"Until that wreck a couple days ago," Dominic said. "Chase Chambers almost died."

"On the track, yes, thing are great," Archer added. "Off the track, they have some security issues they would like us to help them shore up. There is some concern that the accident you mentioned might not have been so accidental. Dominic, Daniel, and I will propose a few new security options for them."

"What do you need us to do?" Snow asked, chucking a thumb back and forth between himself and Big John.

"Mr. Chambers has some concerns about the cause of their recent issues. Snow Security can help secure their office, garage, and secure them on location during race week, but we aren't investigators," Archer explained.

"But I am," Snow said, seeing how the old man's plan came together.

"You are?" Dominic said, surprised by the news. "When did that happen?"

"Last week," Snow said. He smiled and held up his newly acquired private investigator's license. The p.i.'s license had been Archer's idea, a way for him to help out the family business without actually having to work directly under Dominic. Archer had explained that this way, when he asked Snow for a favor, the company could pay him a fee for services rendered.

Plus, with Snow's penchant for getting into trouble, having the p.i.'s license and open carry permit for the Glock that was never far out of his reach could come in handy. Seeing the wisdom in his grandfather's words, Snow applied for the license and jumped through the requisite hoops. The biggest hurtle was that the last decade plus of his life was still considered classified. As far as the world at large was concerned, Abraham Snow didn't exist for the last ten years or so.

To get a private investigator's license, he had to have experience in at least one of four categories. Technically, he had never spent five years as an investigator or as a police officer with the state. He didn't have a degree in criminal justice from an accredited college or university since he had been recruited right after high school. He had never been employed by a private detective agency for at least five years. What he did have was what they called substantively equivalent training or experience. Unfortunately for Snow, most of that experience remained classified.

Snow called in a favor and thanks to a phone call to the licensing board from General Henry Pinkwell, his former boss and a member of the Joint Chiefs of Staff, Abraham Snow's substantively equivalent training or experience was rubber stamped through no problem.

Now, he was a licensed private investigator, like his childhood hero, Thomas Magnum.

If only he could rock the mustache, but such was not to be. He couldn't even pull off a Seventies porn 'stache, not that he wanted to.

"I take it he thinks these accidents are sabotage," Snow said.

"That's one avenue we're considering," Archer said. "We have a few leads and he's agreed to let you investigate. If we can find out who is behind the sabotage, that will make securing the team a whole lot easier."

"And him?" Dominic said, motioning toward Big John.

"He's with me. Big John's my consultant," Snow said as if that was all the explanation needed.

"Consultant?" Dominic wasn't buying it. He had never held his son's friend in the highest regard, especially once he went to jail. Dominic had considered Salmon's incarceration as a foregone conclusion.

"B.J. knows a whole lot more about cars than the rest of us put together," Snow said before his father could object further. "If there's anything amiss, he'll find it."

Dominic pursed his lips and snorted. He wasn't willing to argue the point, especially since Archer would take their side anyway, but at least all of them understood that he was displeased.

The rest of the ride to the speedway was filled with briefings about the Chambers Racing Team's employees, their garage specs, and racing in general.

Archer Snow smiled. This was the closest his son and grandson had come to getting along in a long time. He planned to enjoy it as long as it lasted.

The remainder of the briefing went smoothly. Archer laid out the plan of attack. He and Sisko would meet with the track's owner and the NASCAR representative handling security so they were in the know on the additional security measures Snow Security Consulting would be initiating effective immediately. Normally, this was Dominic Snow's area of expertise, but since he knew more about the racing world than Archer, they would trade places for this case.

Dominic would meet and greet with the client, shake some hands, and take a tour of the grounds. His job was to get a good look at the areas requiring protection, and offer some preliminary security measures on the spot. He would take notes that would be used to form a more intensive plan.

Abraham Snow and Big John Snow would shadow Dominic on his run through. Archer invited them both to offer suggestions, but also made sure they remembered that, family issues aside, on the job, Dominic was their boss and they needed to afford him the respect of his position. Neither Snow of Big John argued the point.

Additionally, as the investigators, they would ask questions, meet the crew working the pits, the truck drivers, and other support personnel it takes to run a state of the art stock car racing team.

Archer had only been to the racetrack once, when he met their client, Grant Chambers, for the first time. That meeting had taken place in a restaurant on the other side of the interstate. Pulling into the facility now, Archer was in awe of its size.

The Atlanta Motor Speedway was huge. The complex sat on 887 acres of prime real estate conveniently located right next to Interstate 75, about 30 miles or so south of Atlanta. Basically, it was its own small city. It housed a 1.54-mile quad-oval track with a seating capacity of 71,000 fans, not to mention those who worked concessions, souvenir booths, and the race teams themselves. AMS opened in 1960 as a 1.522-mile standard oval. Although that was a bit before his time, Snow and his dad had spent many a weekend sitting on those hard aluminum seats.

The facility's head of security, Ian Petty, greeted them in the lobby of the main building. He introduced himself to each man, shaking their hands and adding, "No relation" each time he told them his name.

"I guess you get that a lot, huh?" Dominic said.

"More often than not," Petty said.

"Well, there's a reason Richard Petty is still called The King," Dominic said.

"Of course." Petty handed each man a visitor's pass on a lanyard so they could hang it around their necks. They were accepted with nods and soft thank yous.

"These will allow you unrestricted access to the areas of the track that you inquired. There are offices and sections that are off limits. Of course, the individual race teams have ultimate say over allowing you into their garages or not. We take security seriously here and they trust we will keep their proprietary equipment and devices secure."

"Of course," Archer said. "We're only concerned with securing our clients and their employees. We'll have a small presence here, but most of our work will happen when our clients are off site."

"Fair enough," Petty said. "I have arranged for a guide to transport you and your associates to the pits, Mr. Snow."

"Thank you," Dominic said.

Petty motioned for Archer to join him. "And I'll take you upstairs, Mr. Snow."

"Thanks," Archer said. "You boys play nice now," he said to his kids before they headed off toward the pits.

2

Archer and Sisko followed Petty toward the elevator.

While they waited, Archer asked, "Have your investigators determined the cause of Mr. Chase's crash yet?"

"As best they can determine, it's simple equipment failure," Petty said. "These may be state of the art vehicles, but they are put through their paces on the track. They are built and rebuilt by hand. Mistakes happen coming off an assembly line. In this line of work, there is no assembly line."

"Why are they called *stock cars* if they are anything but stock?" Sisko asked.

Petty smiled. He probably answered this question often. "In the original sense of the term, a stock car is simply a car that has not been modified from its original factory configuration. In the early days of the sport, drivers would race whatever car they could get their hands on. It wasn't until later that the term came to mean any production-based automobile used in racing. These days, stock car is just another term for racecar."

As if on cue, the elevator *pinged* and the door opened.

"We keep it alive because it's part of our name," Petty said. "NASCAR is the National Association for Stock Car Auto Racing after all and we really don't want to change our name to NARCAR."

"I can understand that," Archer said as they stepped into the elevator.

Sisko nodded and followed, satisfied with the answer.

###

Kelly Pratt wasn't a racecar driver, but she certainly drove like one.

The twenty-year old tour guide smiled as she drove the van carrying the visitors out of the tunnel into the pits, kicking up dust as she took the curve far faster than either Dominic or Abraham Snow would have liked. Big John Salmon, on the other hand, was having a blast.

Pratt was a fountain of knowledge. The perky blonde rattled off track facts and driver stats faster than they could keep up with them.

"How long have you worked here?" Snow finally asked when he could get a word in.

"Off and on about ten years," she said. "I used to work summers here with my dad. He worked maintenance for the track until he retired a couple years back. I guess you could say I interned here. Once I graduated from high school, they brought me on full time and gave me a scholarship to help pay for college."

"Nice," Snow said. "You planning to go into the racing business after college?"

"Absolutely. I plan to own my own team one day. I'm working for the track right now, but I've got applications out to several teams who are looking for new crew so I can get hands on experience. You can't be the boss without knowing how everything works, right?"

She parked the van and slid out to open the sliding side door.

"That's always been my motto," Snow said as he stepped out of the van. "Of course, that could be why I always found myself the employee instead of the employer."

She laughed at that.

"From the way you handled this van, I thought maybe you wanted to be a driver," Snow said.

"Nah!" she laughed. "Driving's fun and all, but we've got drivers aplenty. I'm studying for a business degree. I want to know how to run my own race crew."

Big John chucked a thumb back toward the van. "Well, the way you handled this thing, you have a future as a driver if you want it," he said.

"High praise coming from him," Snow said.

"You a driver too, Mr. Salmon?" Pratt asked.

"You kidding? This man can drive anything with wheels," Snow said. "And a few things without."

"Not professionally," Big John added before his friend could continue. "Came close though. Another life."

"It's never too late," Pratt said with a big smile.

"I'll keep that in mind."

Kelly Pratt led them into Pit Row, pointing out interesting spots along the way while dolling out facts and interesting tidbits. She knew the track's history backward and forward.

"The Chambers Team is birthed over here in garages eight and nine," she said when they arrived, pointing out the Chambers Racing sign hanging next to the open garage door next to one another.

"Thank you for the tour, Miss Pratt," Dominic said politely as they reached garage number eight. "I think we can take it from here."

Pratt smiled and nodded. Message received. She pulled a business card from her shirt pocket and passed one to each of them. "When you get ready to head back, just call that number and I'll pick you up and take you back to the office."

"Thanks for the tour, Kelly," Snow said and shook her hand.

Big John nodded and also shook hands.

Dominic was already moving toward the garage. As usual, he was all business and Kelly Pratt was not who he was there to do business with so he moved on.

The garage was exactly what Snow expected. This was not a showplace garage like the ones shown on TV. This was a working garage, much like the one he slept above each night. Big John kept his garage clean, but even the cleanest working garage is going to build up oil, grease, and grime, the lifeblood of the automobile. It was inevitable.

Dominic was shaking hands with a man roughly the same age as him, late fifties by Snow's reckoning. When he and Big John joined them, he made the introductions.

"Abraham, John, this is my client, Grant Chambers."

They shook hands and exchanged pleasantries.

"Welcome to Chambers Racing, gentlemen," Grant Chambers said. He motioned around the garage where three men were huddled in, around, and under a race car with the race team's logo and number emblazoned on it.

He motioned for the man under the hood to join them when he looked up from his work.

"This is my son, Chase. This is his car we're working on today."

"Hi there," Chase said, shaking hands with the visitors with a smile on his face. "Sorry we couldn't meet you up front, but as you can see, we're fighting the clock to get our back up car up to snuff before the race this weekend. We just got the new engine in today. If we want to qualify, we have to be track ready by Friday."

"We heard about the accident," Dominic said. "You're lucky you weren't hurt."

"We've become a bit *accident prone* of late," Grant said, adding air quotes to the '*accident prone'* part.

"We heard that too," Snow said.

"If you have a few minutes, Mr. Chambers, I can go over our security plans with you," Dominic said. "We will start by adding a security team to watch your garage space twenty-four hours a day. That will protect your equipment. After that, we have to secure you and your people. Is there somewhere we can talk privately?"

"I have an office in our trailer," Grant said, motioning toward the mobile car carrier parked outside the garage.

"Perfect," Dominic said. "My associates will take a look around out here, if that's okay?"

"Sure. If you need anything, either Chase or Tommy Yates," He pointed toward a pair of legs sticking out from beneath the race car. "He's my crew chief and can help you with anything you need."

"Thanks," Snow said as Dominic and Grant headed off for their private chat. "Actually, Chase, if I could ask you a few questions, that would help get me started."

"Whatever you need," the driver said. "I'm just the guy behind the wheel though. Dad's the one you'll have to talk to about security."

"I'm not exactly here for that," Snow said. "I'm here to investigate the accidents your team has been having. Snow Security will keep you safe, but I'd rather go ahead and stop whatever's happening from happening again. Do you have any idea who is behind these accidents?"

Chase ran his fingers through his wavy hair, pushing the stray strands out of his eyes. "Nobody springs to mind."

"Any enemies?"

"Well, you can't become a two-time Winston Cup Champion without pissing off somebody," he said with a laugh. "And that's just me. I've lost count of how many times Pop's brought home the Cup."

"Six," Snow and Big John said simultaneously.

"Right," Chase said, grinning. "One more and he ties Richard Petty, Dale Earnhardt, and Jimmie Johnson."

"Good company," Big John said.

"The best. Dad could very well make it if he has a great rest of the season. He might pass them next year."

"So those rumors of his retiring…"

"One hundred percent true," Chase said. "After the current season ends, he plans to announce that next season will be his last as a driver. Sort of a farewell tour. I trust you'll keep that to yourselves, gentlemen?"

"Of course. Client privilege and all that," Snow said. "You mentioned enemies?"

"Enemies might be too strong a word. Competitors, certainly, but I can't imagine any of the other drivers resorting to sabotage. It's just not that kind of atmosphere here."

Snow pointed at the open layout of the garage. "All of the bays are open to one another. What's to keep one of your competitors out of your bay when you aren't here?"

"Professional courtesy."

Snow tried not to laugh. "Are you really that trusting of everyone here?"

Chase looked hurt. The insinuation stung.

"You'll have to forgive my friend, Mr. Chambers," Big John said. "He has trust issues."

"Not without good reason," Snow shot back, ignoring the sudden pinprick he felt around the bullet wound in his chest.

"Regardless, I'm sure Mr. Snow Sr. out there…" He pointed toward the trailer. "…will have one of his guys camped out in here twenty-four hours a day until the race is over. You and your equipment will be safe."

"I wouldn't be surprised," Snow said.

Chase nodded. "Look, in here, we're just neighbors. If I break a wrench, the team in the next stall will lend me theirs just like I would if theirs broke. There's just not that kind of atmosphere in here. Now, you get us in our cars and out on the track and all bets are off, but even out there we watch out for one another. This is a dangerous sport. You have to trust the other drivers out there on that track with you."

"What about off the track?" Big John asked.

Chase shrugged. "The usual stuff. Sometimes egos get bruised and spats happen, but nothing too serious. Schoolyard stuff. Sometimes we get sponsors who aren't happy that we didn't sign with them or the ones who did who feel they aren't getting their money's worth. Reporters, bloggers, journalists who don't make our press lineup have been known to throw a baby tantrum or two. Rabid fans who feel they got brushed off. All of that comes with the territory. All part of the job. Not sure if any of it leads to sabotage though."

"I still have to check," Snow said. "Best to be thorough."

"What about your brother?" Big John asked.

"What about him?"

"I own a TV. I see the news."

"Now, you listen to me," Chase started, anger rising in his cheeks and voice. He pointed a finger toward Big John. "My brother and father may have their problems, but there is no way in hell he would do anything to hurt me or this family! You are way out of line!"

Snow held up is hands. It was now his turn to apologize for Big John. "My friend meant no offense, but we have to be thorough. I wouldn't be doing my job if I didn't look into every possibility."

Snow turned to look at Big John, a scowl on his face. "Although, I would have been a bit more tactful about how I broached the topic."

"Sorry," Big John said.

"It's okay," Chase said, calming down. "I'm very protective of my baby brother."

Snow smiled. "I understand. I have a baby sister I feel the same way about. It's all good. We will need to talk to your staff and your brother though."

"Understood. Actually, here comes Beau now." Chase waved and signaled the younger man over. Hey! Beau, come here a minute!"

"What's up, Chase?" Beau Chambers asked as he jogged over to them. There was no denying that these two were related. Beau was the spitting image of Grant Chambers just as much as Chase.

"I wanted you to meet Mr. Snow and Mr. Salmon. They're here investigating our recent… troubles."

Beau shook their hands in turn. "You think you can get to the bottom of all this?"

"I hope so," Snow said.

"You hope so?" Beau said, his voice rising. "If you expect to get one dime out of this family, you better do more than hope so, mister!"

"Easy now, Beau," Chase said, the voice of calm. "I'm sure it's just a figure of speech, right, Mr. Snow?"

Snow nodded.

"See?"

"Sorry," Beau muttered.

"It's okay. I am actually pretty good at what I do," Snow said. "Do you have any theories on who might be behind your recent… troubles?" he asked, parroting Chase's turn of phrase.

"Oh, I'll do you one better," Beau said. "I know exactly who is behind it!"

"Who?"

"You ever heard of Oliver Simcoe?"

"Doesn't ring a bell," Snow said.

"He's the owner of Simcoe Tech," Big John said. "They build engines, primarily, but occasionally branch out into other components. Big money."

"What makes you think he's behind this?"

"Because," Beau said simply. "Right before our '*accidents*' started, he threatened to ruin my Dad."

3

Abraham Snow hated being lied to.

With Chase Chambers hot on his heels trying to calm him down, Snow burst into the office where his and Chase's fathers were discussing new security measures.

"We need to talk," Snow said.

"You better have a good reason for barging in here like this," Dominic said, barely keeping his anger in check.

Snow ignored him, focused on Grant Chambers instead. "Tell me about Simcoe Tech."

"Simcoe Tech? What do they have to do with anything?" Grant said.

"Your son seems to be under the impression that they are behind your recent troubles," Snow said.

"I see you talked to Beau."

"I did," Snow said. "Is he wrong?"

"Where is he?" Grant asked.

"He's showing my partner around," Snow said. "He seemed to be under the impression that you would rather he not be here for this discussion."

"That's because it's a discussion I'm tired of having and he knows it," Grant said, his voice tinged with the frustration only a parent can have with one of their children.

It was a tone Abraham Snow was all too familiar with, having heard it many times directed at him by his own father.

"It seems odd to me that you didn't mention your problems with them before."

"Because there's nothing to mention."

"Try again," Snow said.

"It's nothing," Grant reiterated.

"Tell us anyway," Dominic Snow said before his son could repeat himself, which shocked Snow no end. It wasn't like dear old dad to take his side on anything.

Grant let out a breath. "Okay. Okay. What do you want to know about Simcoe Tech?"

"Why does your son think Oliver Simcoe is behind the sabotage?" Snow said, emphasizing each word.

"Beau looks at everything in black and white. It either is or it isn't. He's young. He has that right because he hasn't quite learned yet that the world is full of shades of gray. To him, everything happens in absolutes. Good is good. Bad is bad. That's not the way the world works and it damn sure isn't the way business works."

"Maybe it should," Snow said.

Dominic cleared his throat.

Snow shot him an irritated glance.

"Abraham, let's keep it on topic, what do you say?"

"Fine. What shade of gray does Simcoe fall into, Mr. Chambers?" Snow asked.

"Last year, Oliver Simcoe asked me and Tommy Yates to join one of his engine trials. His company designed a new engine that was supposed to be more fuel efficient for less pit stops, more environmentally friendly, which make for great P.R., and faster because every driver wants to win. I was reluctant. I hate these type of trials. Would never do another if I had a choice, but Oliver was persuasive. The money wasn't bad either. We bought a new car and trailer with what they paid for my time."

"Why reluctant?"

"These type of trials are generally a glorified public relations farce. They bring in a guy like me so photographers get shots of me next to a Simcoe engine and a Simcoe logo. The press runs with it, focusing more on me than the engine, which is given a seal of approval by my being there. It also takes up a good deal of time, which I really didn't want to invest. I would rather spend that time with my family."

"But you agreed to do the trial anyway?" Snow said.

"Yes. My wife suggested I do it and use the money for some upgrades the team has needed instead of sinking more of our personal money into it. My wife is the brains in the family. If not for her, I would just be a guy who likes working on cars and driving too fast."

"What did the trial entail?" Snow asked.

"We toured the plant, went over the specs for the new engine, watched a demonstration," Grant said. "I even did a test run on the engine on the track. ESPN, SPEED, FOX Sports South, CNN, and local news had camera crews on hand for that. It was great P.R. for Simcoe."

"And you?"

"Maybe a little," Chambers admitted. "It's part of the job. You can't do this kind of work and shy away from the limelight."

"I take it you weren't impressed with the engine?" Dominic added.

"The engine did what it was supposed to do, but there were some bugs involved that bothered me so I voiced those concerns."

"What kind of bugs?"

"Design flaws. The engine tended to overheat faster than it should have. On the track, in a race that lasts a couple of hours, that can lead to disaster." He pointed in the direction of the track. "A blown engine out there could get somebody killed, maybe even several somebodies. I couldn't sign off on that, not until they fixed those problems. That's what I told them."

"I take it Simcoe disagreed with your assessment."

"You could say that. He threatened to sue me for slander if I said anything about his engine's flaws publicly."

"I take it you signed an NDA," Snow said.

"Yes."

"Non-Disclosure Agreements are pretty common practice in any kind of private trials like this," Dominic said. "The designer generally has some proprietary components included that they don't want their competitors to be aware of in their product."

Snow nodded. He knew that information already, but bit back his response. Dominic brought out the worst in Snow, but the last thing he needed was to get into an argument with his dad in front of the client. "Thank you," was all he said.

"Did Mr. Yates agree with your assessment?" Snow asked.

"I'm sorry?"

"Mr. Yates. You said your crew chief was also part of the trial. Did he agree with your assessment of the new Simcoe engine?"

"No."

"No?"

"No," Grant said, louder this time. "He agreed that there would be more testing before rolling out the engine, but he did not completely agree with my findings."

"Then what happened?"

"Simcoe paid us what he owed for our time and kicked me and Tommy off the trial so we went back to work."

"So, you were both let go from the trial?" Snow asked.

"Yes," Grant said. "Simcoe said we were a package deal."

"Were you paid the full stipend or a partial?" Dominic asked.

"Partial. We were paid for time served on the trial."

"What happened with the trial?" Snow asked.

"It continued without taking my input into account. Simcoe put the new engine in the cars of a couple of the drivers they sponsor. That worried me, but my objections were supposed to be a matter of public record, which I later found out it wasn't. Simcoe had buried my concerns. Those drivers were betting their lives on an engine they believed to be safe."

"But you knew better," Snow added.

"Yes."

"What did you do?"

"Not enough." Grant shook his head. He let out a breath. "I went to the owners and drivers and told them what I knew, what I suspected. They listened, but nothing happened so I went directly to NASCAR with my concerns. Took it all the way up the ladder. I was told they would look into it."

"Did they?" Dominic asked.

"Sure. NASCAR takes driver's safety very seriously. There are very specific guidelines for what can and cannot be used in our cars and safety equipment."

Grant dug through a stack of books on a shelf, held in place by a bungie cord to keep them in place when the truck was moving. He handed it over to Dominic, who was closest to him.

"In there you'll find NASCAR's guidelines. Those are in place to keep the drivers safe. This is a dangerous business, Mr. Snow. Without these guidelines, drivers and crew would all be in danger."

"What happened to the investigation?" Snow asked.

"They did look into it," Chase said. "NASCAR is thorough. They took Dad's concerns seriously…"

"But?"

"But, ironically, off the track, NASCAR's wheels move very slowly," Grant said. "There was a race the same week I made my concerns known. They let the engine stay in the car while they investigated since there was no concrete evidence that they weren't safe. They passed along my concerns to the drivers and owners, but since I had already talked to them as well, it fell on deaf ears."

"I can see where that would be frustrating."

"There was an accident during the race and Danny Jacobs in the number ninety three car's engine exploded. His car flipped end over end.

There wasn't enough left of it to even recognize that it had been a stock car by the time it came to rest."

"I saw that on TV. He survived, didn't he?"

"Yes," Chase said. "I was two cars behind him. If you thought it looked bad on TV, you should have seen it from where I was sitting."

"The fire burned hot," Grant added. "Too hot. Danny was burned bad. He's alive, but in an ICU burn ward. It's still touch and go, last I heard. I talked with his daddy last week. Danny's a fighter, but that family has a long, uphill battle ahead of them. He'll never drive professionally again. For a driver, that's a fate almost worse than death."

"After the accident, did NASCAR pull Simcoe's plug?"

"Yes. The other engines were removed and they were placed under immediate investigation. NASCAR stepped up their investigation."

"Their findings?"

"The investigation is still ongoing, but Simcoe's new engines are on the restricted list," Grant said. "Some teams have even pulled old Simcoe engines in favor of another manufacturer's brand as a safety precaution."

Snow whistled. "That hits Simcoe where it hurts. They could lose… what, millions?"

"Easily," Chase said.

"And he blames you for this?"

Grant choked out a laugh. "Let's just say he's none too happy with me at the moment."

"Did he threaten you like Beau said?" Snow asked bluntly.

"Sort of. He told me he would ruin me."

"You don't consider that a threat?"

"I thought it was his bruised ego talking," Grant said. "Oliver is more bluster than bite. At worse, he might try to sue me, which he is, but sabotage? It never occurred to me to take the threat seriously. It still doesn't."

"It also didn't occur to you to mention this when someone started sabotaging your equipment?" Snow said.

"In all honesty, no," Grant said. "I've known Oliver Simcoe for over twenty-five years. Yes, he can be an asshole at times, but then again, I'm no angel either. He was upset, but the man I know wouldn't resort to trying to kill my son!"

"Maybe you don't know him as well as you think, Dad."

"Don't you start too!" Grant warned his elder son.

"What if they're right, Dad?"

Grant punched the top of the desk and winced as a jolt of pain ran up his arm. "I really don't think Oliver Simcoe is behind this," he said calmly.

"I hope you're right, but I still have to look into him. It could be someone from his company. I'm guessing you don't have a personal relationship with everyone in his employ, do you?"

"No."

Snow's phone chirped. He saw there was a missed call from his sister. He dropped the phone back into his pants pocket and made a mental note to call her back when he was finished with the Chambers' boys.

Snow smiled. "Okay, so let's just all take a breath and we'll see what I can dig up. With my father's recommendations, they'll make sure you and your family is safe while I find out who is targeting you and why."

"Okay," Grant said. "Okay."

Snow turned to look at Dominic. "I apologize for the intrusion."

It's okay," Dominic said softly.

Snow turned and headed toward the door when his phone rang. He fished it out of his pocket and broke into a smile when he saw the caller ID.

"Hey, Sammy," he said playfully as he stepped out of the office in the Chambers Racing Team's semi. "I was just about to call you back. What's up?"

Seconds later, Abraham Snow's world unraveled.

4

Samantha Dean was tired.

The mediation she was working in Dubai had dragged on for over a week. There were long hours spent in the boardroom trying to get one side or the other to agree on anything when all they really seemed to want to do is argue. Not a single one of them had shown so much as an inkling that they truly wanted to solve their problem and she was getting ready to admit defeat and throw in the towel.

The day's session was done and all she wanted was to rest when she stepped into the elevator going down. Her client had provided a car that would whisk her away to her hotel when she was ready to go.

The night before, she had shared her observations with her boss at the Hanson and Diamond Law Firm back in New York where their corporate headquarters resided. Donald Hanson III, whose grandfather had started the firm decades earlier had told her to give it a few more days. If she couldn't get things moving by then, he would fly to Dubai to personally recuse the firm from its obligations as mediator of the dispute.

She walked out of the evening session, exhausted and frustrated, both in equal measure. She had promised a Skype call into the office, but decided that she needed a drink first and then perhaps dinner before admitting to her boss that her efforts had once again failed.

Despite the rough day, Samantha Dean kept up a positive demeanor. So far, she had managed to keep her frustration from the clients on both sides of the table. It was no easy task as there were several times during the session where she wanted to scream at them to just agree, dammit!

Before calling the office, perhaps a Skype call to her husband, Jameson Dean, was in order. Like Samantha, he was also a lawyer, but unlike her high-paying corporate law position, Jameson Dean was a prosecuting attorney for the City of New York. He had a caseload that she did not envy and new crimes were committed every day.

As she stepped off the elevator and headed to the lobby bar, she fished her cell from her pocket and hit a number on her speed dial.

The phone started to ring.

"Mrs. Dean?"

Samantha stopped the call and dropped her cell onto the bar.

"Miss Cordoza," she said as she screwed on a smile and turned to face her client.

"Rough session?"

"Something like that," Samantha said, letting the smile dissolve slowly. "Are you sure mediation is what you need? Nobody is willing to budge. I'm beginning to think you need litigation instead of my services."

"Nonsense. I think things are going swimmingly. I wouldn't be surprised if we reached an agreement soon."

"I appreciate your optimism, Miss Cordoza. I wish I shared it."

"Please, how many times do I have to ask you to call me Daniella?"

"My apologies, Daniella," Samantha said. "I'm Sam."

"How about I buy you a drink, Sam?"

"Sure. Why not? Scotch. Rocks. I'm just going to powder my nose."

Cordoza smiled and nodded.

"Be right back."

"Take your time," Cordoza said as she eyed the mediator's unattended cell phone.

As soon as Samantha Dean was out of sight, she picked up the phone and scrolled through the contacts. She smiled when she fell upon the one that most interested her.

She snapped a photo of the contact information with her own phone then dialed.

He answered on the second ring.

"Hey, Sammy," a familiar voice said playfully on the other end of the line. "I was just about to call you back. What's up?"

"Hello, Agent Snow," she said in her most seductive voice.

"Who is this?"

"Have you forgotten me so soon, Abraham? Or do you prefer James? I know I liked you better as James Shepperd."

James Shepperd was the name Agent Snow had used to gain entry into Miguel Ortega's organization. That was the name she came to know him by. It was the name she had whispered in his ear when they made love. It was all a lie. James Shepperd was as phony as Miguel Ortega.

The irony that she was surrounded by men pretending to be something they were not was not lost on her. She had spent most of her life molding herself into whatever she needed to be to get the job done. To have been so readily fooled by someone else who was pretending to be someone he was not stung the ego.

"Daniella?" Snow said, the pieces falling into place. "Daniella Cordoza?"

"So, you do remember me. I am flattered."

"Don't be. Where's my sister?"

"She's safe. I'm just watching her things while she stops off at the bathroom for a moment. I promise you, no harm will come to your sister if you do as you're told. I rather like her. She's funny and sweet. Please don't make me hurt her."

"You have my undivided attention."

"Excellent."

"What do you want, Daniella?"

"My wants are simple, James. I want you and your friends, that man in Hawaii for example, to stop trying to track me down. Mr. Ortega is content to let this matter drop without retribution provided you stop trying to find me. I'm willing to go along with it too, if you promise to behave. I really don't want to have to kill you. We are off limits. Understood?"

"And you think threatening my sister is going to make me back off?"

"No. Don't think of this as a threat. I just wanted you to know that I can get close to those closest to you. Oh, and now that I know where you are, thanks to your sister's phone, I can keep tabs on you too. Remember that before you do anything stupid."

"I'm warning you…"

"Oh, don't start," Cordoza said. "You leave me and Mr. Ortega alone and we'll leave you alone. Understood?"

She could hear his breathing over the phone. No doubt he was stewing, wondering what play he had left. Finally, he relented and said, "Understood."

"See, I knew you could be reasonable, Agent Snow. I will miss the good times we had, but do as you're told and this is goodbye. We'll never see one another again."

Cordoza clicked off the phone and turned off the ringer before dropping Samantha's phone back on the bar where she had left it. She dialed her own phone.

A man answered on the first ring. "Yes."

"Tell our man we have a location. Atlanta. He knows what to do."

"Understood, Miss Cordoza. I will pass that along."

"Good. Now get everyone back together. We're done here. Time for the last act."

"Understood."

Cordoza saw Samantha Dean approach so she changed her tone, became more cheerful as she spoke into the phone even though there was no longer anyone there. "That's fantastic news! Yes, gather everyone back in the conference room now."

When she saw Samantha's quizzical look, she held up a finger to hold her off a moment and added, "No. I'm with Mrs. Dean now. I'll tell her the good news. Yes. See you in a few minutes. 'bye."

"What good news?" Samantha asked as she took a sip of her drink, ready to relax.

"That was my assistant. The other side has agreed to the latest offer." She smiled "Looks like we've got ourselves a deal."

"Wow," Samantha said. "This is quite… unexpected." *So much for relaxing.*

"I told you we were getting close."

"I'm glad one of us believed that," Samantha said. "Any idea what changed their minds?"

"None, but I guess we'll find out together."

Cordoza held up her glass. "To a job well done."

"I'll drink to that," Samantha said, clinking glasses before downing the remainder of her drink.

Cordoza threw a couple of bills on the bar to cover the drinks and tip. "What say we go up there and get this deal finished. I don't know about you, but I'm about ready to get back home."

"I hear that," Samantha said as they headed toward the elevator. "I'm ready to get back to my husband and our dog."

"I'm sorry I had to pull you away for so long. Family is very important."

"Yes, it is, Daniella. Yes, they are."

"So, I've heard."

As the elevator door closed, Daniella Cordoza smiled.

A job well done indeed.

5

Waiting had never been one of Abraham Snow's best attributes.

Even as a kid his father chastised him for always being so impatient. Now, as an adult, frustration plagued him when things didn't move as quickly as he wanted them to happen.

While still on the phone-- *Sammy's phone*-- with Daniella Cordoza, Snow waved down his father and called him over. Dominic seemed displeased, a common enough thing when the two of them were together, but excused himself from Grant Chambers' office to see what was going on.

Snow held up the small notepad he kept in his front pocket. On it he had scribbled, *Do you have operatives in Dubai?*

Dominic didn't know what was going on, but he nodded and held up two fingers.

Send them to Sam's location. Have them watch. Be discreet.

"What's happening?" Dominic asked.

Snow held up a finger to silence his father. "I'm warning you…" he told the person on the other end of the phone.

Dominic pulled his phone and made the call. Whatever their differences, both he and his son loved Samantha. Neither wanted to see her get hurt.

"Understood," Snow said and ended the call.

"What?" Dominic demanded.

"There's a woman out there named Daniella Cordoza, who doesn't like me trying to find her or the man she works for. She wants me to back off and made her point by calling me from Sam's phone."

"Is she…?"

"Sammy's fine. This was a warning for me to back off. She won't hurt her."

"Are you sure?"

"Hurting Sam won't get her what she wants."

"What does she want?" Dominic asked.

"Me. Gone. I guess that's something she and you have in common, huh?"

He meant it as a joke, but the look on Dominic's face told him that his father took it as anything but humorous.

"Now you listen to me," Dominic said, his tone strictly professional. "I may not be thrilled with your grandfather bringing you into the family business and you and I may not be close, but you are still my son. No friction between us will ever change that. I don't want you gone. I just don't want you here."

"Whatever," Snow said as he sent a text.

"Who are you texting?"

"Sam wasn't the only one she threatened. My friend Brooks is in danger. I'm letting him know he's under surveillance. If he hasn't spotted it already, I want to give him a head's up."

The phone dinged as a new text arrived.

It was a single letter. *K*

Now that Brooks was in the clear, he called Big John.

"Ham?"

"I gotta cut things short, buddy. You ready to go?"

"You take off. I'll catch a ride back unless you need me to come with," Big John said.

"You on to something?" Snow asked.

"Maybe. Just talking to Beau. We'll chat later."

"Okay. Stay frosty and call if you need me."

He ended the call then pulled out the business card Kelly Pratt had given him. She answered on the first ring.

"Kelly, this is Mr. Snow. We're going to need that pick up a little earlier than expected."

"On my way," Pratt's cheerful voice called.

"Your guys got eyes on Sam?" Snow asked Dominic as he ended a call.

"Yes. She's fine. This Cordoza woman, is she still there?"

"My men are in observe mode," Dominic said. "Unless somebody tries something, Samantha won't even know they're there."

###

Big John Salmon was having a great time.

Beau Chambers started by giving him a tour of his family's team garages and then introduced him to some of the other drivers and mechanics for some of the other race teams. As a race fan, he loved being immersed in the culture and not being treated like a fan, but as Beau's guest. They were more themselves when the fans weren't around, cutting up and using raucous humor.

The Chambers garage was a flurry of activity as they worked to get Chase's back up car ready for qualifying. The new engine was being installed and, as so often happens with cars, nothing was going smoothly. Tommy Yates and his team were working in shifts, along with Grant and Chase Chambers. For whatever reason, they had left Beau out of the lineup, though he and Big John did offer to pitch in and help.

Big John was no stranger to the kind of frustration the team was feeling. He had battled many an engine himself to get it installed correctly. One day, he hoped someone would design a smart engine that did the job without being so clunky and hard to handle. Modern engines had too many moving parts, each one having the potential to break down and kill the engine cold.

Big John enjoyed being part of the pit crew, even if only temporarily. Tommy Yates, the crew chief, really knew the Chambers cars backward and forward from engine to tailpipe and back again. He'd been working in racing teams for nearly thirty years and had some great stories to tell about *the good ol' days*. For a moment, John wondered what his life might have been like if he had zagged when he was younger instead of zigging like he did. Driving had been a dream and racing was one of those big life goals he set for himself, but instead he had taken up a different kind of driving profession. Big John became a car thief, and a damned good one. Before he was busted, there wasn't anyone who could boost a car faster or smoother than him.

Getting caught was the splash of cold water that sent him on a straighter, narrow path. After serving his time, he got out with the promise that he would not return to his old life nor would he ever go back inside. Jail was not anyplace he ever planned to end up again.

For the most part, he had kept those promises.

Sure, he still liked to drive faster than the law allowed, but other than a few minor traffic infractions, he hadn't stolen so much as a grape in the supermarket in the last few years.

Big John liked Beau Chambers' style. The heir to the Chambers' racing heritage was several years younger than him, but otherwise, they were a lot alike. They hit it off instantly.

When the team called it a night. Instead of heading back to their trailers, out came a deck of cards and handfuls of singles. Beers were opened and bets made. Big John wasn't much of a gambler so he excused himself from the game. He stepped outside to call for a ride home when Beau Chambers stopped him.

"Let's go take a walk," he said.

"How do you like running short track?" Big John asked as they walked through the pits.

"It's okay. I mean, any time I get to drive fast, I'm happy, but I've got the itch to move up."

"There's going to be three Chambers' boys competing for the Cup at the same time?"

"Doubtful," Beau said, suddenly very interested in a small rock he kicked across the pavement.

"Why not?"

"Ah, the old man doesn't think I'm ready yet. You know how it goes. I'll get there, but if I keep on waiting for my daddy to give me a spot on the A-Team, I may lose my chance. I might have to take matters into my own hands. Maybe find a team outside the family."

"You can do that?"

"Sure. I'm only under contract to my Dad's team a season at a time. I can jump to another team anytime I want, but... well, as corny as it sounds, I don't want to break up this team. I want to be out there side by side with Grant and Chase Chambers, the three Chambers boys working together, a real racing dynasty."

"Have you told your dad that?"

Beau choked on a laugh. "Until I'm blue in the face. I love my Daddy. He's a great man and he's great at what he does, but when he looks at me he stills sees a little kid. He doesn't see the real me. Hell, at my age, he was already racing, but he thinks I'm too young to be out there."

Beau kicked another rock, watched it bounce across the pavement.

"All I want to do is drive, man. I'm just looking for my shot. It shouldn't be this hard."

"Yeah. I understand that," Big John said. "I used to run local heats on Saturday nights at a little dirt track near home. They've since paved it. Not the same, but I still enjoy popping in to watch every now and then."

"You don't drive anymore?"

"Not on a track, no."

"What happened? Don't tell me you grew out of it."

Big John laughed. "Naw, man. Nothing like that. I made some bad choices as a kid. Did five years for boosting cars, did some evading arrest, that sort of thing. Ain't nobody letting a guy with my rap sheet behind the wheel of one of these beauts," he said, pointing toward the stock cars.

"Sorry, man. How long you been breathing fresh air?"

"A little over two years," Big John said. "Ham's grandfather hired me to work on his personal cars. He's got some real sweet rides. He collects some, flips others. Right now, we're working on restoring a '57 Ford Fairlane that some lady found in an old barn. There's a lot to do to get her humming again, but we're in no rush. I love tinkering with those old beauties."

"Nice that he trusts you."

"Yeah. Mr. Snow's been a good friend. Hell, he's a better grandfather to me than my own was, so yeah, I got lucky."

"You ever get the itch?"

Big John stopped. "Itch?"

Beau shrugged. "To steal a car."

"Sometimes." Big John snorted a laugh at a memory. "I was pumping gas the other day and saw this sweet, sweet ride pull in. Jackass gets out, ignition running, and takes off inside without so much as looking back."

"Dumbass deserves to have his car stolen."

"That's exactly what I was thinking," Big John said.

"What stopped you?" Beau asked.

Big John shrugged. "Would have been too easy."

"Is that the real reason?"

"No," Big John said with a smile.

Beau returned the smile. He understood.

"You and I are a lot alike," he said. "How about I buy you a drink, Mr. Salmon?"

"Shouldn't we be getting back?"

"Nah. You saw how they were. Once they start playing poker, they're done for the day. Plus, they really don't want me in there. The only reason they didn't ask me to leave is because you were there."

"How nice of them," Big John said, dripping sarcasm.

"Welcome to my world," Beau said. "Now, about that drink?"

Even though he didn't drink anymore, he figured he would enjoy the conversation. "Sure. As long as you call me John. Or Big John."

"Deal."

6

Abraham Snow was tired.

He hadn't slept a wink until he received word from his father that Samantha's plane was safely in the air and headed back toward United States airspace and then he was up and down so much he didn't get much rest. It was an eighteen and a half hour flight with a three hour layover in London, but there was a Snow Security contractor on the plane to keep an eye on her just in case Daniella Cordoza decided not to keep her end of the bargain and leave Samantha alone.

Snow wouldn't relax until his little sister was safely back home, but he had never been so happy that his family's company handled clients all over the world. It was just dumb luck that there was a team on the ground in Dubai that was able to be re-tasked and sent directly to her location. Ah, the wonders of modern technology.

Sam's plane was due in Atlanta the next day. She was going to spend the night in Atlanta so she could visit with the family before flying home to New York the day after. Snow had offered to pick her up at the airport, but Dominic had already beaten him to the punch. They were all going to have dinner together instead.

Snow quickly volunteered to give her a lift back to the airport for her flight to New York. He missed having her closer to home. She must have felt the same way the past ten years or more that he had been away.

Now that Cordoza knew he was living in Georgia, the last thing he wanted to do was make it easier for her to pinpoint his exact location, but he also refused to hide from her. He would have to be more careful going forward.

Snow silently chided himself. Since he had returned home and retired from his former life as an undercover operative for Uncle Sam and Mother, his personal security habits had atrophied. Now that he was no longer looking over his shoulder at every turn or having to be careful not to let an alias fact slip, he had allowed himself to get comfortable. That comfort put his sister and friends in the crosshairs.

His promise to Daniella Cordoza to the contrary, Snow could not let that stand. Finding her and her boss, the man using the alias Miguel Ortega, was even more imperative than before. He would not be able to relax until this problem was behind him.

To that end, he had placed a call to his and Brooks' former boss, Elizabeth Walker. She had been their handler for a time then eventually

Brooks took over for her as she moved up the ladder within the organization.

Walker was fierce, good at her job, and more importantly, Snow trusted her. After his retirement went into effect, she became his official liaison to Mother in case they needed to consult with him on an old case or for whatever reason he might need to get in touch. No one ever fully retired from Mother and Snow knew that as well as anyone. If not for the bullet he'd taken that came only a half an inch from hitting his heart forcing him to the sidelines, he had little doubt his request to "pull the pin" as retirement was called in the business would have gone through so smoothly.

Oh, sure, he could pick up the phone and call General Pinkwell if the need arose, but that was more of an off-the-books I need a favor scenario. It was not a well Snow wanted to use more often than he needed to. The General had been kind enough to help him out with getting his private investigator's license, which was a big help. Snow promised to take the general and his grandfather out for a big, juicy steak dinner the next time he was in town as a thank you. It was an offer he knew the general would not be able to refuse. General Henry Pinkwell and Archer Snow went back a long ways, back when Archer worked for Mother himself, something Snow was surprised to discover.

Walker had agreed to do some digging on the Ortega case, which was still ongoing. She agreed to get back in touch soon and they would meet. Now all he had to do was wait.

Waiting was not something he did well so Snow poured himself into his work. With the help of a research team at Snow Security, he was running background checks on Oliver Simcoe and the other members of the Simcoe engine trial. Beau Chambers' theory was thin, but it was worth checking out just to be sure. He also had them checking out any competitors or media who might have run afoul of the race team in the past six months. While the brain trust over at Snow Security did their thing and Big John hung around the track with his new friend, Beau, Snow called Simcoe Tech and made an appointment to speak with the head man himself.

He was kind of surprised when they agreed to meet with him.

A very pretty receptionist with a southern drawl so sweet he could feel a cavity forming greeted him in the lobby when he arrived at the glass and steel architectural monstrosity that was Simcoe Tech's corporate office. His apartment would have fit in the lobby alone at least three times, maybe four.

The receptionist told him that Mr. Simcoe would be with him in "*just a minute*."

An hour and a half later, when Snow's patience was completely at its end, the man's aide, a *yes man* named Harold, finally decided to make an appearance. He brought with him an assortment of excuses, none of which interested Snow in the least.

"Mr. Snow. Hello. Apologies for the delay. Mr. Simcoe's day is simply crazy. With a big race this weekend, there's so much to do. I'm sure you know how it is," the aide said in a manner that told Snow that he didn't really think he did. *How could anyone's time be as important as Mr. Simcoe's*?

"Lucky for me I made an appointment then," Snow said matter of fact.

"Well, you see…" the aide started.

Snow had no intention of letting him continue.

"No. You see," Snow said, raising his voice so that others milling about the lobby or in the open walkways- *gotta love those open* floorplans- above could hear him. "I made an appointment to talk to Mr. Simcoe about the sabotage of the Chambers Racing Team and the attempted murder of one of NASCAR's all-stars!" He was practically shouting at this point.

Snow lowered his voice and looked the aide square in the eye. "Shall I keep going?"

The blood was all but drained from the poor aide's face. "I think you made your point," he stammered. "Uh, this… uh, this way, please."

Snow followed the aide to a private elevator that took him directly to Mr. Simcoe's office. The man was sitting behind his large red mahogany desk, fingers steepled in front of him as he stared daggers at Snow across the gulf between them. If he hadn't gotten the message loud and clear from his aide, Simcoe was determined to make sure Snow knew he was not welcome.

For his part, Snow didn't really care.

"Thank you for agreeing to speak with me," Snow said politely after he was ushered across the large office to a cushioned chair across the desk from Oliver Simcoe.

"I'm a very busy man," Simcoe said. "You've got one minute."

"Did you try to kill Chase Chambers?"

Silence fell over the room. Oliver Simcoe gave off an air of superiority. He was in his early fifties and had developed a hefty midsection that strained against the buttons on his shirt. The suit he wore was expensive, but a few years old. That told Snow he didn't waste money if he didn't need to, smart in business. His hair was graying, but still dark on top. His beard had long since turned white. Sitting behind his fancy desk, Simcoe looked as though someone had just kicked him in the chest while his assistant appeared to be on the verge of a full-blown panic attack.

He assumed that was his doing.

Snow leaned forward in his chair, hands pressed above his knees. "Well, did you?"

"How dare you?" Simcoe said. He too leaned forward, placed his elbows on his desk. "Just who the hell do you think you are to come in here and accuse me of something so heinous?"

"That's not a no," Snow said. He sighed. "I was really looking for a no here, sir."

"Of course, I didn't try to kill him, you moron," Simcoe said through grit teeth.

"But you threatened Grant Chambers."

"So what? I threaten a lot of people. That's business."

"And people wonder why nobody likes you," Snow muttered.

"I don't care if anyone likes me," Simcoe replied.

Snow shrugged. "Well, you can see how threatening Grant Chambers might make you a suspect, don't you?"

"Look. Yeah, I threatened Chambers. I didn't want him to run around blabbing about the imagined safety issues he thinks he saw in my new engine design. He signed a NDA and I wanted to remind him what would happen if he broke it."

"And what would that be?"

"That I would sue his ass off, which, by the way, is exactly what I'm doing. He broke the non-disclosure agreement he signed. He knew better, but he did it anyway. Now there are consequences to be paid."

"Is he fighting it?"

Simcoe snorted a laugh. "Of course, he's fighting it. He'd be stupid not to, but let me let you in on a little secret, Mr. Snow." He smiled. "I like it when they fight. That means I get to fight too."

Simcoe's smile widened as he leaned back in his chair, feeling superior.

"And I like to fight. What's more, I like to win. You let Grant Chambers fight. You let him spin tales about sabotage to garner sympathy. It won't matter. By the time I'm through with him, I'll own that little racing team of his and he'll be back pumping gas at the local corner gas station in whatever piss-ant little town he gets to call home by the time I've taken everything he ever owned. Then, then you'll know what a threat looks like, Mr. Snow."

Snow pursed his lips, nodded.

"What about Tommy Yates? You suing him too?"

"If it were just up to me, you bet your ass I would," he said. "But Tommy Yates is an old, washed up relic of NASCAR's *glory days*. He's been a worker bee all his life. The old bastard doesn't have more than a couple of nickels to rub together. Suing him costs me more money than it's worth."

"How very magnanimous of you," Snow said without trying to hide the sarcasm.

"You might want to take a lesson from all this, sonny. I'd be careful how you fling accusations around, if I were you, Mr. Snow. I've got enough lawyers to sue the lot of you."

Snow stood and made a show of dusting off his jeans. "Well, lucky for both of us you aren't me."

Simcoe chuckled. "You think I'm bluffing?"

Snow shrugged. "Don't really care. You feel the need to come after me, be my guest. I don't own anything, but let me warn you that digging into my life too deep has consequences."

"Now who's threatening who?"

"Oh, no threat, Mr. Simcoe. Just friendly advice."

Snow turned his back and headed toward the door where the aide waited.

"Oh, there is just one more thing," Snow said before reaching the door. He turned to face Simcoe, still sitting at his desk.

"Oh?"

"Danny Jacobs' accident? Has NASCAR determined the cause of the engine explosion yet?"

"That investigation is still ongoing. My engine was not responsible."

"You sure about that?"

"Absolutely."

"And yet, NASCAR pulled all of them until further notice?"

"Standard procedure. We are cooperating with NASCAR's investigator's fully and are even running independent tests on our own. Tests we will share with NASCAR when they are completed, just in case you were wondering."

"I actually was, yeah," Snow said.

"Faulty tech is bad for business, Mr. Snow. I'm in the business of making money for myself, my company, and my shareholders. Putting defective engines in cars with my name on them and sending them out there to explode on world-wide television is not good for business. I want to make sure these engines are safe. If they aren't, we'll find out."

"And if they are?"

"Then I'll pull them myself."

Snow stared at the man, not sure whether to believe him or not.

"Just stay away from the Chambers family," Snow warned.

"I'm not a bad man," Simcoe said as he pushed himself to his feet. At a heavyset six two, he was tall and imposing, a mountain of a man. "If your client keeps his mouth shut, then we'll be good. That's all I've ever asked."

"Okay," Snow said. "I'll pass that along to him."

"Thank you."

"Now, if I find out it was you, or one of your people behind this, I will rain holy hell on you and your company."

He smiled.

"Just so *we* understand each other."

Simcoe motioned toward the exit, the meeting adjourned. "I think we understand each other just fine, Mr. Snow."

"I'll see myself out, Harold," he told Simcoe's assistant as he left Oliver Simcoe's office.

Back on the road, Snow ran through the meeting again.

The conversation with the head of Simcoe Tech had been enlightening. Snow wasn't convinced that Simcoe was behind the sabotage like Beau Chambers was, but he couldn't rule out any of Simcoe's underlings taking matters into their own hands. Simcoe was the head of the company tree, but there were certainly those on lower branches who had a lot to lose if the engine was permanently shelved.

Snow had the team at the office looking into the person who originally designed the engine and the team who put it all together once Simcoe secured the designs. Any one of them could find themselves unemployable if their engine design turned out to be flawed, especially if there were fatalities. They had gotten lucky with Danny Jacobs' accident, although the driver might see things differently. He had been injured, but not fatally. The latest report showed his condition improving steadily. NASCAR officials gave every indication that he would be back behind the wheel before the season was over.

He was lucky.

Would the next driver be as lucky?

Snow couldn't be sure. He'd only spent five minutes with Oliver Simcoe, but that was long enough to realize that the man cared very little about anything accept his bottom line, despite his claims about putting the drivers first. He also struck Snow as an angry man, easily agitated and prone to violence. His police record, which he had pulled before the visit, backed that feeling up. Assault, battery, fighting, usually involving alcohol, women, or business disagreements. It was mostly minor, but it did create a pattern of behavior that painted Oliver Simcoe as a violent, dangerous man.

He might not be guilty of sabotage, but he would recommend that Dominic put someone on him when he and Grant Chambers were in the same vicinity, most likely at the track or industry events. A fistfight was not out of the realm of possibility.

Snow was already thinking ahead to his next move. The plan was to join Big John at the track and talk to Kelly Pratt and her friends working at the track. They often saw things when no one thought they were looking. He hoped they might shed some light on the situation.

His thoughts were so wrapped up in the case that he didn't notice the blue panel van pull out of Simcoe Tech behind him nor did he notice when it made the next three turns behind him.

He was being followed.

7

Big John Salmon felt weird not driving.

With Snow off interviewing a potential suspect, John caught a ride in to the Snow Security office with Archer Snow. Archer very rarely drove himself anywhere on business, but the old man was not so spoiled that he didn't do his own driving between the office and his home out in Sommersville County.

Archer was a good driver and Big John sensed a kindred spirit in his employer. In his heyday, Archer Snow was reportedly an ass kicker and risk taker of the highest order, something John understood all too well. He never felt more alive than when he was risking life or limb on some hair-brained stunt. Between what he remembered of Archer growing up and the stories he heard from Snow and from Archer himself, it was hard not to like him. Now that he was living out his golden years, that charm that had served him so well when he was younger had been amplified. Some of the things Archer was allowed to say without fear of reprisal was staggering to Big John.

He once told Archer, "*I would get arrested if I said half the stuff you do*."

Archer only laughed at the notion.

The drive in was without incident. Atlanta's start and stop traffic patterns made the drive irritatingly longer than it should have been, and Big John was not looking forward to the slow crawl from Atlanta to the speedway in Hampton, but there wasn't much he could do about Atlanta's crappy traffic. There was no getting around it.

Unless you were Archer Snow.

"What do you say we take the helicopter the rest of the way?" Archer said with a child-like grin when they parked at Snow Security.

"Sure as hell beats the alternative, Mr. S," he said.

"Just got to pop into the office and check on a few things."

They took the stairs to the lobby side by side. The two of them definitely made an interesting pair.

Archer turned 70 on his last birthday, but he had more energy than many twenty year old's did. He was tall, but shorter than John. His hair, which had long ago turned white had been long and stringy, usually shoved under an old cowboy hat. He looked like an old cowboy working the range. At least until recently when he cut his hair close. The trim actually made him look a bit younger, but definitely more business-like.

He wore slacks and shirtsleeves under a jacket. He didn't wear a tie, but there was one folded in his jacket pocket should the need to wear it arise. He always seemed to smile.

Big John, on the other hand, wore jeans and a T-Shirt beneath an unbuttoned plaid colored shirt. Big John stood six foot-five, which is mostly how he got the nickname. He was also broad shouldered and built like a linebacker for a pro football team. He was pure muscle, having come out of prison trim and with very little body fat. Big John had a big, boisterous laugh, but there were times when he tried to crawl back in the shell he had constructed around himself in prison. They had been fairly close when John was a kid, but Archer had given him a second chance after he got out and Big John looked at the man like a surrogate grandfather of his own. In the past few years, they had become inseparable.

"Take your time," Big John said. "I'll see how the researchers you loaned me and Ham. See if they turned up anything."

"Good idea. Where is Abraham this morning, anyway?" Archer asked once they were alone in the elevator.

"He's interviewing a guy that Beau Chambers thinks might be behind the sabotage."

"Oh?"

"Yeah. CEO of a tech firm, Oliver Simcoe."

"I've heard the name. From what I hear he's a shrewd business man, like those shark people you see on TV."

Big John smiled. "Takes shrewd to recognize shrewd, I suppose," he said.

"Damn right," Archer said, playfully elbowing him on the arm.

Once in the office, Archer went in one direction and John in another. He stopped by the research team to see if they had dug up any useful information that would lead to a saboteur. Here was a lot of data, but nothing concrete that led to a definitive suspect. It did narrow the pool, but not by a lot.

When Archer finished his business, John was waiting for him the lobby.

With a little small talk between them, they headed toward the roof where the old man's private helicopter waited. Archer had his pilot's license and was certified to handle the chopper. John had no qualms about climbing aboard.

"Man, if I were you, I'd fly home every night," Big John said once they were airborne.

"Where's the fun in that?" Archer said.

###

They arrived at the speedway in good time.

Since Archer had called ahead, Kelly Pratt and her van were waiting for them at the helipad. After a round of *greetings*, *hi there*, and *good to see you again*, she drove them to the pits.

They stopped at the garages holding the Chambers Racing Team.

Archer and Big John shook hands with Grant and Chase Chambers and Tommy Yates. They were holding their morning meeting over a cup of coffee and some type of friend food sandwiched between two slices of bread.

"How did things go last night?" Archer asked.

"Without a hitch," Grant said after washing down the last of his breakfast. "No problems here or back home. I talked with my wife this morning and she said your men were there and not getting underfoot."

Archer smiled. "We should put that on our brochures."

They laughed.

"You seen Beau this morning?" Grant asked his eldest son.

Chase looked at his watch. "Nope, but it' nowhere near noon yet so if I had to guess, I'd say he's passed out in his trailer."

"That boy," Grant said, clearly agitated.

"Take it easy, Pop," Chase said. "Tommy and I don't have him working on anything important. Asleep, he stays out of the news."

Grant started to say more, but stopped himself out of respect to their guests. John could tell that this was an old argument and one that would be solved in a single sitting. Tommy Yates shook his head, turned and headed back to the garage. He too had probably witnessed this topic of conversation before.

John had spent the day before with Beau Chambers. He liked him. Beau reminded him of himself when he was in his twenties, full of piss and vinegar and ready to take on the world. Back them only three things mattered to him: fast cars, fast women, and a cold drink. If there was a way to enjoy all three at the same time, so much the better.

All that changed when he was arrested and then eventually sentenced. Five years in a place he never wanted to return had helped him kick the booze and the smokes, age had helped him enjoy women who lived life a little slower, but fast cars… that was a vice he could never bury.

Being here at the track, surrounded by the sounds and smells of the cars, watching the qualifying laps as the cars zoomed past him at top speed. It was both sad and exhilarating at the same time. There was still a yearning to climb behind the wheel of a stock car and join the pack as they fought their way to the front in search of that all-important checkered flag. He doubted that longing to be a race car driver would ever go away, even if it was a dream he could never fully realize.

There was also a twinge of sadness because it was his own foolishness that had screwed him out of his dream. Oh, sure, back then he had shouted at the unfairness of it all and blamed anyone he could outside himself. Being on the inside gave him a lot of time to think on what he had done and contemplate what would happen after.

Big John Salmon walked out of prison a changed man. Like so many others, he swore that he would never find himself on the inside again. The odds of an ex-convict being arrested again were pretty low. He planned to beat those odds, but it was not easy. He lost count of the number of times a cop knocked on his door whenever a car in the vicinity was stolen or even broken into. If not for Mr. Snow offering him a job in his garage, things could have easily gone a different way.

Archer Snow had saved him, showed him a better way.

Big John was determined to help Beau Chambers the same way.

"Where's his trailer?" John asked.

Chase pointed to three campers clustered near one another. Beau's is on the right with the bike leaning against it. Mine is in the middle. Dad's on the other side."

"I'll go say good morning," Salmon said.

"Good luck," Chase said. "A freight train running through an atomic explosion wouldn't wake that boy up."

"I'll take my chances."

"Tell him I said he's late for work," Chase said.

Salmon was halfway across the infield when the motor home's door opened. *Oh, good. He's awake*, he thought as he started to say hello.

The legs that stepped out did not belong to Beau Chambers. She was blonde, her hair was long and straight, but slightly mussed, but that only added to her appeal. Tall and leggy, the bottle blonde wore a short white dress so thin it was hard for her to keep any secrets, like a lack of underwear. Her arms were also bare and she carried a pair of white shoes with six inch heels and red bottoms. Salmon was pretty sure they were an expensive brand, but shoes were not his forte as his forty-dollar tennis shoes clearly demonstrated. She was early twenties, he guessed. Pretty in that thin fashion model way.

The second set of legs out the door belonged to Beau. He was wearing jeans over boots, but instead of a shirt, he wore another girl. Her legs were wrapped around his bare midsection and her arms around his neck while she twirled her fingers through his chest hair and nuzzled his neck. She had long, dark hair that flowed in curls down her back from beneath his cowboy hat. She also wore Beau's flannel shirt over her skimpy black dress and she still had her heels on. She also looked like a model who stepped out of Sports Illustrated.

All three of them were giggling like teenagers when Beau slipped the brunette off his back and slapped her behind as she scurried away toward the tunnel that would take them back toward the parking lot.

He did not get his shirt back, but he did reclaim the hat, which he slipped back on as though he had just won the rodeo.

Everyone in the pits was looking in their direction.

Including the photographers and fans with phones who started snapping away.

"I guess TMZ has their top story for tonight," Grant said. He was angry and turned and headed back into the garage.

His older son chose not to follow that example.

"Hey!" he shouted and the cameras were now pointed in his direction as Chase Chambers stormed across the space between the garage and the trailers.

Once there, he grabbed his brother by the arm and pushed him hard against the trailer he called home while on the road, tipping over Beau's motorcycle.

"What in the hell is wrong with you?" Chase shouted. "Don't you think we have enough problems right now without you doing something stupid like this?"

"Oh, come on, Chase," Beau said, still clearly buzzed from the night's drinking and debauchery. "Are you telling me you never took advantage of all the trim being thrown at you out here? Are you telling me Dad didn't? Hell, isn't this how you and your wife first hooked up? I seem to recall she liked to shimmy around here in her tight ass cut off shorts too."

"You shut your damned mouth!" Chase shouted.

Beau reared back as if he was going to take a swing at his brother.

Chase pushed him harder against the metal before he could throw a punch. "At least I had the good sense to keep it quiet, you dumbass!" He pointed toward the people watching. "Your giggling little slap and tickle fest there is probably already on the internet!"

"So what? Tell me there ain't a man out there wishes he was me right now. Did you see those two?"

"I did. So did Dad. So will Mom." Chase eased off the pressure and lowered his voice. "Look, buddy, I don't care how many girls you feel the need to bang! Hell, bang 'em all for all I care!" He took a breath, tried to catch his. He lowered his voice and added, "Just try to show some discretion, okay?"

Beau let out a breath. "Sure. I'll keep things on the down low. Just for you."

"That's all I ask," Chase said, suddenly looking older than his years.

Beau saw Big John standing nearby, offered a half-hearted smile. "You got something to add?" he asked his new friend.

"Nope," Big John said.

"Good."

Beau looked at the crowd watching and filming the entire encounter. He told them where to go then flipped them off then headed back inside his trailer.

Shaking his head, a frustrated Chase Chambers walked back to the garage.

Big John stood the bike back up and made sure nothing was broken. Thankfully, it was only a little scratched up. Nothing too serious. After leaning it back against the trailer, he stared at the closed door for a moment, weighing his options and wondering what he should do. He was an outsider, a stranger to this family and to this sport. Sure, they got along after the met yesterday, but did he really have the right to talk to Beau about his problems?

He didn't have an answer, but one thing he did know was that if somebody didn't talk to that young man soon, it might be too late.

Steeling himself, Big John knocked on the door.

Beau pushed the door open hard, ready for another fight. Clearly, he was expecting his brother based on the surprised look on his face when he saw Salmon standing there.

"What do you want?"

"Just wanted to see if you were okay," John said. "Maybe get some more insight on who is trying to sabotage your family's team."

Beau moved inside. "Come on in, but be warned, I am in no mood for a lecture."

Salmon stifled a laugh then climbed the steps inside the trailer. "That's okay. I'm not the lecturing type."

Once inside, Beau offered him a beer. When he declined, Beau pulled one from the refrigerator and popped off the top.

"A little early, isn't it?" Salmon asked.

"Hair of the dog," Beau said in that cocky way that told Salmon this was an excuse he used often.

"Isn't that for when you're starting to sober up and the hangover kicks in?"

"Semantics," Beau said playfully. "You can't get hangovers if you don't stop drinking, right?"

"You don't get NASCAR contracts either."

The pointed comment hit home. Beau got to his feet in a shot and pointed toward the door. "Now don't you start in on me too, man. I get enough of that bullshit from my two dads out there. I sure as hell don't need it from you."

"Then what do you need, man? You told me you wanted to drive."

"I do. Those cars out there… they call to me. Do you know what that's like?"

"Yes," Salmon said, his voice somber.

"You've never touched the life, John," Beau said, anger rising. "You talk about what you missed out on, but you really don't know because you've always been on the outside looking in! Everyone thinks it's all sunshine and roses on this side of the fence and that's what you think too, don't you?"

"Nah, man. Like everything else in life, the thing you want, you have to work your ass off to get it. That *good things come to those who wait* line is pure B.S. Good things come to those who get off their ass and work for it. This takes work, but it also takes common sense, man. Getting caught on film with beautiful women might make you famous, but it won't make you a champion," Salmon said.

He pointed toward the door.

"Not out there."

"What do you know?"

"I know I fucked my own chance up. Nobody else. Just me. Take it from experience, man. I see you making the same mistakes I did."

"And if somebody like you had told you all this when you were where I am now, would you have listened?"

"Probably not," Big John said. "I was pretty stupid back then, kind of like you're being now."

"I am not stupid. You've never seen me in one of those cars. I'm damned good."

"Then get out there and show them."

"My Daddy don't care!"

"Then to hell with him," Salmon said. "If your father won't sign you, take your skill elsewhere."

Beau snorted a laugh, turned to look down the hallway toward the now empty bed. "It's funny. You say your mistakes are what keep you from driving one of these beasts. Well, try being the son of Golden Grant Chambers. Ain't nobody going to give me a shot without his say so and he ain't interested in giving in."

"Have you asked?"

"Yeah."

"No," Salmon said, leaning forward. "Have you really asked?"

"You just don't know, man. You haven't lived this life, grown up in it only to be told to sit on the sidelines in front of millions of people."

"Maybe you're right," Big John said. "Maybe you do have more to lose than me, but that's because you have more."

Beau spun back to face him.

"Ah, that touched a nerve, did it?"

Big John stood to his full height, his head almost touching the ceiling.

Beau shot daggers at him, angry, hurt.

"Slice it any way you want, Beau, the only thing keeping you out of a race car is you."

"You're full of shit," Beau said.

Salmon shrugged.

"But you might be right."

Big John took the beer bottle out of his hand.

"Balls in your court, kid," Salmon said. "What are you going to do about it?"

8

Sammy Betts was disappointed that he wasn't allowed to drive.

Usually, when he was paired up with someone in town on business, they always let him drive. Now this new guy though. No, sir. He was adamant that Sammy ride shotgun. Since he needed the money, Sammy wisely buttoned his lips and climbed in the passenger seat.

When the guy they were following, Abraham Snow, pulled into a service station to fill up, the van drove past and pulled over into a fat food restaurant down the street, but still close enough to surveil the gas pumps.

"Is that him?" Sammy asked from the passenger seat.

The driver pulled a photo up on his phone and showed it to his passenger.

"What do you think?"

"I think it's him."

"I'm so glad I brought you along," the driver said disapprovingly. "I'd hate to think I've been following the wrong guy all day."

"Sorry," Sammy said.

"Listen and learn," the driver said. "You have to be sure of your target before you start anything. We don't get paid for '*well, that kind of looked like him*', now do we?"

"No, Mr. Morgan."

"That's right. You want to be a professional hit man, boy, you have to be a professional first and foremost. There's no doing this job halfway. You get me?"

"No halfway. Right. I got it. Sorry," Sammy Betts said.

"And stop apologizing so much."

"Sorry," Sammy said.

The driver rolled his eyes.

Sammy Betts was a local boy. He was little more than muscle for hire, but the locals trusted him and he was good at taking orders, if not too bright. When The Connector, a local temp service manager for homegrown talent, called and told him there was a hitter in town who needed some local color to help him navigate, Sammy jumped at the chance.

Sammy was mostly muscle. He hit people and, if they were smart, they stayed down. He liked what he did, hurting people for fun and profit, but to be a hitter, that was the prestige. He was eager to learn from the visiting pro, a hitman of some renown named Richard Morgan.

Morgan was the real deal. He had over twenty confirmed kills to his name, probably more that weren't officially sanctioned, Sammy assumed. The man was as cool as a cucumber. He didn't raise his voice or threaten or bully, not like some of the jackasses Sammy had been teamed up with in the past. No, this guy… he was bon-a-fide badass. He didn't need to flaunt it.

Sammy knew he could learn a lot from this man.

"He's on the move," Morgan said, snapping Sammy back to the here and now.

The target came out of the convenience store with a soda and a bag of potato chips. Not a very healthy meal, especially if it was going to be his last, but Sammy couldn't be worried about things like that, especially considering he had a bowl of cereal and a beer for breakfast and a pack of stale powdered donuts and a soda for lunch.

The candy-apple red 1961 Chevrolet Corvette convertible the target drove was a thing of beauty. It also made him really easy to follow. Morgan pulled the van out into traffic behind him, careful not to get too close.

"Where does this road go?" Morgan asked.

"We're pretty far off the beaten path here," Sammy said. "This road leads back to the interstate, but we've got about twenty miles of pretty empty countryside before we get there. He's taking the scenic route."

"Perfect."

"Not really," Sammy said. "He'll see us."

"Watch and learn, kid," Morgan said. "Your education is about to start."

For a couple of miles, they kept a considerable distance, but eventually traffic thinned out and they were the only ones on the road. Up ahead there was a curve.

"You ready?" Morgan asked.

"Always."

"Hang on."

The van accelerated and closed the distance between the two vehicles quickly. The driver of the convertible noticed them. Morgan noticed him check and then move the rearview mirror to get a better look.

Morgan floored it and the van leapt into high gear. From the outside it didn't look like much, but under the hood, the van was a behemoth. Even that old muscle engine car the target drove couldn't outrun him for long.

The van clipped the driver's side rear bumper, giving it just enough of a nudge to spin the car into a slide.

The driver recovered quickly, which was a surprise.

He's had training, Morgan realized. *I guess I'm going to really have to earn this one.*

Another nudge and the convertible was sent into another slide.

This time the driver was unable to compensate quickly enough.

The Corvette screeched over asphalt then ripped up chunks of grass and gravel from the side of the road.

The driver jerked the wheel hard, but it was too late.

The Corvette slid off the road into an embankment, hitting hard and bringing the car to a dead stop, half on and half off the road.

The driver was stunned, his head lying against the steering wheel.

Richard Morgan stopped the van a few feet away.

"You're up, kid?" he told Sammy Betts.

"Up for what?" the confused local asked.

Morgan put a clean gun in the boy's hand. "Take this gun, walk over there, and put a bullet in the back of that man's head."

"What if he moves?"

"Then shoot him in the side of the head."

"I… uh…"

The hitter let out a breath. "Look, kid. You told me you wanted to learn how to do what I do. This is the second lesson and already you're messing it up. The first rule is 'be professional'. Second guessing yourself is not professional behavior, Mr. Betts. The second rule is you have to pull the trigger. If you can't do that then what good are you to me?"

"I guess none."

Morgan pulled his own gun, a .45 Magnum, and pointed it at Sammy's head. "Let me put it another way. Either you get out there and finish the job or I'm going to shoot you then go out there and shoot him. Then, I'm going to come back here and shoot you again. Understood?"

Sammy Betts nodded.

"Then get your ass out of the van," Morgan said.

###

Abraham Snow hurt all over.

Lifting his head off of the steering wheel eased some of the pressure, but the world was spinning around him. With an easy tenderness, he touched the spot that throbbed the hardest and winced on contact. There was blood on his fingers, though not a lot, thankfully.

Disoriented, he wondered briefly where he was then started piecing the fragments of the past few minutes back together. He remembered filling up with gas then heading back toward the interstate, taking he long way around. Long rides through the country have always been a good way for him to loosen up and let his mind work through problems while the rest of him relaxed.

There was a van.

It sped up.

The van hit me.

Twice.

Bastard ran me off the road.

That snapped him back to the present.

In an effort to clear the cobwebs, he shook his head and instantly regretted it. The world around him was off center and he was seeing double.

He heard the van's door open, saw the passenger get out.

The enemy was carrying a gun in his hand, had it held at his side.

Snow pulled his cell from the console and typed a 9-1-1 text, hoping it went through and was readable because he couldn't clearly see the screen.

A familiar stabbing pain through the chest caused him to seize up and the phone fell out of his hand to the floorboard as he collapsed over into the passenger seat while still belted into his own. Snow clutched his chest, hoping the pounding would subside. He'd felt this way before, after he had been shot in South America. The doctors had warned him that too much exertion might reopen the wound or, worse case scenario, cause a heart attack.

Please, God, don't let this be a heart attack!

Snow's options were not good. Heart attack or being murdered by a kid with a gun. Neither sounded very appealing.

Snow released the seatbelt and eased more into the passenger seat. He opened the glove box and pulled out the trusty Sig Sauer he kept there for emergency situations. Having pissed off a cartel enforcer or two had left him with something of a persecution complex. Like a good Boy Scout, Snow preferred to be prepared, just in case he ran afoul of any old enemies. The gun held ten .357 bullets and Snow kept it loaded.

He chambered a round.

"Hey!"

Snow froze.

"You alive in there?"

Snow turned to look, but couldn't see the man with the gun. He was close though.

He opted not to answer the question. No sense giving anything away. If the shooter thought he was dead, he would approach with his guard lessened.

He would find a not so toothless target waiting for him.

Still laying across the seat uncomfortably, Snow pointed the gun toward the driver's door. His body screamed with each movement, his arms felt like they were wrapped in lead, but he somehow found the strength to hold the gun on target and waited.

He did not have to wait long.

The kid couldn't have been more than twenty-five, Snow figured, but he was old enough to hold a gun.

"Don't," Snow warned.

He didn't listen. Nervous and trembling, the gunman lifted the weapon, aimed it toward his target. He hesitated.

Snow didn't. He squeezed the trigger twice and the would-be gunman's chest exploded as two slugs hit him center mass. It was a textbook shoot, exactly as Snow had been trained to make.

By the time the shooter's lifeless body hit the asphalt, Snow was already on the move. Using his feet and legs, he pushed himself fully into the passenger seat. Whoever the shooter was, he wasn't working alone. Snow had seen him slide out of the passenger side of the van. That meant that there was at least one more out there, the driver.

What's he waiting for? Snow wondered.

It was a risk, especially as wobbly as he was at the moment, but Snow pushed himself up, using the seat to steady himself. He had the gun pointed toward the van. He couldn't see the driver from this distance, thanks to the sunlight reflecting off the windshield. His cell phone rang. He ignored it.

"I can't convince you to surrender, can I?" Snow shouted at the driver.

The van leapt forward with a jerk as the driver punched the gas.

"Guess not," he said.

Like an out of practice gymnast, Snow pushed himself fully into the passenger seat. He landed off balance with a pained *Uhnf!* at the same moment the van hit the car on the driver's side, knocking him off balance.

The gun fell from his hand.

A gun came out of the window and the van's driver opened fire, his shots going wild.

Snow mentally counted off the rounds as he scrambled to reclaim his dropped weapon. Not knowing what kind of gun the driver was using, he could only guess how many rounds it held before he would have to reload.

He found his gun, grabbed it.

At the first pause in the shooting, Snow popped up, one foot in the floorboard and his left knee resting on the seat as he leaned against its back to steady his aim.

"Don't!"

The driver was reloading, but froze at the shouted command.

"Toss it," Snow ordered.

The driver sent the handgun sailing out the window into the ditch off the side of the road.

"And your back up," Snow added.

The driver smiled, reached for a weapon Snow couldn't see from his current angle.

Oh, I don't like this!

The driver lifted his left hand, palm open as if to surrender.

He right hand came up holding a gun.

He pointed it at Snow.

Without hesitation, Snow put three slugs through the windshield.

The driver slumped forward, dead, his head hitting the steering wheel.

Snow hoped that there wasn't anyone else in the van because he wasn't sure he could handle another one. Heart pounding, head beating in time to see which would explode first, Snow slumped down in the seat. He was spent.

His cell rang again.

Despite the protest lobbied by his aching limbs, he stretched forward and grabbed the phone.

"Snow," he said weakly.

"Snowman?" Mac's familiar voice shouted from the other side. "What's going on?"

"Mac?"

"I'm on the way, buddy. Got you on GPS locator. Hold tight."

"Not… not going anywhere."

"You need anything? I got local unies and an ambulance en route."

"Gonna need a bus. Got t--two bodies."

"Stay with me, buddy!" Mac shouted, concerned. "Snowman! Ham?"

There was no answer from the other end of the line.

Abraham Snow had passed out.

9

"How long?" Tom McClellan asked the pilot.

He was in a helicopter, heading north of the city to find his friend after his 9-1-1 text. Thanks to his resources as an FBI agent, McClellan-Mac to his friends- was able to track Abraham Snow's location via his GPS locator that embedded in the text. It was a trick Mac had mentioned to his friend over beers and burgers one night.

At the time, Snowman had called it "*a neat trick*" and said he'd have to remember that in case he ever needed it.

And now he had.

"We're coming up on the signal," the pilot called.

"There!" Mac pointed.

His friend's car was sitting just off the road along with a van and one body lying in the middle of the road. Local law enforcement was on the scene, turning around traffic and clearing space for the helicopter to land. An ambulance and a paramedic truck were parked nearby.

"Agent Daniels, I want names on the two shooters down there," Mac told the agent he had brought along for back up.

"You got it, Mac," Agent Kira Daniels said.

The pilot brought the bird down gently in the center of the two-lane blacktop.

Mac jumped out as soon as they touched down and ran over to Snow's car, pulling his credentials from his jacket as he got closer. He winced when he saw the damage to the car.

He walked up to the local uniformed officer who looked to be in charge. Agent Daniels headed toward the crime scene with her kit.

"Tom McClellan. FBI." He held up his badge. "I'm looking for Abraham Snow. This is his car."

"Yes, sir, Agent McClellan." He pointed toward the paramedic's truck. Mr. Snow is with the medics. He told us to expect you."

"He's okay?"

"He seems to be, sir."

"Thank you," Mac said and headed toward the paramedic's truck. "Snowman?" he called.

"Here, Mac."

His friend was sitting on the edge of a gurney one of the medics, an aggravated woman whose name tag read *Martin* checked his blood pressure.

"What's the verdict, Doc?" Mac asked.

She looked at the newcomer, uncertain who he was or if he belonged there.

"It's okay," Snow said before she could ask to see his ID. This is my buddy, Mac. Mac, say hi to Dawn."

"Miss Martin," Mac said with a charming smile.

"How do you know her last name?"

The medic tapped her plastic name badge.

"Oh," Snow said and laughed. Then he winced.

"Some detective," Mac joked.

"You really his friend?" Martin asked.

"I am."

"Your friend needs to go to the hospital. He's banged up pretty good, but there's some arrhythmia that has me concerned."

"I'll make sure he gets looked at. He was shot in the chest about eight or nine months ago," Mac told her. "If you ask, I'm sure he'll show you the scar. He's quite proud of it."

"Want to see?" Snow said.

"No thank you," Martin said. She looked at Mac. "He refuses to let us take him to the hospital. I'll release him to you if you want to take responsibility for him, but I think you're crazy if you do."

"Sure. Not the first crazy thing I've done for this boy."

"It's your funeral, she said, rolling her eyes. "Or maybe his."

"I'll take my chances."

She handed over a release form and Mac signed it.

"You're a lucky man, Mr. Snow," she said as she helped him out of the back of the truck.

"So I have been told. Thanks, Doc. Thanks."

"Thank you," Mac repeated. He looked at Snow. "Are you okay?"

"Did you see the car?" Snow said, changing the subject. "Grandpa's gonna be pissed."

"Archer's just going to be happy you're okay," Mac said.

"Probably, but he loves that car."

"Almost as much as he loves his grandson," Mac added.

"Maybe."

"What happened?" Mac asked, walking his friend toward the crime scene.

"Van ran me off the road," Snow said. "Then this guy tries to shoot me so I shot him first."

"As you do."

"Right," Snow said. "So then, the guy driving the van floors it and tries to shoot me, which seems like overkill, but maybe not since I'm still here."

"So, you shot the driver too?"

"Yep. Tossed a gun into the ditch over there. I guess he thought I'd assume he only had the one and drop my guard when he drew on me with the one he had hidden. His mistake. It was a clean shoot."

"I'm sure it was," Mac said. "Still, there's procedure to follow. You'll have to hand over your gun."

"Sheriff already bagged it," Snow said. He pointed toward the man in question.

"Good. I'll talk to him."

"Agent McClellan."

"Abraham Snow, meet Special Agent Kira Daniels. Kira, Snow," Mac said by way of introduction. They shook hands.

"What did you find?" Mac asked Agent Daniels.

She held up a portable finger print scanner. "Guy on the pavement is a local hire, a wannabe trying to make his bones."

"The driver's the pro, I take it," Mac said.

"You were right," Daniels said. "The driver has a sheet longer than my arm. Name's Richard Morgan according to his fingerprints. ID has another name on it."

"Morgan? Why does that name sound familiar?" Mac asked.

"Yeah. It rings a bell for me too, Snow said.

"This guy's a celebrity in the hitman world. He's been tied to at least twenty or thirty high profile hits around the world. They hung the nickname, The Collector on him because he cuts off the victim's index finger. We assume that's to carry it back to whoever hired him as proof of the hit. He's based out of Greenville, South Carolina."

"A hub of scum and villainy to be certain," Snow joked.

"Maybe hitmen like to live in nice, quiet places when they aren't out murdering people," Mac said.

"Maybe."

"Go ahead and call it in," Mac told Daniels. "Use your cell, not the radio. Let's keep it quiet until we see how the chief wants to handle it. Have our South Carolina office follow up on that address."

"On it," Agent Daniels said and walked away to make the call.

"Bad guy," Snow said as he watched them load the hitman's corpse into the ambulance.

"Apparently, not bad enough," Mac said. "You are about to make a lot of law enforcement agencies happy. They can take this guy off their most wanted list."

"I'm more interested in who sent him after me and why."

"I take it you have some suspicions?"

"I've pissed off my fair share of scumbags when I was on the job," Snow said. "Thing is, though, none of them knew my real name or where to find me. I always used an alias when I was undercover and I've not used that alias since I came home. There's no way they could have tracked me that way. No, this was somebody after Abraham Snow."

"Who have you pissed off since you got home?" Mac asked.

Snow laughed.

"What are you working on now? Could this be connected with that?"

"I doubt it," Snow said. "I'm looking into a case for Archer. Someone sabotaged one of his client's race cars. I was here talking with the prime suspect, a guy named Oliver Simcoe."

"You think he could have hired this guy?"

"Simcoe's a dick so it wouldn't surprise me if he hired someone, but I just met him for the first time an hour ago and he didn't know I was coming. These guys had to have followed me from his office. No way he put this all together that fast."

"Then who, Hambone? Who?"

"Daniella Cordoza."

"That's the one who shot you, right?"

"No. That was her boss. Or one of her bosses. She could pull this together quick, she knows my name, and as of yesterday, she knows where I live."

"Come again?"

"She knows I'm in Georgia."

"How pray tell does she know that?"

"She called me."

"Called you?"

"Yeah. Called me on Sammy's phone."

Off his friends stunned look, Snow held up a hand to stop the questions before they could start.

"She's fine. Cordoza hired her firm and used her to get my number and location out of Sammy's phone. She's on the way home now, under guard. She has a layover here tonight and will head back to New York tomorrow."

"What did the lady say when she called you?"

"She offered a truce. Told me she wouldn't come after me if I didn't come after her. I told her okay."

"Did you believe her?"

"Hell no." He pointed toward his wrecked car. "And you wonder why I have trust issues."

"The kind of work you did, I'm surprised you trust me."

"Never assume," Snow said with a smile and twist of his head.

"What now?"

"I've got a call in to someone who can help. We've got to put Ortega and Cordoza out of commission."

"Come on," Mac said. "Let's get you checked out at the hospital then I'll take you home."

"Good. I could use a nap."

10

That night, the Snow family gathered for dinner.

As he did any time all of his brood were in town at the same time, Archer invited them all to a nice meal at a fancy downtown eatery. Until this year, it was an impossible task with Abraham being MIA. Archer had tried to keep track of him, thanks to his connections with General Pinkwell and Mother, the organization his grandson worked for as Archer once did himself, but they were tight lipped. All they would tell him was that his grandson was alive and well.

Now that he was home, getting his son and three grandchildren in one place was something special. It was harder to see the others as Dominic's sister had moved to California after marrying. Archer used to see the grandkids every summer, but now that they were older with families, jobs, and lives of their own, he rarely saw them.

As the only girl in the bunch, Archer had always doted on Samantha. They all did. She was the glue that kept them all together and kept Dominic and Abraham from throwing punches at one another.

Everyone had a good time and when the night was done, Snow gave his baby sister a lift back to her hotel. Her flight was leaving the next morning to take her back to New York. Once they were at her hotel, he asked her about Daniella Cordoza.

"How do you know her?" Sam asked.

Snow laid it all out for her. He told Sam about his last undercover mission, at least the parts that were not still classified, and how Daniella Cordoza works for an organization run by several men all using the alias Miguel Ortega. He told her how one of the men using the Ortega alias shot him and how he and Cordoza left him for dead on a tiny airstrip in South America. He skipped ahead to her stealing Samantha's phone and using it to call him and threaten her life.

"That bitch," Sam said once he finished.

"You'll get no argument from me, sis."

"She used me. More over, she used my firm. When I get back, we're going to…"

"Nothing," Snow said. "You're not going to do anything. I'm telling you this because it's dangerous. Stay away from her."

"No way. I'm going to sue her ass. She can't get away with this."

"Sammy, please," Snow said. "We're working on it. She's already sent one person after me and she threatened you."

"I am not going to run and hide."

"And I don't want you to. I want you to go about your business as usual. Dad's going to have a couple of his guys keep a discreet watch over you the next few days just to be safe, but I'm pretty sure you were just a means to an end. Now that she's found me, there's no need for her to bother you again."

"I don't like this."

"Neither do I, sis, but it's got to be this way. Do it for me, huh?"

"Fine," she said, pouting. "You want to stay here tonight?"

"Nah. I'm good."

She let out an exasperated breath, a trait she picked up at an early age when dealing with her male relatives. "Look, there's no sense driving all the way home and then all the way back to take me to the airport tomorrow. There's plenty of space on the fold out couch."

Snow smiled. "As appealing as that sounds, there's a nice big king sized bed in the room I'm renting next door." He chocked a thumb toward the adjoining door.

"You think you're pretty smart, don't you?"

Snow smiled. "Yeah. I do."

Samantha laughed.

"Get some rest. We'll grab breakfast before I take you to the airport."

"Sounds like a plan. Goodnight, Snowball."

"'night, Sammy."

###

Being a p.i. is a lot harder than it looks on TV.

After dropping his sister at the airport and making sure the two men shadowing her from Snow Securities arrived, Abraham Snow pointed the car he borrowed from his grandfather toward Atlanta Motor Speedway. As suspected, Archer had not been upset about the convertible and promised that as soon as they could get it in the garage, Big John and his boys would have it looking as good as new.

His focus had naturally slipped off the case, but now that his sister was safe, there was nothing he could do bout Daniella Cordoza until he heard back from Elizabeth Walker. He did not expect that to happen for a few days yet.

All he could do until then was focus on the job at hand and keep an eye open for anyone following him or other trouble. Cordoza was not the kind of person to give up after one setback, if indeed she was the one who hired Richard Morgan to kill him. It very well could have been the man he knew as Ortega, but he rarely did anything during the time Snow was undercover where she was not involved or at the very least, consulted. Snow very much doubted that had changed in the eight months since he'd last seen either of them in person.

Mac had the FBI digging through Morgan's place in South Carolina. It was a small farmhouse style home on a rather large parcel of land, nice and secluded. The feds were digging through the place to see what they could find. They had already discovered enough evidence to close eight unsolved murder cases. This would be a big win for Mac and the FBI and they were welcome to it. Snow had asked that his name be kept out of it, but that notion was torpedoed quickly.

The identity of the saboteur was still a mystery to him. He doubted Oliver Simcoe was directly responsible, but there was still the possibility that he was indirectly responsible or had hired someone to do the deed. He couldn't rule that out yet.

Outside of Simcoe and his employees, of which he had read Snow Security research files on until the wee hours of the morning, that left the others who were part of the engine trials. Archer's research team was pulling information on all of them as well. So far, no one had leapt out at him as a great suspect.

Once he got to the track, he was going to talk to some of the other drivers, get their take on things. Maybe someone had seen or heard something that would point him in the right direction.

The track was abuzz with activity when he arrived. The big race was only days away and the drivers were finishing up qualifying to determine their starting position in Sunday's race.

There was a race on Saturday as well, this one featuring up and coming drivers. Grant Chambers' son, Beau, would be racing in that one. Grand and his older son, Chase would be competing in Sunday's race. That was three opportunities for the saboteur to strike.

Dominic had seen to the driver's security, but Snow wondered if anyone was watching the crew.

Snow called Archer when he reached the parking lot. Crowds had already begin to arrive for the next day's race or to watch the qualifying heats. The speedway also had space available for people to park their

RVs and campers for those who chose to arrive early and stay after the race ends.

Kelly Pratt was waiting for him when he arrived.

"Don't you ever go home?" Snow joked as he got in the van with her.

"Are you kidding? On race week, I practically live here. I rented a motor home so I wouldn't have to go home."

"You really love this stuff, don't you?"

"Yes, sir."

"Do you know why I'm here? Why the guys who rode in with me the other day are here?"

"I heard you guys were private security for the Chambers team after their incidents."

"Mostly true. I'm trying to find out who's behind their troubles."

"Are you saying their accidents weren't accidents?"

Snow shrugged.

"I can't believe that. Who do you think did it? Do you have any leads?"

"The very question I was about to ask you," Snow said.

"Me?" The look on her face was a mixture of fear and disbelief.

"Sure. Nobody knows this place like you do, Miss Pratt. You're here all the time, know everybody. Have you seen anything suspicious?"

"Not really," she said. "I mean, there was that argument Mr. Chambers had with that guy from the engine manufacturer. I'm sure you heard about that."

"I did."

"The brothers don't get along very well. They've gotten into it a few times." She cast a sideways glance at him. "I'm not going to get into trouble telling you this, am I?"

"No. I promise to keep your name out of it."

Whew! "I can't afford to alienate any of these guys. I still hope to work for some of them one of these days."

"Mum's the word," Snow said with a disarming smile. "What were Chase and Beau fighting about?" he asked, steering his source back on track, pun intended.

"The usual. Beau wants to run in the big race, but they don't have enough cars for that. Plus, it takes a lot of juice to get a seat at the table. Beau can't get out of the Busch League and it frustrates him. Or at least that's what I hear. My friend, Sally, she's a… oh, what do they call 'em?" She waved her hand, trying to recall the right words. "Booth babe. Yeah. That's it. Booth Babe. They put her in skin tight suits that leave *nothing* to the imagination and she goes around with samples of some kind of energy drink she and the others in her crew pass out."

"How does Sally have insight into Beau Chambers?"

"Oh, they were sleeping together," Pratt said matter of fact.

"Really?"

"Yeah. Both of them are… well, let's just say they both get around. It was only a matter of time before they hooked up."

"Sounds like a soap opera around here," Snow said.

"Honey, you don't know the half of it," Pratt said, smiling.

As they drove onto the pits, she told him all the latest track gossip.

11

Abraham Snow walked Pit Row alone.

After thanking Kelly Pratt for her insights, he asked that she let him off away from the garage area so no one would know she had talked to him. He told her it was a precautionary move so no one would have reason to think he had asked her any questions. She bought it and wished him luck before heading back.

In truth, he needed time to process the facts at hand, which were slim at best. Either the Chambers team was just unlucky or someone was sabotaging them. If it was sabotage, Simcoe, or someone working for him was the most likely target. And then there was Beau Chambers and his temper. When he had talked to Big John, he'd heard about the problems between the brothers. Kelly had only confirmed it.

Brothers fighting was nothing new. Snow and his brother, Douglas, had certainly had their fair share of dust ups over the years, especially when they were kids. He was about to write it off as sibling rivalry, but he kept coming back to how badly Beau wanted to move up to the big leagues. The only way he was going to get his shot was if a space opened up.

He kept coming back to the same question. If Chase Chambers had been seriously injured in that wreck, who would have driven in the race on Sunday? The only answer that he could think of was Beau. The real question was, was Beau capable of trying to hurt his brother for a shot at driving in the bog race on Sunday?

There was really only one way to find out.

"Oh, there you are, boy," Archer Snow's distinctive voice called out.

Snow saw his grandfather across the pits, talking with the client. Archer's cowboy hat made him stand out in a sea of ballcaps.

"Good morning," he said as he arrived. "Everything go okay last night?"

"No problems on our end," Archer said. "This place is secure. How about your part?"

"Not so much."

"What's your next move?"

"I've got to talk to Beau. Have you seen him?"

Archer pushed his hat back and scratched at his newly trimmed haircut. “I saw him and John running around here somewhere. The team is getting things ready for Chase’s qualifying run a little later.”

“He’s running today?” Snow repeated.

“Yeah. They’re doing second round qualifying now. He should be up any time now.”

“’Scuse me, grandpa. I need to find Beau.”

Snow jogged toward the garage with Archer just a couple of steps behind.

“What are you thinking, boy?”

Snow turned to face Archer. “If there’s going to be another attempt on Chase’s life, what better time to do it than during qualifying?”

“And you think Beau…”

Snow shrugged as he ran. “I hope not, but it fits.”

Archer pointed into the garage. “You go that way. I’ll search over here.”

“Watch yourself, old man.”

“Yeah, yeah,” Archer said, humored by his grandson’s concern.

Snow ran through the garage, followed by shouts from mechanics, crew, and drivers alike as he pushed his way through the crowds. He did not see Beau Chambers anywhere so he pulled his cell phone and used speed dial to call Big John Salmon.

“Ham!” he shouted over the noise of cars revving and engines purring. “Where are you?”

“Just what I was about to ask you. Are you with Beau Chambers?”

“Yeah. He’s around here somewhere!”

“Where are you?”

“Pit Row! We’ve come to watch Qualifying!”

“Stay put! I’ll be right there!”

Snow headed back the way he came, this time more careful of the crews working in the garage stalls. He got back to the Chambers’ garage right after Archer did.

“Any luck?”

“He’s with Big John,” Snow said, trying to catch his breath. His chest ached. He knew better than to exert too much energy. His doctor had warned him repeatedly. Being banged up from the car wreck wasn’t doing him any favors either. “They’re watching Chase qualify,” he said once his breathing returned to normal.

Archer watched his grandson closely. He was still concerned that Abraham took too many risks considering his condition. He didn't say anything because he understood. He too had been young and stubborn once. Now, he liked to tell people he was just stubborn.

"How did Chase do on round one?" Snow asked as they walked toward pit lane.

"Now bad," Archer said. "The kid can drive."

"No problems with the car?"

"Not that I noticed."

Snow's face crunched up. Archer recognized the look.

"What's got you stymied, kid?" he asked.

"If you were going to sabotage the car, qualifying would be the best time, right?"

"That would depend on how I was going to sabotage it," Archer said.

They turned around and walked back toward the now empty garage.

"Anything look out of place to you?" Snow asked once they were back inside.

"No. Of course, I've spent most of my time with the NASCAR brass or with Grant. I haven't been in here much."

Snow scratched at his chin. "Something's off. I just can't quite put… my…"

His voice trailed off then Snow sprinted across the garage to a crate near the far wall. He lifted the lid, which was only lying across the top.

Archer joined him a second later.

"What is it, son?"

"Proof of sabotage," Snow said, dropping the lid.

"Beau?"

"I don't think so."

"What is it?"

"See for yourself," Snow said.

Archer looked into the crate and saw an engine.

"This doesn't look like a new motor," he said. "When we buy new engines at home, they come in a crate similar to this one, but this engine has been used. It's been run before."

"Yeah. I'm guessing yesterday," Snow said. "Then, probably last night, it was removed from the car and replaced by another one."

"By who?"

"I have a pretty good idea," Snow said. "Call Dad and have him meet me at pit lane. Then find out who was in here last night. That's our saboteur."

"You know who it is, don't you?"

"Yeah, but I hope I'm wrong."

Snow ran out of the garage toward pit lane.

###

Snow's chest felt like it was going to explode, but he couldn't slow down.

He had to lean against a tool chest when he arrived until he could slow his breathing to something akin to normal levels. There was nothing good about getting shot, but the shortness of breath and fatigue that was now a constant companion were damned annoying and inconvenient.

He wondered if he would ever feel completely normal again.

A crew member from one of the other teams stopped to ask if he was all right, but Snow thanked him and sent him away.

The crowd was large, NASCAR officials, press, crews, sponsors, and investors were all on hand to watch the festivities. Even Oliver Simcoe and a small entourage of his underlings were on hand. There was no time to deal with Simcoe at the moment, but Snow decided he would get to him soon enough.

Then he saw Big John and Beau nearby and pushed forward.

He caught up with them just in time to see Chase Chambers' car speed away from the pit wall in a cloud of white smoke from burnt rubber.

"Dammit!"

"What's the matter, Ham?" Salmon asked.

"We need… need… need to stop Case."

"Why?" Big John asked, holding his friend by the arms to help stabilize him. "We need to get you to a medic," he said.

"No. We have to stop Chase."

"Why?" Beau asked.

"Car's not safe."

"Sabotage?" Dominic Snow asked as he joined them with Archer and Grant Chambers in tow. Grant had a headset around his neck for talking with his driver while on the track.

"Did you authorize an engine change in Chase's car?" Snow asked Grant.

"No. The one we had was running fine. Why?"

"Last night, someone swapped out your engine and replaced it with another," Snow said.

"Why would they do that?" Grant asked.

"I think your engine was replaced with one from the Simcoe trials."

"No way!" Grant said. "I would never authorize that."

"But you weren't in the garage last night," Dominic said.

"Who was?" Big John asked.

"Tommy Yates," Archer said.

Yates was watching the qualifying, headset on and stop watch in hand. Each of then turned to look in his direction.

"You need to stop Chase before that engine overheats!" Snow shouted at Grant.

Chambers pulled the headset back on. "Chase! I need you to come in right now!"

No response.

"Chase?"

"What's wrong?" Archer asked.

"He can't hear me."

"Is there another way to signal him?" Snow asked.

"Have the flagman signal him to stop," Big John said.

"Do it," Grant told one of his crew.

"Will that work?" Dominic asked.

"It's a longshot," Grant said, looking for his son's position on the track.

Snow started moving toward Tommy Yates. He figured that Chase would have thought something was wrong if all communication with pit row ceased. He hoped Tommy still had an open line to the car.

Grabbing him by the collar, Snow spun Yates around to face him. "Call him back in. Now!"

"It's too late," Yates said. "I'm so sorry, but it's too late."

"What did you do?" Grant shouted.

"I'm sorry, Grant," Yates said, suddenly looking older than his years. "They didn't give me a choice."

"Who?"

"It was Simcoe, wasn't it?" Snow asked.

Yates nodded.

"Oliver Simcoe told you to hurt my son?"

"No," Yates said. "Not hurt. He just wants to prove that his engine works."

"But it doesn't work," Grant said. "You saw it."

"I don't think it's as bad as you do," Yates pleaded.

"And you're willing to risk Chase's life to prove it?"

"I'm sorry," Yates said.

"Not as sorry as you're going to be," Archer Snow said as he had Daniel Sisko take him away to be held for questioning.

"We've still got to find a way to contact Chase," Dominic said.

Big John looked around and realized they were missing someone. "Where's Beau?"

As if on cue, Beau Chambers roared past them down pit lane on his motorcycle and onto the track.

"There's no way he'll ever catch up to him," Dominic said.

"I wouldn't be too sure," Big John whispered, never taking his eyes off the track.

At the end of pit lane, Beau took a hard right and headed toward turn four, where his brother would in seconds be heading right toward him.

Beau watched as the car driven by his brother entered turn four at top speed. One of Chase's go to moves was to enter the turn high and then drop down to the lower bank and picks up a couple of extra tenths of a second. It was a tried and true move, but also one that put him from one side of the track to the other. If he didn't see Beau approaching in time, there would be no way for the motorcycle to get out of the way in time.

In a collision between a stock car and a motorcycle, the car wins every time.

Beau had grabbed a yellow flag that was rolled up in his hand. It was dangerous to drive at these speeds one handed, but he let the flag fly loose so he could warn his brother.

"He's going to get himself killed!" someone shouted.

"I wouldn't bet on that either," Big John said.

12

There's more to driving a racecar than driving.

As he entered turn four, Chase Chambers was focusing on his driving and the car. The car was performing well, but there was a vibration in the engine he hadn't felt the day before. He wasn't concerned, but it would have to be checked out. He would have Tommy take a look at it when he finished qualifying. Hopefully, it wasn't anything severe. He tried to call it in, but the radio was also on the fritz.

That was unusual.

With two issues noted and recent events still fresh in his mind, he started to feel concerned. Chase considered aborting the rest of his run and heading down pit lane instead of taking turn four, but then he decided to stick it out and not run the risk of not qualifying. He needed to place for Sunday's race if he had any hope of holding on to his points standing.

A quick glance in the direction of the pits showed a large crowd gathered, more so than he was expecting. Something was going on and he was cut off from it, but there was no time to worry about that.

The car hit turn four at top speed and Chase took the car high on the embankment as he entered the turn then dropped toward the low side.

That's when he saw something that wasn't supposed to be there.

Chase didn't recognize his brother from that distance thanks to the vibrations of the car and the heat off the track, but he did notice the motorcycle and the swatch of yellow the driver waved back and forth to get his attention.

That yellow flag meant caution and that meant slow down.

Before he was even fully conscious of it, Chase throttled back and hit the brakes, gently at first, careful not to lose control of the car and left the track into the grass that separated pit lane from the track. He knew from experience that the grass would help slow the car's momentum.

The car slid on the grass and slammed into the retaining wall before bouncing away to come to a final rest in the grass.

Small streams of smoke rose from beneath the hood.

The motorcycle was the first to arrive and Beau Chambers ran over to help his brother out of the car after dropping it on the grass.

"Come on!" Beau shouted. "We have to move!"

They ran away from the car and leapt over the retaining wall.

The engine exploded with a loud POP! that sent smoke into the air without destroying the car. If the engine had exploded at full speed, the results could have been disastrous.

The Chambers boys each let out a breath.

Chase slapped his brother on the shoulder. “Thanks, bud.”

The brothers hugged as the rest of the assembled crew and emergency teams arrived.

###

Oliver Simcoe and his aide headed toward the limo they had arrived in.

At first, Simcoe wasn’t sure why his aide so strenuously suggested that it was time for them to leave, but with all of the chaos happening around the pits, he agreed.

“What did you do?” Simcoe asked as soon as they were inside the car.

“I did what you wanted, sir,” Harold said.

“How’s that?”

“I was going to prove your engine worked.”

“Well, I guess you proved Grant Chambers’ point instead, didn’t you?” Simcoe said as he slammed a fist into the door.

“I’m sorry, sir.”

“Sorry! How did you get my engine in that car?”

Harold smiled. “That was actually easy, Mr. Simcoe. The crew chief, Tommy Yates had some pretty deep gambling debts. I bought out his marker in exchange for getting the engine in the car for today’s qualifying round.”

“What were you thinking?”

“I was thinking that once the engine sailed through qualifying, we could move forward, get back on track, uh, so to speak.”

“Are you serious?” Oliver Simcoe’s face burned crimson. “You’ve ruined me. Once that detective starts questioning Yates, he’ll point the finger at us and that’ll be all she wrote for us.”

A knock at the window interrupted him.

Abraham Snow stood next to the limo. Behind him stood two uniformed police officers.

Simcoe rolled down the window.

“We should talk,” Snow said.

"Not right now," Simcoe said. "Call my office for an appointment."

"I'm afraid we'll have to insist," Snow said.

With a resigned sigh, Oliver Simcoe opened the door.

###

Abraham Snow loved the races.

Sitting with Archer, Dominic, Big John, and Daniel Sisko under an awning, Snow sipped at his overpriced beer and watched as a car zoomed past on the driver's qualifying run. The smell of gas, grease, exhaust, and burnt rubber filled the air. It was a fragrance that reminded him of a simpler time, a time when he and his father weren't at one another's throats.

"I still can't believe it was Tommy Yates behind everything," Big John said.

"Well, Harold James and Oliver Simcoe had their hands in it too," Snow said. "Yates was in deep with some not-so-nice people. He owed them a lot. Harold took advantage of that and offered him a way out."

"But why would he take it?" Big John asked. "I watched him with the crew, the family. He loves those guys."

"Desperation can make a man do almost anything," Dominic said before taking a sip of his beer.

"Amen to that," Snow said. "Plus, you have to remember that Tommy didn't think there was anything wrong with the engine. That was Grant."

"He was right about the engine though," Archer added.

"He was indeed," Dominic said.

"Will Chase be able to race Sunday?" Snow asked.

"Yes," Archer said. "John and I helped them find another engine to get them through this race."

Snow smiled. "I bet you did, grandpa."

Archer and Snow clinked their bottles, water and beer, respectively, and grinned like school kids.

"Well, the saboteur is in custody so I guess I'm out of a job," Snow said. "What about you guys?"

"We'll stay on protection detail until the race concludes and Grant gets back home," Dominic said. "Speaking of, he offered up passes for Sunday's race for anyone who wants one. Abraham? John?"

He held out the passes.

Snow took them both and passed one over to Big John.

"Thanks, Dad."

Dominic cracked a smile. "Any time."

The clinked bottles then sat back and watched the rest of the qualifying lap in silence.

Snow smiled. It was a good day.

###

Kelly Pratt arrived promptly to pick them up.

Before heading home for the evening in Archer's helicopter, Abraham Snow, Archer Snow, and Big John Salmon said their goodbyes to the Chambers' boys. Daniel Sisko would stay behind with Dominic Snow and then drive him back to the office.

"Thanks again for all your help," Grant said, shaking their hands.

"Happy to help," Snow said. "I'm sorry it turned out to be someone so close to you."

"Same here."

"I do have a favor to ask," Snow said as he motioned for Kelly to join them.

"Grant Chambers, I'm not sure if you know Kelly Pratt or not, but she has been a big help to us while we've been here. She's looking for a racing team to intern with and I think she'll be a great asset to whichever team snaps her up, but she's not had a lot of luck. I wondered if maybe you might have a place for her while you're reorganizing your team?"

Grant smiled. "A pleasure to meet you, Miss Pratt. After you drop Mr. Snow and his party off at the helipad, come on back by and we'll talk."

"Thank you, Mr. Chambers. I appreciate that. Will be back in a jiffy."

Snow and Grant shook hands again before they headed out to the van.

Beau Chambers was waiting outside.

He shook hands with each of them and thanked them again for what they did for his family.

Big John handed Beau one of his business cards for Archer's garage. "In case you want to come out and see our operation or just call if you ever need to talk. I've been told I listen pretty good."

Big John clapped the young driver on the shoulder before joining his friends in the van.

"He going to be okay?" Archer asked.

"Yeah. I think so."

"I'm sorry if this was tough for you. I didn't think about what you gave up when I asked you to come along," Snow said. "I really just thought you'd enjoy being here."

"Think nothing of it, Ham. I had a great time," Big John said sheepishly. "I'll admit, it stung at first, being here, but at the end of the day, it ain't nobody's fault but mine. Hell, I've got it good compared to most. I've got a job a love and great people in my life. What's to complain?"

"You're a good man, John Salmon."

"I know."

They laughed.

Ten minutes later, they were airborne and headed for home.

"I don't know about you guys, but I'm starving. I could go for a big juicy T-Bone. What do you say, boys? My treat."

"Sure," Big John said.

"I could eat," Snow said.

"I wonder if they'll let me land this in the steakhouse's parking lot?" Archer wondered aloud.

13

Sunday's race went off without a hitch.

Unfortunately for them, neither Chase or Grant won the race, but Chase finished in the top ten, Grant in the top five. There had been no more accidents reported and everything seemed back to normal for the Chambers Racing Team. Snow Securities would keep them on as a client, but in a less hands on, guards on duty sense. Dominic was supervising a team that would upgrade the security measures at the Chambers' farm and garage in the coming days.

Surprisingly, he had asked Big John to join him on the job.

Snow tried not to take it personally that he wasn't invited. He had enjoyed the race and had even enjoyed spending time with Dominic. They had always put their shared animosity aside for NASCAR. Apparently, it was one of the few things they still had in common outside of family.

Monday came around and help felt horrible. Too many beers and too much time in the sun. He was tired and sunburnt, but more importantly, still recovering from the attack on his life. The pain in his chest was still there, though less severe. He promised Mac that he would place a call to his doctor on Monday and he had done so earlier and left a message. It would be the evening, if not the next day, before he expected a return call.

He also called Samantha to check on her.

Sammy was her usual self, the strongest of the Snow clan. Nothing ever seemed to faze her, not even coming face to face with the woman who was partly responsible for almost killing her brother. Of course, since he had kept those details away from her, she didn't have to be.

After a short chat with her before she headed into a meeting, Snow slipped on some shoes and made his way down to the garage. The '61 Corvette convertible had been towed to the garage from the accident site after Mac and his FBI techs finished going over it. Archer and Big John were standing by the car, looking it over.

"What a mess," Snow said when he saw it. "Is she salvageable?"

"It's going to need some work, but I think it's doable," Big John said.

"I am sorry about your car, grandpa."

Archer looked perplexed. He touched his chest with both hands. "My car? I seem to recall giving this beauty to you when you got out of the hospital."

"And I remember saying thanks, but no thanks."

"And yet you drove it anyway," Big John muttered.

"You told me you'd keep it."

"I believe I said we'll see," Archer said. "Besides, I'm older than you and I'm your landlord so all decisions made by me are final."

"Is that so?" Snow asked, laughing.

"My house. My rules."

"Uh, huh."

Archer took Snow and Big John out for lunch so they could talk over the repair schedule, but Snow knew the old man simply enjoyed their company. Not that he minded. He enjoyed hanging out with them as well.

After lunch, Big John went back to work in the garage and Archer headed into the city for a meeting at the office. He invited Snow to come along, but he decided to skip it this time. The weekend had ended on a positive note between him and his father. He didn't want to risk upsetting that balance on a Monday.

That meant the rest of the day was wide open.

He played video games, strummed on the guitar a little, and even tried to do a little reading, although that led to a mid-afternoon nap.

The sun was just starting to inch toward the horizon when he woke. There were no missed calls and no new messages waiting for him. No emails either. He tossed the phone on the couch and flipped on the TV to watch the news.

As usual, there was little of interest to him, except highlights from Sunday's race. The kerfuffle during qualifying had not even made the network news. A few sports channels had covered it, although none of them treated it as anything other than an accident. Beau Chambers' stunt was chalked up to just another of those impulsive outbursts the troubled young driver was known for and no one had bothered to correct the reports. It was easier to let the matter rest than to drag NASCAR and the family through the mud so Beau took the hit.

He was more popular than ever.

When the phone rang, Snow clicked off the news and picked up the phone. The caller ID simply read: WALKER.

"I was beginning to think you forgot about me," Snow said by way of greeting.

"Good to talk to you too, Snow," Elizabeth Walker said.

There was no animosity in the words, just the playful jibes of old friends. Walker had first met Abraham Snow on an undercover mission. For three months, she played girlfriend to his alias, James Shepperd while shacked up together in London and later on a cruise ship. When you work deep cover, there's no turning the aliases on and off and the two of them became quite intimate.

Once the mission was completed, she was reassigned to another department for another mission and he went on to the next mission. It was another year before they saw one another again, only this time she wasn't playing the love interest.

This time she was his boss.

Salmon Brooks had been Snow's handler, but as he moved more and more back into fieldwork, Elizabeth Walker replaced him as Snow's handler. When Brooks and Snow were partnered up, Walker became his handler as well.

She was good at her job and kept them safe, not an easy task considering their line of work. Aside from a slight miscalculation involving Miguel Ortega, she had been batting a thousand. Of course, he was fair enough to admit that he hadn't seen Ortega figuring out his true identity and shooting him coming either so they chalked that one up as the exception that proved the rule.

Now that he was retired, Walker was his liaison to Mother. She was in charge of the investigation into the Ortega organization, a group that was far more difficult to track than they had first thought. It was Snow who had first deduced that Miguel Ortega was nothing more than an alias used by multiple leaders in the organization. That made pinning any of them down easy. Miguel Ortega could be in multiple places at one time, which made making a case in court all but impossible.

Snow was convinced that there was someone at the head of the organization pulling the strings, but he never discovered that person's identity. He was well on his way when his cover was blown and one of the Ortega's shot him three times, two of the in the chest.

Walker was helping him work those leads.

"You and I should chat," she said. He could hear a rumbling noise that told him she was on the move, probably in a bulletproof SUV or town car that a howitzer couldn't penetrate.

"Learn anything new?" Snow asked.

"I think we should get together and chat," she said, sidestepping the question. "What day are you free?"

"I'm free whenever you are. When will you be in town?"

"Soon," she said.

He hadn't expected more since they were talking over an unsecured line.

"My schedule is wide open. Call me when you have a date and time and I'll meet you," Snow said.

"I've got a few things to tidy up here before I head down there for some work stuff. How about sometime next Friday? We can grab lunch before our chat."

"It's a date," he said, smiling, knowing that she wouldn't be.

Walker was a funny lady, but on the job, she was all business. He respected that about her. "*Chat*" was one of the code words they used back in the day to mean debrief. That she used it three times meant that she must have had something big. "*Sometime next Friday*" meant this Friday, just a few days away.

"Until then, stay frosty, Snowman."

"Always."

And then she was gone.

Snow held the phone for a moment and wondered what was happening that she wasn't telling him. His status with Mother was retired, which meant he was on the outside looking in. It was lucky they were keeping him as in the loop as they were and they were only doing that much because it looked like Ortega and Cordoza were still gunning for him.

Were they after him now because he was the one that got away or had his and Brooks' off books investigation actually yielded some results? It was the only reason he could think of that they would still be trying to find him.

Snow pulled his copy of the Ortega and Cordoza files from a box hidden in the back of his closet and spread them out onto the kitchen table. He started pouring over them, re-reading each file and trying to look at it from a fresh perspective. Somewhere in there was a vital clue, something he and Brooks had overlooked.

He was determined to find it.

When he finished going through everything, the sun was just beginning to rise.

A fresh pot of coffee later and he stood on the balcony wearing only a pair of shorts while overlooking the lake. The answer was there. He could feel it, but it continued to elude him. It was still early, but he texted Brooks with a message to call him. A message came back: *L8R*.

Snow smiled at Brooks communication skills. Later, they would discuss the problem and try to come up with a solution. He wouldn't tell him about his meeting with Walker until he was sure there was something worth sharing. In their line of work, retired though they both were, compartmentalizing information was a skill that helped keep them alive. Even as a civilian, it was a hard habit to break.

Snow was tired of running.

He had run all the way back to Georgia, but that was as far as he would go. He would hide from Ortega and Cordoza no longer. They were still out there and he was more determined than ever to find them and bring them to justice. They would pay for not only what they had done to him, but for their many crimes.

Stretching away the fatigue, Snow headed out to the lake for an early morning swim.

He was looking forward to a beautiful day.

EPILOGUE

Elizabeth Walker flashed her badge at the door.

The guard stepped aside with only a "ma'am" to indicate her arrival. Inside, a man wearing an inexpensive suit and tie met her. She showed him her badge as well.

"Agent Walker," the man said. "Detective Charles."

"Has he been moved?"

"No, ma'am. Our office received word that you were on the way and to leave everything as is until you arrived."

"I appreciate your cooperation, Detective."

"Of course," Charles said. He motioned toward the hallway. "It's this way."

Walker followed the detective down the hallway to a bedroom at the end of it. It was a small apartment, probably a safe house or stash house from the look of it. She had seen this kind of place before, had even spent more than her fair share of nights in places just like it.

The smell was the first thing that hit her when she entered.

"Cocaine," she said before covering her nose and mouth.

"Yes." The detective pointed to a stack of drugs inside an open closet. Several of the bags had been ripped open and the white powder was everywhere.

Including all over the body lying in the center of the room.

The man was lying on his back, a pool of blood thick in the carpet around his upper body. A urine stain surrounded his lower extremities. The unique smell of the corpse did not mix well with the cocaine scattered across the room.

"Your vic was shot three times at close range. It won't be official until the M.E. does her things, but I'd say cause of death is the bullet through the heart."

"That'll do the job," Walker said.

Also in the room was a small folding table lying on its side, two chairs, one of which was broken, and a pizza and bottle of red wine that had both been knocked to the floor.

"Looks like one hell of a fight," Charles added.

"Has CSU taken their photos yet?"

"Yes, ma'am."

"My team is on their way up. They will take custody of them to protect chain of evidence. Once that happens, I will need your people to vacate the premises. This is now a matter of national security."

"Looks like a drug deal gone bad to me," Charles said. "Or drug dealers having a falling out."

"I'm sure it was designed to look that way," she said.

"Sorry?"

"Time to walk away, Detective Charles."

Irritated, but knowing he didn't have any wiggle room to argue the point, Detective Charles nodded then turned on his heel and walked away. He muttered something under his breath as he walked away.

Walker ignored him. She had gotten used to being called names when she stepped in to take over a crime scene. It was nothing new.

She knelt next to the body and waited for her crime scene tech from her division to arrive.

"We have a name for the stiff?" Technician Mike Horton asked as he set down his gear.

"Not a real one."

The tech took fingerprints with a digital scanner and uploaded them to VICAP immediately. "You know this guy, Chief?"

"Yeah. I do," Walker said. "An alias at least."

"Who is he?"

"His name is Miguel Ortega."

Abraham Snow will return in SERIES 1. VOLUME 2.

SPECIAL THANKS!

There are some folks I'd like to give a BIG THANK YOU for helping make it happen.

If not for my pals, Gary Phillips and Paul Bishop mentioning my name to the right person and the right time, I might never have gotten Snow off the ground. They, along with authors John Hartness, Sean Taylor, James R. Tuck, Derrick Ferguson, and Buzz Dixon also said some nice things about Snow, which you can see on the back cover. I am thrilled to have Dennis Calero's art grace these covers. Thanks, guys.

Also, a HUGE THANK YOU to my Patrons for supporting my work on Patreon. I appreciate each and every one of you and I hope you enjoyed getting copies of Snow's adventures a few days before everyone else. There are perks to being a Patron and you are the greatest. Lil' John Nacinovich, Robert McIntyre, John Kilgallon, Darrell Grizzle, Andrea Judy, Shannon Muir, Richard Ewell, Jeff Allen, and the Rad Ranger himself: Sean R. Reid. Rock stars one and all.

MEET BOBBY NASH

Although he doesn't run around getting into a lot of adventures like Abraham Snow, Bobby Nash spends his days writing about heroes who do. Bobby is an award-winning author of novels, comic books, short stories, novellas, graphic novels, and the occasional screenplay for a number of publishers and production companies.

Bobby is a member of the International Association of Media Tie-in Writers and International Thriller Writers. On occasion, Bobby appears in movies and TV shows.

He was named Best Author in the 2013 Pulp Ark Awards. Rick Ruby, a character co-created by Bobby and author Sean Taylor also snagged a Pulp Ark Award for Best New Pulp Character of 2013. Bobby has also been nominated for the 2014 New Pulp Awards and Pulp Factory Awards for his work. Bobby's novel, Alexandra Holzer's Ghost Gal: The Wild Hunt won a Paranormal Literary Award in the 2015 Paranormal Awards. The Bobby Nash penned episode of Starship Farragut "Conspiracy of Innocence" won the Silver Award in the 2015 DC Film Festival. Bobby's story in The Ruby Files Vol. 2 "Takedown" was named Best Short Story in the 2018 Pulp Factory Awards, one of five nominations for The Ruby Files Vol. 2 (created by Bobby Nash & Sean Taylor). Bobby's digest novel, Snow Drive was nominated for Best Novel in the 2018 Pulp Factory Awards.

For more information on Bobby Nash and his work, please visit him at www.bobbynash.com

###

Learn more about SNOW, his friends, and adventures at http://ben-books.blogspot.com/p/snow.html

MEET DENNIS CALERO

Snow cover artist, Dennis Calero is an American comic book artist and illustrator, known for his work on titles such as Spider-man Noir, X Factor, Legion of Superheroes, Kolchak, and Doctor Who.

Learn more about Dennis Calero and his amazing art at http://denniscalero.com

#####

Thanks, Dennis. I couldn't have done it without ya, brother.

Bobby

BOBBY NASH'S
SNOW
THE ESSAYS
BEN
BOOKS

HALFWAY TO THE FINISH LINE

A Snow Series 1, Vol. 1 Essay by Bobby Nash

I can't believe how far we've come.

When I started writing SNOW FALLS, I had not envisioned seeing us where we are today. Snow has changed publishers and the idea of breaking it into series are the biggest changes, but I think they are good changes.

By the time you read this, SNOW TRAPPED, the fourth book in series 1 should be out and making the rounds. Snow Trapped kicks off part two of the first series and points us toward a resolution to Snow's over-arching storyline. Who betrayed Snow to the Ortegas? Who hired the hitman who came after him? Who killed… well, you know who dies at the end of Snow Drive?

All of these questions point us into Snow Trapped as Snow tries to get some answers. He also finds himself in the wrong pace at the wrong time on the wrong day. He has the worst luck, doesn't he?

I would like to take a moment to thank those who have been following Snows adventures. Writing this series has been one of the highlights of my career and I hope to write him for a long time to come. To that end, I've already started plotting series two.

I just need to finish writing series one first.

For those of you reading this who are new to Snow's adventures, I bid you a fond welcome and hope you enjoy the ride.

In the pages following this are my essays about writing each book as they appeared in the original releases, left mostly unaltered, which is tough. You know how we like to tinker and rewrite. I think they share some insights on what I was thinking when they came together. I hope you enjoy them.

I do have a small request.

If you like what you read, please tell a friend and leave a review. Reviews are an author's lifeblood. Reviews make it easier for others to find our books and each one is greatly appreciated.

If you want to get a sneak peek on upcoming releases and behind the scenes insider information, please join us on Patreon at www.patreon.com. Patreon acts like a subscription service. Each month, subscribers get an ebook or two and new releases when they come out, sometimes sooner.

A BIG THANK YOU to a few folks who helped make this all happen. Paul Bishop, Gary Phillips, Jeffrey Weber, and Dennis Calero have been part of Snow Falls since the beginning. Even though the original plan did not work out as anticipated, I never would have started writing Snow without it and these characters that I love would exist only in the back of my mind, which is no place for them to live.

Thanks for sticking with us on our journey. Let's do it again real soon.

Keep watching the forecast.

Bobby

WHEN SNOW FALLS

A SNOW FALLS ESSAY BY BOBBY NASH

SNOW FALLS is one of my favorite stories. I fell in love with the characters, especially Abraham Snow and his grandfather, Archer. By the way, Archer seems to be the fan favorite from this story, which pleases me greatly. SNOW started as an idea for a TV series. Since I don't have any TV connections, the odds of that happening seemed unlikely. Then, I had a wild idea of filming it myself in short 10 - 15 minute installments as a web series then collecting it as a movie. Sadly, I didn't have the funds of manpower to make that happen either.

In 2012, I was invited to join a start up ebook publisher, a sideline for a well-known music producer. The plan sounded solid and I dusted off the idea for SNOW, which was called HUNT'S BOUNTY at that time and, after making quite a few adjustments, pitched it as SNOW FALLS. It was accepted. Sadly, as sometimes happens in business, things go KA-BOOM! and that's what happened with this new venture. As a result, SNOW fell into limbo, even though story #2 was written and ready to go and stories 3 and 4 have been plotted.

I love TV P.I.'s and SNOW is my throwback to the TV series of the 70's and 80's that I loved. You'll see a lot of Magnum p.i., Rockford Files, A-Team, and Simon & Simon in these stories. Most of all, they are meant to be fun and I hope that comes through.

So, why the name change from HUNT'S BOUNTY to SNOW FALLS? Just a whim, really. I had created the character with a last name of Hunt. In his first story, which I started writing, he is a soldier who loses his legs while trying to diffuse a bomb. Now, walking with prosthetic legs and a cane (very much inspired by actor Jim Byrnes from Highlander), Hunt assembles a team of former soldiers to form a bounty hunting business and bring crooks on the run back to justice. Like Snow, the titles would have Hunt in there somewhere. Hunt's Bounty, Hunt's Revenge, Hunt on the Run, Hunt For Justice, you get the idea. I still think Hunt has legs, pun intended, and who knows, maybe I'll dust him off and get his story told as well.

For now, however, the focus is getting SNOW back on track. There's also plans for a Sheriff Tom Myers series as well, featuring the sheriff of Sommersville County from the novels EVIL WAYS and DEADLY GAMES! He'll move to the forefront in his own adventures.

Watch out. There's a SNOW STORM on the horizon.

Keep watching the forecast.

Bobby

BREWING UP A MOB WAR
A SNOW STORM ESSAY BY BOBBY NASH

I write a lot of pulp fiction.

Pulp has made something of a comeback in the last decade and I was lucky enough to be involved in one of the first new properties that helped launch what has been called the New Pulp movement. I'm not here to debate the usual question about what is or is not pulp or anything like that. I've been part of that conversation plenty.

I'm sure you're wondering what pulp has to do with SNOW STORM, right? Well, I'm sure there are those who would say that the Snow books, SNOW FALLS and SNOW STORM could certainly be considered pulp. Yes, there are definitely pulpy bits in these tales, but that's not really why we're here either.

The pulp heroes of yesteryear often found themselves going up against mobsters, gangsters, and the occasional madman bent on world domination. As I started writing tales of pulp heroes and villains for a variety of publishers, I kept dreaming up stories with mobsters in them. I hit upon what I thought was either a great idea or utter lunacy. I leave it to history to determine which category best describes my plan.

I set about creating several mob families, the Tommasso family, the Prince family, the Bester family, the Roarke family, and the Manelli family. Since I had already put in some work on these groups, I figured it couldn't hurt to reuse them from time to time. Since the stories take place over a lengthy span of time, I had to roughly plan out where each would be around that time. What followed was an idea for a mob war that is playing out in the background of many of my stories featuring pulp characters, told out of order, but that will hopefully make sense as things unravel.

It's the Manelli's and the Roarke's that tie this in to SNOW STORM as we finally see who wins this mob war that has been playing out off and on since the 1930's. I'm not sure if anyone has noticed, but up until I mentioned at a con last year, I don't think I had ever told anyone what I was doing, certainly not a room for of people.

Do you have to read everything I've written to understand what's going on?

No. Like I said, the mobster's stories are part of a larger tapestry, but you don't have to read them all to know what's going on.

Now, if you want to read everything I've written, please be my guest. I won't try to stop you. Ha! Ha!

I love TV P.I.'s and SNOW is my throwback to the TV series of the 70's and 80's that I loved. You'll see a lot of Magnum p.i., Rockford Files, Matt Houston, and Simon & Simon in these stories. Most of all, they are meant to be fun and I hope that comes through.

The focus for this year is getting SNOW back on track and with this second release, we are already on our way. The next book, SNOW DRIVE, will not be out in March, however. I have a few other projects on deadline then back to Snow. Look for it in a few months. After that will either be SNOWED IN (which I really wanted to call snow hard ***but called Snow Trapped instead***) or SNOW BUSINESS (the seeds of which were planted in this very story). I just have to figure out which one should happen first.

There's also plans for a Sheriff Tom Myers series as well, featuring the sheriff of Sommersville County from the novels EVIL WAYS and DEADLY GAMES! Once I get them on the schedule, Tom Myers will move to the forefront in his own adventures. And since it was revealed in this story that Snow and his pals went to school in Sommersville, could a crossover be in the cards? Anything's possible.

I would love to hear your thoughts on SNOW STORM and SNOW FALLS. Reviews are an excellent means of finding out what readers like and don't like, plus it helps move the book along in the rankings and we could use all the help we can get. As always, keep up with SNOW NEWS at http://ben-books.blogspot.com/p/snow.html.

Oh, and before I sign off, I received a couple of questions about getting Snow's adventures in paperback. That is in the works now. Most likely, what will happen is that we will release a paperback containing 3 or 4 Snow adventures in one collection. I'm still working out the logistics on that to make it an affordable package.

Will keep you posted.

Keep watching that forecast.

Bobby

PEDAL TO THE METAL
A SNOW DRIVE ESSAY BY BOBBY NASH

If you've read the essays in the back pages of SNOW FALLS and/or SNOW STORM, then you know that I love TV Private Eyes. You've also read how Abraham Snow is my throwback to the TV series of the 70's and 80's that I loved so much then and still love revisiting today. You'll see a lot of Magnum p.i., Rockford Files, Matt Houston, and Simon & Simon in these stories.

One of the aspects of those old shows that appealed to me then as now is the characters. Watching a TV series like magnum p.i., for example, I bought that these guys were friends. There were many moments that felt like we as the viewers had just stumbled upon them living their lives before this plot stuff happened.

I wanted to recapture that feel with Snow and his friends and family and boy, has it? In writing their adventures, I feel like a voyeur, watching to see what they do next. I can't imagine Snow without Big John or Mac at his side and Archer Snow certainly refuses to sit on the sideline. Even characters like Samantha Dean, Snow's sister, keep pushing themselves into the limelight. At the beginning, she was never intended to appear in each book as she has so far. You probably hear writers all the time talk about how our characters take on a life of their own. It's true.

The book you hold in your hand is proof.

Some of my fondest childhood memories involve going to the races with my dad. R.O. and I used to go down for qualifying, hit the souvenir booths, and watch some racing. My favorite driver as a kid was Richard Petty, The King, good ol' #43. I even had a scrapbook. Sadly, I've never met Mr. Petty, but I did visit his museum once. It was an incredible trip.

Having Snow and his dad bond over the races was simple. It made sense. Having Big John tag along was simply icing on the cake. It also gave me a chance to dive deeper into Big John's past and see how his driving dreams crashed and burned when he went to prison. I even came up with a plot for a future book based on one line of dialogue in this book. I love it when that happens too.

I'd also like to give a shout out to the real life Richard Morgan, owner of Richard's Comics and Collectables in Greenville, NC for volunteering to be killed off in Snow Drive. We were talking at the SC Comicon earlier this year when he told me he had been killed off in a comic book and a movie and wouldn't it be nice if he could be killed off in a novel. As luck would have it, I had this assassin in mind and he hadn't been named yet so I figured he would get a kick out of it.

The next book is called SNOW TRAPPED and it will premiere fall 2017. I'll post all the details in the usual places as soon as I have them. This one went through a couple of name changes, the last one as I was putting together the ad you'll see in a couple of pages. It has been Snowed In, Snow Trap, and Snow Hard (as the plot would make clear why), but SNOW TRAPPED won the day.

SNOW BUSINESS will follow winter 2017.

I would love to hear your thoughts on SNOW DRIVE as well as SNOW FALLS and SNOW STORM. Reviews are an excellent means of finding out what readers like and don't like, plus it helps move the book along in the rankings and we could use all the help we can get. As always, keep up with SNOW NEWS at http://ben-books.blogspot.com/p/snow.html.

Oh, and before I sign off, thanks again for checking out Abraham Snow's adventures. I love hearing from you and I'm glad you're enjoying them. I am having a great time writing these characters and hopefully we can get the sales up so I can keep on writing them so please, tell your friends. Word of mouth is a great way to get the word out about SNOW.

Keep watching the forecast.

Bobby

ALSO BY BOBBY NASH

Evil Ways
Deadly Games!
Earthstrike Agenda
Domino Lady: Money Shot
Alexandra Holzer's Ghost Gal:
The Wild Hunt
Snow Falls
Snow Storm
Snow Drive
Snow Trapped
Fightcard: Barefoot Bones
The Adventures of Lance Star: Sky Ranger
85 North
Frontier
Sanderson of Metro
Shadows on the Horizon
The Ruby Files (Vol. 1 & 2)
Domino Lady: Sex As A Weapon

And many more. Visit Bobby at www.bobbynash.com for a full list.

WHERE FICTION LIVES

BEN-BOOKS.
BLOGSPOT.COM

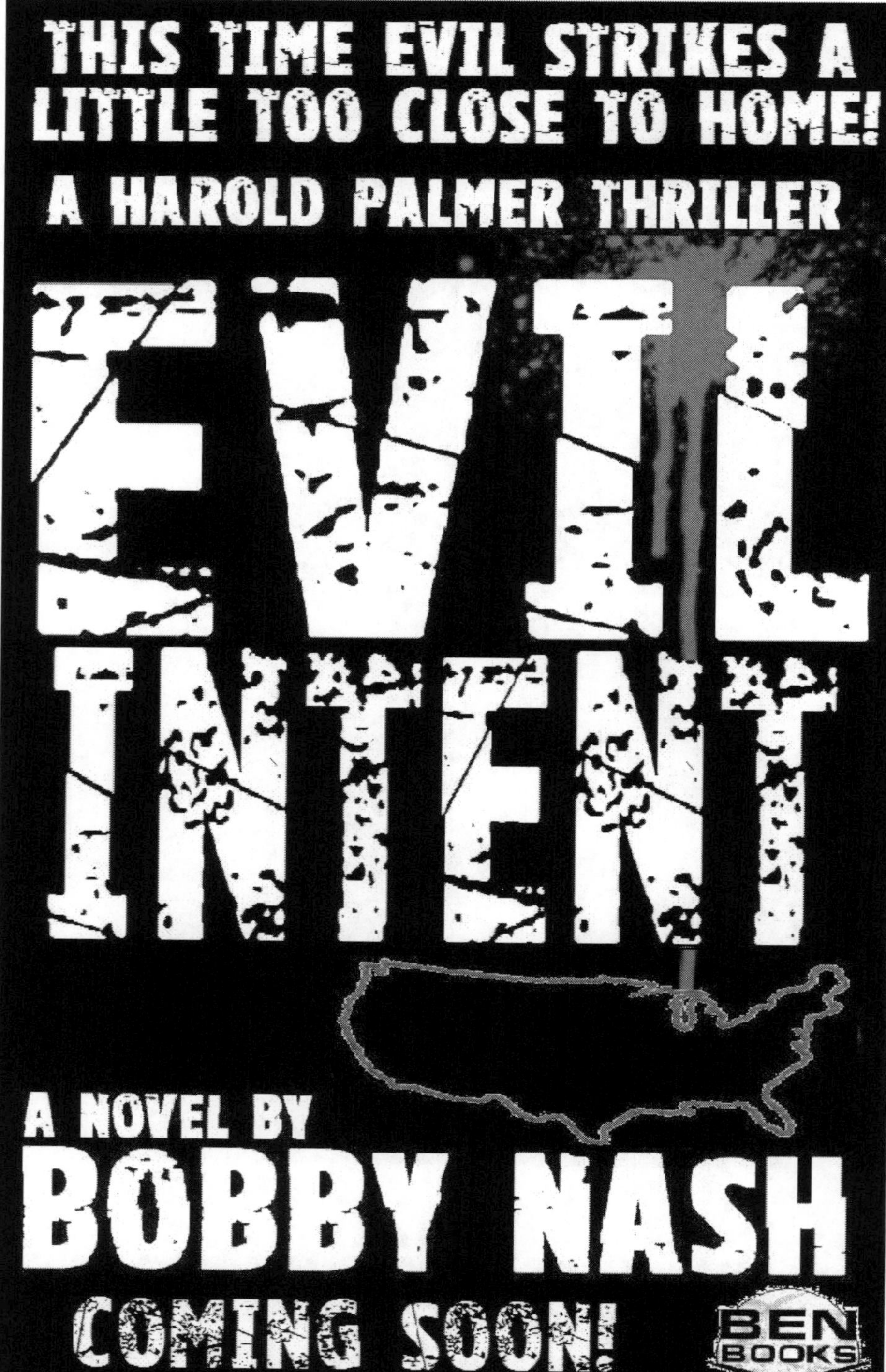
THIS TIME EVIL STRIKES A LITTLE TOO CLOSE TO HOME!
A HAROLD PALMER THRILLER
EVIL INTENT
A NOVEL BY
BOBBY NASH
COMING SOON!
BEN BOOKS

JOHN BARTLETT AND BENJAMIN WEST ARE BACK
AND THIS TIME THE GAME IS MORE PERSONAL!
DEADLY
DEALS!
COMING 2019
NOT FINAL COVER
A NOVEL BY
AWARD-WINNING AUTHOR
BOBBY NASH

ABRAHAM
SNOW
WILL RETURN
BEN
BOOKS